THE DROVING LAD

"Is this the farm of Drumbeg?" the man asked

THE
DROVING LAD

Kathleen Fidler

illustrated by Geoffrey Whittam

CANONGATE · KELPIES

First published 1955 by Lutterworth Press
First published in Kelpies 1989

© 1955 Kathleen Fidler

Cover illustration by Alexa Rutherford

Printed in Great Britain
by Cox and Wyman Ltd, Reading

ISBN 0 86241 254 4

CANONGATE PUBLISHING LTD
17 JEFFREY STREET, EDINBURGH EH1 1DR

Contents

Chapter		Page
	How the Story Began	7
1.	A Stranger Comes to Drumbeg	11
2.	Adventure on the Moor of Rannoch	34
3.	The Stranger at the Ford of Frew	62
4.	The Falkirk Tryst	88
5.	The Return of Simon	116
6.	Colin Strikes a Bargain	137
7.	Pursuit in Carlisle	159
8.	The Cattle Stampede	175
9.	Escape from Catterlen	192
10.	The Barnstormers	213
11.	Catterlen Again	234
	How the Story Ended	254

How the Story Began

Old Colin Cameron, the Highland cattle drover, sat nodding in the firelight of his farm kitchen at Drumbeg, his newspaper upon his knee, his spectacles upon his forehead. On the hand-pegged cloth rug before the fire his grandson Ian was stretched, trying to read a book by the light of the flames, for it was the year 1863 and the farm-house had no gas lighting. Suddenly the door opened and in came Beth Cameron, Ian's grandmother.

'Just what I thought you'd be doing, the pair of you!' she scolded. 'Are you both trying to spoil your eyesight?'

'I think Grandfather was asleep,' Ian chuckled.

'Eh, what is that now?' Colin said, waking with a jerk. 'Just closing my eyes so I could think better, that's all I was doing.'

Mrs Cameron lifted the glass chimney from the lamp, turned up the wick, and lighted a taper at the fire and put it to the wick.

'Now you can see better to *think*,' she teased her husband gently. 'Very important thinking it must have been for you to close your eyes to do it, surely?'

'Aye, wife, so it was,' Colin replied, lifting the *Glasgow Herald* up again and re-adjusting his spectacles. 'I see in the paper that the new railways are going to be extended soon to Oban and then to Ballachulish.'

'My! Think of that now! A railway coming so near to us here in the West Highlands, no less!' Mrs Cameron exclaimed.

'Aye, wife, changed days, changed days indeed!' Her husband shook his head. 'Soon we shall be putting the cattle on the train and sending them straight from here to the London market, instead of driving them down over the hills to Falkirk in a big herd.'

'Why, if that happened there'd be no cattle market at Falkirk!' Mrs Cameron said, almost with dismay. 'Imagine it! No Falkirk Tryst!'

'Aye, it'll come to that some day,' Colin predicted.

Ian looked up anxiously from his book. 'Why, Grandfather, do you mean you won't be driving your cattle to the fair at Falkirk again? You won't be taking the beasts along the drove roads any more?'

'No, Ian laddie, the railway won't arrive at Ballachulish all in a jump!' his grandfather laughed. 'It's driving the cattle to Falkirk we'll be for many a long year yet, I'm thinking.'

'Oh, I'm glad of that,' Ian said in a voice of great relief.

'Why, my lad?' his grandfather asked with an amused smile, as if he knew the answer well enough.

'Oh, Grandfather, have you forgotten that you promised that I should go along with you and Father and John the herdsman, to drive the cattle to Falkirk Tryst as soon as I was big enough?'

'Aye, but it's a wee while you have to go yet, Ian. It's hard tough work being a drover,' his grandmother reminded him.

'But I'll be twelve next birthday,' Ian protested. 'How old were you when you first went with the cattle to Falkirk Tryst, Grandfather?'

'Not much older than you, Ian,' Colin Cameron admitted. 'I was very close on thirteen years.'

'There! You see, Grandmother!'

'Yes, but your grandfather was brought up on a farm and he had been handling cattle ever since he could walk, almost.'

'Aye, that's right, Beth, and bulls too,' Mr Cameron chuckled.

'Bulls?' Ian asked, much impressed.

'Aye, bulls!' his grandfather told him. 'Why, it's just fifty years to this very month since I led Torcull the Black down to the cattle fair at Falkirk. Yes, it was in the year 1813, I remember.'

'Torcull the Black?' Ian asked, puzzled.

'Yes, he was one of the finest bulls that ever came out of our farm at Drumbeg.'

'Tell me about him,' Ian begged.

'Och, it's a long time ago and a long story too. Fifty years since I was a lad setting out on my first drove. Ah-ha!' old Colin sighed.

'Will you tell me about it, Grandfather, *please*?'

'You may as well be telling him, Colin, for Ian will be at you now till you do,' Mrs Cameron laughed.

'Please, Grandfather!'

'Ah, well then,' Colin Cameron gave way good-naturedly. 'Sit you down on this stool here beside me.' He sat for a moment or two looking into the glowing fire as if he could see pictures there, then he began talking very quietly.

'When I was lad our farm at Drumbeg was not such

a big one as it is now, stretching along the shores of Loch Leven, but it was a good one as the Highland farms go. Though there was not a deal of work for the plough to do, there was good rich pasture along the waterside and Drumbeg had always a fine herd of cattle. Indeed, my father, James Cameron, had an eye for a good animal and a name throughout the West Highlands for breeding good bulls. Aye, we were proud of our bulls at Drumbeg.' Colin Cameron nodded his head and paused to light his pipe and puff at it for a minute or two as he sat there, lost in thought.

'Go on, Grandfather,' Ian urged.

'It was a busy life but I loved my work among the animals,' his grandfather continued. 'For all their spread of horns and fierce rolling eyes, they were quiet obedient creatures enough when you knew how to handle them. Though my father could be thrawn at times, I liked working for him and with Angus, my elder brother. Aye, I looked up to Angus. In the spring and summer, too, there was often the come and go of drovers and buyers from the south to strike a bargain with my father and to buy our cattle. Many were the merry tales and the singing in our farm kitchen then at nights. Sometimes my father took a drove of cattle himself to the south, and how I always longed to go with the drovers.'

'Like I do, Grandfather,' Ian put in quickly.

'Aye, like you do, Ian,' his grandfather agreed with a smile. 'Little did I think though, one day, when a stranger came riding up to Drumbeg in the warm September of 1813, and a knock came to the door, that when I went to answer it, I was opening the door to adventure. . . .'

A Stranger Comes to Drumbeg

The thick-set horseman in tight-fitting riding breeches and top boots came slowly along the lane from Ballachulish by the shores of Loch Leven. As he rode he glanced curiously at the cattle in the low pastures, almost as if he were weighing them and pricing them in his mind. He reached the grey stone, thatched farm-house, and reined in his horse for a moment while he looked at it, almost as if he were weighing that up too, its poverty or its wealth, then he shrugged his shoulders and dismounted close by the door nearest to the out-buildings, and tapped loudly on it with the stock of his riding whip. The door was opened by a well-built sturdy lad of twelve.

'Is this the farm of Drumbeg where Mr James Cameron lives?' the man asked him.

'Yes, sir, it is,' the boy replied and waited.

'Is Mr Cameron at home then, my lad?' the man asked a trifle impatiently.

'Yes. He is at the byre milking the kye.'

'I would like to have a word with him. My name is Laidlaw.'

'Will you please be stepping this way to the byre then, sir,' the boy said, leading the way round the side of the house.

As they went a herd of young bullocks peered at

them through a tangle of tawny brown hair and shook their heads and lowed in the meadow next to the farm.

'You have a good herd of cattle this year?' Mr Laidlaw commented.

'Yes, we have done well with the beasts indeed,' the lad told him in a grave grown-up fashion.

'You will be Mr Cameron's son, no doubt?'

'Yes, I am Colin Cameron.

'I hear you have a fine bull here at Drumbeg.'

'Aye, we have a few bulls, but no doubt you will be meaning Torcull the Black,' Colin said with an air of pride.

'No doubt I am,' Laidlaw replied dryly with a little smile. 'Is your father thinking of selling the bull?'

'That will be for my father to say, sir,' Colin answered him a little stiffly. 'It is not for me to be talking of what is in my father's mind.'

'A true cautious Highlander, I see,' Laidlaw remarked with a faint sneer.

'And you, I take it, sir, are a cattle buyer from the Lowlands?' Colin retorted quickly.

'I wouldna say but what ye're right,' Laidlaw replied easily.

They reached the byre, and Colin thrust his head over the half-door and called to his father. 'Father, here is a gentleman, a Mr Laidlaw, wishing to speak to you.'

'I will come,' Mr Cameron said, rising from his milking stool and wiping his hands on a towel. 'Do you take over the milking of Brown Jennie, Colin.' Colin took his place on the milking stool while James Cameron came forward to the stranger. 'Well, Mr Laidlaw, what can I be doing for you?'

'I am a cattle buyer from the south, Mr Cameron,' Laidlaw told him. 'I hear ye have a herd o' cattle that I might think o' buying from ye for the October Tryst at Falkirk if I like the look of them well enough and we can agree upon a price.'

This was rather too brisk an approach to the matter of buying and selling for the Highland farmer and he answered a little stiffly: 'I have not the honour of your acquaintance, sir.'

'Laidlaw's the name, William Laidlaw,' the other replied curtly.

'It is not a name I have heard,' James Cameron said, stroking his dark beard. 'Have you been to buy cattle before in this part of the country, Mr Laidlaw?'

'No, I have not, but a man must extend his trade,' Laidlaw said impatiently. 'I have heard Drumbeg is a good cattle farm.'

Cameron cast him a quick inquiring glance. 'And who told you that I had a good herd of cattle for sale?'

'Och, one hears a thing here and there at an inn, maybe, or at another farm. A buyer has to keep his ears open,' Laidlaw told him vaguely. Then he added in a businesslike tone, 'Now, if it's convenient to you, I'll take a look at the cattle.'

Cameron was in no hurry, however. 'Bide a moment, Mr Laidlaw. When I have sold my cattle before, it has usually been to Mr Barlow of Cumberland or his topsman, people I know well.'

'Thomas Barlow will not be coming to these parts this year,' Laidlaw said offhandedly.

'Did you learn that, too, at the inn?'

'Maybe I did! Maybe no'! I canna mind,' Laidlaw

said shortly. 'But if you want to sell me your beasts, you'd better be letting me see them while it's still daylight.'

'Aye, you shall see them, surely,' James Cameron replied in a smooth voice. 'They are in this field beside the byre. Come a step or two this way.'

As they passed one of the out-buildings, the door of which was open, Laidlaw stopped suddenly. 'Bide a moment, farmer. Is yon the bull I've heard tell of, in this cattle pen here?'

The farmer nodded. 'No doubt. That is my prize bull.'

'The one named Black Torcull?'

'Aye. It seems to me, Mr Laidlaw, ye have heard a plenty about Drumbeg,' the farmer said shrewdly.

'It is my business to learn these things and I am interested in bulls,' Laidlaw told him. 'I like the look of this one.'

'Do ye now?' Cameron said in a dry voice.

'Aye, he's a good shape, a full broad chest, a straight flat back and a small head. His eye's lively, and he's got a good thick shaggy black coat, forbye. Aye, he'll do. What will you be asking for him, now?'

'I had rather you would be naming the price you are prepared to pay, Mr Laidlaw. That is the way I have always done business before.'

'Well, shall we say twenty-five pounds?'

'Twenty-five pounds for a bull which has so many good points! Come now, Mr Laidlaw.'

'Maybe I was a thought too generous in my praise of the beast,' Laidlaw said sourly. 'I can get plenty bulls at twenty-five pounds anywhere in the Highlands.'

'Maybe, maybe, but not like Black Torcull,' Cameron said with a smile. 'I shall not sell him at twenty-five pounds.'

'Don't place too high a value on the animal, Cameron. I tell ye, I've no need to look far for a good bull, but I've a fancy for this beast, and so I'll raise my price to thirty pounds, if ye'll take ten pounds in gold now and the rest at the Falkirk Tryst.'

'I would not be selling him for thirty pounds either,' James Cameron said decisively. In the byre, Colin, who had stopped his milking to listen to his father's bargaining, breathed a sigh of relief. 'But what will you be offering me for the stirks in yon field?' his father went on. 'I shall not sell my bull unless I sell the herd too.'

'So that's the way of it? Take one, take all?' Laidlaw exclaimed, slightly exasperated. 'Well, then, I'll give ye four pounds apiece for the beasts. That's a fair price.'

'I did hear that at the cattle fair at Muir of Ord stirks were fetching eight pounds apiece, aye, and more,' Cameron told him.

'Good news travels fast among the farmers in the Highlands, it seems.'

'Indeed, sir, do we not all know that England is at war with Napoleon Bonaparte and will pay good prices for salt beef for the navy!'

'You must remember, too, that I have the cattle to drive to the Tryst at Falkirk and all their expenses on the way,' Laidlaw pointed out. 'It is not *all* profit to me, you know, what with fees for grazing the animals on the road, and tolls to pay at the bridges and the market taxes too.'

'I am knowing that well, but for all that there is a big difference between four pounds and eight pounds, now, Mr Laidlaw.'

'You Highlanders drive a hard bargain,' Laidlaw exclaimed in annoyance. 'Listen then, I'll make ye an offer of five pounds each for the stirks and thirty guineas for the bull. I'll pay you twenty pounds now for a token payment and the rest at the Falkirk Tryst in October. And that's more money than Drumbeg has seen for many a long year, I'll warrant,' he added with a sneer he did not attempt to conceal.

This was too much for James Cameron's Highland pride. The hot blood mounted in anger to his face. 'It's not for you, a stranger, to be speaking about the wealth or the poverty of Drumbeg,' he told Laidlaw stiffly.

'Och, plague take your Highland ways, man!' the buyer cried, losing control of his temper. 'Five pounds apiece for the animals and thirty guineas for the bull. Will you, or will you not take it?'

'I will not be taking it, Mr Laidlaw,' the farmer said coldly. 'Neither your price nor your manners please me. Besides, I know well what my bull is worth.'

'Do ye now?' Laidlaw retorted. 'But before you can get your fancy price, you have first to find a buyer for your bull. I've told you that Thomas Barlow, the Cumberland buyer, will not come to Drumbeg this year. Neither he nor any other buyer!'

'And how do you know that?' James Cameron asked sharply.

'Because I have bargained with your laird over at the big house and only *I* shall have the right to buy from the farms on his land this year. So, if you don't sell to me, you'll sell to no one!'

'Rather than sell to you, I will sell to no one!'

With an effort the buyer spoke in a more reasonable tone. 'Now, man, come off your high horse. That will benefit nobody, least of all yourself. Ye'll be wishing ye'd thought better of it and sold to me when the winter comes and ye've got nothing to feed all that herd of stirks.'

'No, I shall not be thinking better of it, Mr Laidlaw,' Cameron said obstinately, with the air of a man who has something up his sleeve.

'Och, man, talk sense. Thirty-five pounds for the bull then, we'll say.'

'No, Mr Laidlaw, it is not a fair price and well you know it.' James Cameron remained firm.

'It's my last offer. Will ye, or will ye not take it?' Laidlaw demanded.

'I will not take your offer, and if you think to have got the rights of buying from me by driving a bargain with the laird who owns my land, that trick will do you no good, sir.'

'What do you mean? The laird'll take no promises to pay the rent when it falls due.'

'No, but he'll take my gold in payment, no less,' Cameron said confidently.

'Where will you get the gold if no buyers come to Drumbeg for your cattle?' Laidlaw asked him with a twisted smile.

'From the Tryst at Falkirk,' Cameron told him. 'It will not be the first time I have driven my cattle to

Falkirk to sell them. No, nor the last either. I am a free man and the laird cannot sell my right to take my own cattle to the market.'

'So that's the card you've had up your sleeve all this while?' Laidlaw cried angrily. 'So you'll not sell?'

'No, Mr Laidlaw, I'll not sell. You see, I am a drover as well as a farmer. And I would say this, too, to you. Till today I have always been accustomed to do my business with *gentlemen*. Good day to you.'

Laidlaw turned on him in a black fury. 'You'll live to regret the day you turned down my offer, James Cameron. If you think you'll get yon bull safely to the market at Falkirk, you'll soon find your mistake. Mark my words! I'm an ill man to make into an enemy.'

'I think as little of your threats as I do of your offers, sir.'

'You'll think more before long,' Laidlaw snarled at him.

'Good day to you, Mr Laidlaw,' Cameron repeated firmly.

'Och, plague take you and your bull too! Where's my horse?' Laidlaw exclaimed rudely, and crossed the yard to where his horse was fastened to the hitching post. In a moment he had mounted, ground his spurs cruelly into his horse's sides, and with a frightened neigh the animal plunged and was away with a flurry of hoofs.

Cameron dusted his hands one against the other as though getting rid of something obnoxious, and turned into the byre again. 'Well, that's one rogue sent about his business. Have you finished the milking, Colin?'

'Nearly,' Colin replied. 'Father, is it true that Mr Barlow will not be coming to buy your herd this year? Is it true what yon fellow said?'

'Aye, it's true enough, but it's no news to me. Mr Barlow sent me word himself that he could not be riding to Drumbeg this year. He has injured his foot and will come to Falkirk by stage coach.'

'Then will you be able to sell the herd?' Colin asked anxiously.

'We'll need to, my lad, to pay the rent.'

'Then you meant what you said about going to Falkirk Tryst?' Colin inquired eagerly.

'I did. I shall set off in a two-three days to be in time for the October Tryst at Falkirk.'

'Father, could I be going along with you this time to drive the herd? I would like fine to have the charge of Black Torcull,' Colin begged eagerly.

James Cameron shook his head with decision. 'No, no! It is not to be thought of.'

'But Black Torcull is very obedient to me. I can handle him well. He is a good-tempered bull, really,' Colin pleaded.

'Aye, I'll grant you that you do handle him well, but droving is a hard business both for man and beast. Besides, we might be going further than Falkirk if Mr Barlow wants us to take the herd for him to England, which well he might, and him with an injured foot,' his father pointed out.

'I could do it, Father, I know I could,' Colin declared. 'And I have never been to Falkirk Tryst. Will you not let me go along with Angus?'

Though his father smiled at him, he still shook his head. 'No, Colin lad, there will be work for you on the farm. With myself and your brother Angus and old Donald away at the droving, there will be few enough left on the farm as it is to help your mother.'

'Oh, it is always "another time" when I ask, and I'll be thirteen before the year is out,' Colin said with rebellious disappointment.

'Oh, well, you've many a long year before you yet. That's enough now.'

'There's one thing I would like to ask,' Colin said rather diffidently.

'What is it, then?'

'Will you be getting as much for the bull at Falkirk — as much as Mr Laidlaw offered you, Father? I could not help hearing what he said as you stood by the byre. It was thirty-five pounds, was it not?

'Aye, that was his price,' Cameron nodded.

'That's a terrible great sum of money,' Colin said with awe.

James Cameron laughed aloud. 'Aye, maybe you think so, lad, but I know my bull is worth far more. It was the bull yon fellow really came after, not the stirks. I could see through him well enough.'

'Then — then —' Colin hesitated, then the words came out with a rush, 'what *is* Black Torcull worth, Father?'

'You may as well be knowing,' the farmer decided, after stroking his beard for a minute. 'A hundred and twenty guineas, no less.'

Colin let out a long low whistle of surprise.

'Aye, you may open your eyes, laddie,' his father chuckled. 'But that's right enough. Mr Barlow offered me eighty pounds for that bull last year when he was but half grown, but I said I would take a chance on him being worth more this year. I promised Thomas Barlow, though, that I would give him the first chance of buying Torcull. Thomas Barlow is an honest buyer. I have done business with him these many years and I can trust him.'

Colin looked at his father slightly puzzled. 'Then you would not have sold the bull to Mr Laidlaw all the time?'

'That I would not!'

'Then why — why —?' Colin began.

'Why did I seem to bargain with him?' His father finished the question. 'Ah, you've a lot to learn about the business of buying and selling cattle, my laddie. It's aye safe to let a man name his price, even though you do not mean to take it. But yon fellow Laidlaw was a rascal. He knew well enough that Black Torcull was a prize animal, but he thought that I knew less than he did. That is where he made the first mistake.'

'I was hoping you would not sell our bull to him.'

'What? For a quarter of the price put into my hand, less than ten pounds, maybe, and he leads away my prize bull? No, no, I am not so stupid as that. I'd have whistled long enough for the rest of my money from yon fine fellow, and if I went to look for him at Falkirk Tryst, is it likely he would have turned up to pay me? No, I have heard of his kind before. Come now, give me the milk pails while you go to water the bull and feed him. Remember to shut the door of the bull-pen when you have finished.'

James Cameron stopped and picked up a full milk pail in each hand and began to walk towards the house while Colin went to feed Black Torcull. This was the part of his work he loved best on the farm for he was very proud of the bull, and of the way he could handle the fierce-looking animal. He and Torcull the Black seemed to understand each other, and as Colin took water to him, he talked to the bull in a caressing voice.

'It's the grand bull you are, Torcull the Black. There has never been one like you at Drumbeg before. Fine would I like to walk with you to the Tryst at Falkirk, aye, and to England too. I'd be proud to be seen leading you. There will not be another bull like you at the Tryst.' Colin sighed a little, wishing that his father would relent and let him go to Falkirk with the herd. 'Good night to you, Torcull the Black,' he said, rubbing the bull's neck affectionately. Torcull gave a bellow, not loud, but as if speaking back to the lad. Colin laughed. 'It's saying good night to me you are, eh, Torcull?' He drew his brows together in a little frown. 'Wait! I will do a thing I have never done before on our farm at Drumbeg. I will lock the door of your bull-pen.'

Colin locked the door of the small stone out-house, and looked at the key in his hand. 'There was something told me to do that,' he whispered to himself, 'but I will not tell my father and brother for fear they laugh at me, but the key shall go under my pillow tonight. Good night, my bonnie Torcull.' He turned away from the bull-pen and went across to the plain farm-house and to the supper which his mother had prepared for them of kail brose.

That night Colin woke with a start. In the box bed

in the kitchen, a wooden bed built into an alcove in the wall where he slept with his brother Angus, Colin had had strange disturbed dreams of the black bull. He peered into the blackness of the room lit only by the red embers of the kitchen fire and at the square of the window, a dark blue against the night sky. He still felt uneasy, though he knew now that he had been dreaming, and at last he rose and crossed the kitchen and flattened his nose against the window-pane, trying to see the bull-pen across by the byre. Suddenly he stiffened and listened. From the farm-steading came stealthy sounds. One of the farm dogs gave a low growl and a sharp bark. In a second Colin was back at the bed and shaking Angus urgently by the shoulder.

'Angus! Angus! Wake up!' he cried. 'There's someone moving about by the byre.'

Angus turned over sleepily. 'What is it? What is it?' he mumbled. 'Surely it isn't time to get up yet?' He yawned and prepared to turn over again. Colin shook him harder.

'Angus, *will* you wake up? There's someone in the farm-yard who has no right to be there. *Wake up!*'

'Och, stop shaking me! What's to do?'

'Come to the window,' Colin said, pulling at his arm. Angus jumped out of bed and followed him. Colin pointed through the window. 'There! Over there! Over by the bull-pen! Look! Wait, the moon's coming from behind the cloud. See! Three men!'

Angus stared through the window. 'What are they doing? They're surely not trying to get into the bull-pen?' In his still sleepy state it took him a minute to take in what was happening.

'They've come to steal Black Torcull,' Colin cried. 'Quick! Quick! We must wake Father.'

They ran into the inner room and tugged at James Cameron's shoulder.

'Father! Father! Wake up! There are thieves after the bull.' In an instant James Cameron was fully awake. He leaped out of bed.

'Thieves! Let me get at them! Fling on your clothes, lads, and come with me. Where's my thick stick?'

The boys hastened to obey him and flung on kilts and jackets. Barefoot they ran with their father to the door and helped him to draw the bolts quickly. Mrs Cameron jumped up too. 'What is it, James?' she called after her husband.

'Cattle thieves, wife! Bide you there in the house,' her husband called back at her over his shoulder. Then, roaring: 'What are you doing there, you rogues?' he rushed out of the house, followed by the two boys. Before the thieves had hardly time to turn round from the bull-pen he was among them, wielding his stick with fury.

'Take that, and that, and that, you rascals!' he cried, dealing blows right and left.

'Stop! Stop! Mercy!' one of the men cried, shielding his face with his arm. Out of the corner of his eye, Colin saw one of the other men raise a weapon to take aim.

'Look out behind you! There's one with a pistol, Father!' he cried.

Like a wild-cat James Cameron leaped about and struck the muzzle of the flintlock pistol downwards. But quick as he was, he was too late to stop his attacker firing at him. The direction of the shot was deflected from his heart to his leg, however, and the bullet entered his shin below the knee. With a sudden cry of pain he sank to the earth. Angus hurled himself upon his father's assailant; he managed to squirm away from Angus's grasp, but not before Colin had dealt him a shrewd blow with his father's stick. Then the thieves fell back before the furious onslaught of the two boys.

'Run for your lives, men!' one of them cried, and they turned and fled. Angus took a step or two after them, then turned back to where his father was lying on the ground. Colin was already kneeling beside him.

'Father! Father! Are you badly hurt?' he cried.

'The villains have got me in the leg,' James Cameron groaned. 'I think the bone is broken. But guard the bull, lads. Do not let them be taking the bull.'

'The men have gone, Father,' Angus told him. 'They've run away. They had no liking for your stick about their shoulders.'

Mrs Cameron cane running from the house. She went white when she saw her husband lying on the ground. 'Is your father hurt, Angus?'

'The thieves have shot him in the leg,' Angus told her, wild with rage against the men.

'Oh, oh, James!' Mrs Cameron ran to him.

'Now, don't take on so, wife,' Cameron tried to calm her. 'It could have been far worse if I had not managed to strike down the pistol. Help me into the house, lads.'

Very gently the boys lifted their father and he placed his arms about their shoulders and was half-supported, half-carried into the farm kitchen. Mrs

Cameron hurried in before them and poked the fire to a blaze and set the kettle on it.

'We'll need hot water and bandages,' she said.

Grunting and groaning with pain, James Cameron swung into the kitchen and the boys lifted him into the box bed in the alcove by the fireplace.

'Does it hurt much, Father?' Colin asked anxiously.

'Not more than I can thole,' his father said, setting his lips together. He sank down thankfully upon the bed.

'Put the pillow under his head,' Mrs Cameron directed Colin. 'Now, let me look at that leg,' she said. Her face puckered in a serious frown. 'Bring the lamp nearer, Angus.' She looked more closely at the wound. 'Aye, the bullet's smashed the bone, right enough, and I fear it's still stuck in the leg. It'll need a doctor to get it out, I'm thinking.'

By this time old Donald the herdsman, had appeared from his bed in the barn and was peering bewildered through the door, while Betty, the milking lass, had come running from the cottage where she lived with her father Calum, the shepherd, and young John, her brother. Old Donald came forward and looked at the leg too.

'Was it thieves, master?'

'Aye. After the bull,' Cameron said. The old man needed no further explanation. He had lived in the days when there had been much cattle thieving in the Highlands, when one clan stole from another and thought it a brave thing to do, though those days were now past.

'Aye, the master will be needing a doctor. The bullet's ower deep in to get it out with a knife.'

'There's Doctor Mackinnon at Ballachulish. I'll saddle the horse and fetch him,' Angus offered.

'Aye, do that, Angus,' Mrs Cameron agreed. 'I'll bandage the leg above the knee so that he doesn't lose too much blood, but be as quick as you can.'

Angus wasted no time and in a minute or two his horse was heard coming from the stable and soon he was away down the road at a canter. Though he made as much haste as he could, it seemed a long time to the watchers waiting by the injured man before he returned with Doctor Mackinnon riding his big roan horse.

The doctor looked from one to another of the anxious faces in the lamp-light but he did not delay to ask any questions. He knelt beside Cameron and called for a bowl of hot water and some pieces of linen. Mrs Cameron had all ready and brought them to him. Very gently and tenderly the doctor swabbed the wound with the linen and hot water till he could see it clearly.

'Aye, the bullet's deep in, close to the bone,' he said. 'It will have to come out or the leg will never heal. The bone's broken too. Now, Cameron, can ye lie still, man, and grit your teeth while I get the bullet out. I'll have to probe for it, but I'll try to be as quick as I can.'

'Go on, doctor, I'll thole it,' the man said bravely. 'Hold me down on the bed, Angus, so I don't give a jump when the doctor probes, and you and Colin hold my hands, wife.'

Dexterous and quick as the doctor was, the touch of the probe in the wound made the perspiration break out on James Cameron's head and he turned sick and faint. Just when he felt he must cry out, the doctor gave an exclamation of triumph. 'Here it is! Here's the bit of lead that causing all the trouble.' He held up a small round bullet. 'You can let go of your father now Angus. The rest will be plain sailing after this. First to clean the wound with the water and linen. Aye, ye've healthy flesh, James Cameron. Ye'll soon heal,' he comforted the farmer.

'That's grand news,' Cameron managed to say.

'Now, hand me your father's stick, Colin. I'll use that for a splint. That'll keep the leg stiff till the bone's joined again.'

He bandaged the leg deftly to the splint and then rose to his feet.

'There, man, the leg's in a splint and well bandaged. Ye've stood that well, James Cameron. Ye're a tough man.'

'Thank you, doctor,' James Cameron replied a little faintly. 'It was good of you to turn out of your bed in the middle of the night to come to Drumbeg.'

'All in the day's work for a doctor, Mr Cameron, all in the day's work, or maybe I should say the night's work,' the doctor chuckled. 'Whiles I think I sleep more in the saddle than in my bed.'

Mrs Cameron had been busy preparing a meal for the doctor before he should go and she set it before him on the well-scrubbed table.

'Here's meat and drink for you, sir. It was very good of you to come,' she said gratefully.

'My duty, ma'am,' the doctor replied. 'I only wish I had hold of the black-hearted wretch who fired the shot at your good man. Cattle thieves, did ye say? Could you tell who they were, Cameron?'

'No, more's the pity. It was ower dark,' the farmer said.

'I do not think they sounded like men from Lochaber or Appin,' Angus remarked thoughtfully.

'No, neither do I,' Colin agreed with his brother.

'Mm, that's a strange thing now, cattle thieves,' the doctor commented, rather puzzled. 'A hundred years ago, no, even fifty, there were plenty of cattle thieves in the Highlands, but not since the new roads were built by General Wade.'

'Aye, but one hears of a case still now and again among the farmers when one goes to the cattle fairs. I heard of one last time I was at Falkirk Tryst,' Mr Cameron told the doctor. For a moment he looked startled, then he exclaimed: 'The Tryst, now! I wonder! There was a fellow here yesterday, a buyer from the Lowlands called Laidlaw, who was trying to get me to part with my bull. When I would not sell to him, he lost his temper and made all kinds of wild threats. Could he have been one of the thieves, now?'

'He could have been, Father. One of the thieves was a small man like him,' Colin declared.

'Aye, and Laidlaw threatened me that my bull would never reach Falkirk Tryst. Ah, well, we shall see. Tomorrow I start the droving down to Falkirk and I have half a mind to take a musket with me this time,' Cameron said.

Doctor Mackinnon stared at him. '*You'll* start the droving, James Cameron? *Tomorrow*?' he asked with surprise.

Cameron gave an impatient shrug with his shoulders. 'Well, maybe not tomorrow. I will give my leg a two-three days to heal.'

'A two-three days? Come, Mr Cameron, talk sense! Bones do not knit together in a two-three days,' the doctor warned him.

'I could follow the drove on my pony. I would not be *walking* after them, man!' Cameron protested impatiently.

'Now, listen to me, James Cameron,' the doctor said and his voice was very stern. 'If you set that foot to the ground inside a month, you'll be lame to the end of your days. You heed what I'm saying.'

The farmer stared at him aghast. 'A month, doctor! But in a month the Cattle Tryst will be over at Falkirk. I'll be too late to sell my bull then to the man I promised.'

'Well, it's either go lame for life or keep that foot off the ground. But if I were you, I'd leave the droving to these big strong lads of yours for once,' the doctor advised. 'Well, I must be on my way. Thank you for the meal, Mrs Cameron. I'll look in again in a day or two to see how the leg's healing.' He picked up his bag and nodded to them all. 'Now, you think over well what I've said to you, Cameron. Good day to ye all, for it will soon be here.'

Hardly had the door closed behind the doctor than James Cameron exclaimed in annoyance: 'That's a nice thing, now, that I cannot be taking my cattle to the market. You would think yon rascal Laidlaw had planned it so that I should not sell my bull. But I will not be beaten!' he said, pursing his lips and thrusting his chin out.

'Now, husband, mind what the doctor told ye.

Are ye wanting to go limping all your life?' his wife scolded.

'Wheesht, woman! Wait till you hear what's on my mind,' her husband exclaimed impatiently. 'I would not have that honest man, Thomas Barlow, think I had played him a false trick over the bull. Angus, you must take the cattle and the bull to Falkirk Tryst. Old Donald Maclean, the herdsman, can go with you.'

'I'll go gladly, Father, if ye'll trust me with the beasts,' Angus agreed, but he looked a little troubled. 'But the bull now?' he went on. 'The bull is work for one man alone.'

'Aye, I have thought of that,' his father answered. 'Colin shall go with you. He is good with the bull.'

Colin stared at his father, his mouth opening slowly, his eyes shining with delight, unable to believe what he had heard. To go as drover's lad and take the cattle to the Falkirk Tryst! It had been his dream so long.

'But Colin's ower young to walk barefoot over those long hill roads,' Mrs. Cameron objected.

'Oh, no, I'm not, Mother!' Colin cried, fearful lest his father should change his mind. 'Oh, Father, do you mean it? I am really to go to the Tryst at Falkirk?'

'Yes, my lad. After all, it is time you learned something of the droving. But mind well, you will answer to me if there is any mishap to Black Torcull,' his father warned him sternly.

'I will look after him with my own life,' Colin promised fervently.

Angus had been staring thoughtfully through the window as though puzzling something out. 'I cannot think why the thieves did not manage to get the door of the bull-pen open. They must have fumbled with it so long that they wakened Colin and gave us time to rush out at them.'

'That was because I locked the door of the bull-pen last night,' Colin explained with some natural pride that his action had defeated the robbers. 'The key is still under my pillow,' he said, producing it.

'What made you do that?' Angus asked, surprised. 'We have never locked our cattle up before at Drumbeg.'

'I did not like that cattle buyer from the south who came here yesterday,' Colin confessed, a little red-faced. 'There was something inside me like a voice in my head that told me to lock the door. Please do not laugh at me,' he added fiercely, but the others did not even smile.

'We are not laughing at you, Colin,' his father told him solemnly. 'It was a wise thing you did, and there is no doubt that prevented the bull from being stolen. You will do, my lad. I can see you are to be trusted with Black Torcull.' He turned to Angus. 'Now, Angus, you will start with the drove tomorrow. Listen to me carefully, now. You will go by way of King's House and Inveroran, Tyndrum, Glen Dochart, and Glen Ogle. . . .' The lovely Highland names fell like music from his lips, as the two boys came closer and sat beside the bed and listened, with old Donald nodding his head in agreement as he sat by the table. The candles burned low and guttered in their sconces as the daylight crept over the hill to the east and touched the window-pane to misty grey as James Cameron instructed his sons about the drove and the roads they were to take, at which places to rest and which places to avoid. Still the boys listened and there was no thought of sleep with them. The cows lowing in the byre stirred Angus to attention.

'Listen! The cows! It's daylight and milking time,' he cried. 'Come along, Colin.'

'Aye, you'd better be at the work, for you're a pair of hands less the day, more's the pity.' James Cameron said, sinking back on the bed with a slight groan.

'Go now and when you come back I'll have your porridge ready for pouring,' Mrs Cameron told them.

'Aye, and while you are taking it I will tell you about the tolls to be paid at the bridges and where you must take your stance at the Falkirk Market,' James Cameron said, his thoughts running ahead to the droving and the Tryst.

Colin snatched up a milk pail and hurried to the byre, his heart dancing with joy, for was not he going on the long drove to Falkirk, maybe even to England, and was not he to be trusted with Black Torcull, the best bull that had ever come out of Drumbeg?

Adventure on the Moor of Rannoch

The following morning Colin and Angus were up before the dawn and had rounded up the hundred stirks or young bullocks that they were to take to the cattle fair at Falkirk. It was a bright day in late September and the sun rose in a windless blue-grey sky. It would be nine or ten days before they reached the flat pastures at Stenhousemuir near Falkirk where the market was held, for they could not hurry the beasts. The drove roads led up hill and down dale over the grassy slopes where cattle could feed as they went along. Every drover liked to bring his animals into the market in fine condition, well fleshed, for then he would get a better price for them, so that meant the herd must feed well on the road and never be driven over fast or over far. James Cameron stressed this to his sons when they came to take leave of him. The hardy little Highland pony had been saddled and the two dogs, Sim and Rob, were crouched on the ground behind the herd, panting with their tongues lolling out of their mouths, impatient for the word of command that would set them moving the herd along.

'You are ready for the road then, Angus?' James Cameron asked, giving a sigh, for he hated to miss the October Tryst at Falkirk.

'Aye, Father. Old Donald and I will look after the stirks and Colin will lead the bull.'

'Good. Do not drive the beasts too fast, now, or they will lose flesh and then you will not get such a good price at the market. Ten to twelve miles a day is plenty. Take old Donald's advice. He knows the road well and where best to pasture the beasts. Give them a good midday rest, now.'

'I will do that, Father.'

'When you reach the cattle fair seek out Mr Thomas Barlow, the Cumberland buyer. They will tell you where to find him at the Falkirk Bank, for he does his business with them. Give him my respectful compliments and tell him what befell me that I cannot come to the Tryst.'

'Yes, I will mind what you say,' Angus replied, listening attentively.

'Show Mr Barlow the bull. My price is a hundred and twenty guineas. Ask Mr Barlow to name his price first, but do not sell the bull at a less price than I said.'

'It's aye safe to ask a man to name his price first, eh, Father?' Colin put in with a roguish look.

His father gave a chuckle. ''Deed it is! He might name a better price than the one you have in mind. You're learning fast, Colin, but see to it that you watch Black Torcull like the gold he is worth.'

'I will, I promise you,' Colin told him.

'It may be that Mr Barlow will buy the drove of stirks too,' his father continued. 'If he does, he might ask you to take them to England for him. It might be as well to oblige him, for he has always been a good customer, but see he pays you drovers' wages for it.'

'But how will you manage on the farm if we are long away?' Angus asked anxiously.

'Och, there is still Calum and young John. We shall be all right, for the harvest is in and there will no longer be the big herd to look after.'

Mrs Cameron came bustling in from the farm steading. 'I have packed oat-bread and cheese and oatmeal into the pony's saddle-bags for the journey,' she informed the boys. 'If there is not enough, then you must buy more at the farms on the way.'

'I cannot spare you but the one pony. I must keep the other here, for as soon as yon doctor says I can put foot to ground I shall need the pony to take me about the farm to see what is doing. Ten miles a day along a grassy road will not weary you overmuch, anyway,' Cameron said.

'Och, I shall have the bull to lead. I shall not want to be sitting on the pony,' Colin said proudly.

'Be taking care, now, Colin, and do not let the bull be leading *you*!' his mother warned.

'Aye, and when you sell the bull, take good care of the money you get for him, Angus,' his father said with some anxiety.

'Would you like me to put it in the bank at Falkirk?' Angus suggested.

James Cameron hesitated, a frown on his face. 'I have never been used to the ways of banks,' he said. 'It seems a chancy thing to be giving up your money to a stranger and only getting a piece of paper in return for it. I would rather you put it carefully in your sporran or at the bottom of the saddle-bags when you are droving.'

'Do you wish me to take gold or banknotes?' Angus asked.

'I like well to take gold, but this time you will only have the one pony and it might be ower heavy to carry. No, you can take notes, but never let them out of your reach, though.'

'I will be careful, Father,' Angus gave him his word.

'That is all, then. You will rest tonight at the Moor of Rannoch, near King's House, the inn there.'

'Yes,' Angus nodded.

'Will you not wear shoes as you do to the kirk, Colin?' his mother asked him, looking sideways at his bare feet. 'The roads might be rough.'

'Och, all my life I have run barefoot about Drumbeg. I'll be happier without them,' Colin said impatiently.

'The lad's feet are hard enough,' Cameron agreed. 'Well, if ye're quite ready, God speed ye all, and see ye sell the beasts well. Call up the dogs now.'

Colin whistled up the dogs. 'Come up, Rob! Up, Sim!'

The dogs needed no second bidding. In an instant they were running about behind the herd, urging them towards the farm road. Colin took a firm hold on Black Torcull's halter, and gave him a pull, and obediently the black bull began to shamble slowly behind the herd. Mrs Cameron ran after Colin and gave him a last embrace. 'Good-bye and be careful, now, Colin. Do as Angus bids ye. Good-bye, my laddie.'

She stood in the farm door looking after him a little anxiously and sadly as Colin set out with the herd on his first droving to the south, proudly leading Black Torcull. The sky was blue overhead and the road soft and grassy beneath his feet, and after he had given a backward wave to his mother, Colin whistled softly to himself as he and Torcull plodded after the herd. For a while the road wound by the shores of Loch Leven, then, after a time, it struck sharply inland into the Pass of Glen Coe.

That was a place to strike chill to the heart, with its tumbled heaps of ruined cottages and the mountains crowding dark above them. At a point where huge rocks almost barred the road, a torrent of water came tumbling down the glen with a roar like thunder. The cattle crowded together and jostled one another as if even they were a little afraid. Colin was careful to keep Black Torcull well behind and out of reach of their tossing horns.

The gentle lowing of the herd and the calls of Angus and old Donald to the dogs were music in Colin's ears. They came out of the pass into the wild open beauty of the Moor of Rannoch with the setting sun glinting on its many tiny lochans or lakes and its running streams. It was here where they were to make their camp-fire that night and to rest the herd, close to the lonely inn of King's House. The dogs had little trouble in rounding the animals up, for the cattle were too tired to stray far, and even Torcull the Black did not snort quite so fiercely as usual.

Angus circled his arm around his head and shouted to the dogs. 'Up, Rob, up! Bring them in, Sim.'

Barking and snapping harmlessly at the heels of the stragglers the herd dogs brought them up into a circle on the moor, and the beasts stood there patiently, nodding their heads with the wide sweep of horns and lowing now and again.

'Well, that's the herd gathered, Donald,' Angus said with satisfaction, as Colin brought up the rear with the bull.

'Aye, they'll do well enough here. This is where the master always halts them,' Donald replied. 'They will not be straying far for they are weary and there is good grass in this place. Now I will light a small fire for us to cook our oatmeal.'

Angus laughed. 'Trust an old drover like you to make himself comfortable, Donald! Did you bring the wood for the fire with you, for there is nothing but wet peat here?'

'I saw to it there were some sticks in the pony's pack, and I gathered some twigs on the way too, and here is a *dried* peat I brought with me from the farm,' the old man chuckled.

Colin viewed all these preparations with wonder. 'Surely you have not brought peats to last us all the way to Falkirk, Donald?' he asked.

'Losh, no, lad!' Donald exclaimed. 'Further on there are woodlands when we leave the moors, but this fire will give us a little cheer on windy Rannoch. Now, where's the flint and tinder in my sporran?' Donald produced them and by striking the flint against the steel made a spark which ignited the tinder. Stooping down, the old man gathered a tuft or two of dry grass and set it alight, added the twigs and one or two of his sticks, and soon had a fire blazing away. When it was going well he took the porridge pot from the saddle-bags and the oatmeal, and taking water from a little stream close by, he soon had the water boiling and put in handfuls of meal and stirred it with a stick. This was their supper for the night, with a crust of oat-bread and cheese, but they were used to such simple fare when droving. As they ate the dusk began to steal among the hollows of the hills.

'We must watch the herd all night, especially the bull,' Angus said. 'We don't want to lose any of our beasts to cattle thieves who might steal up in the darkness and drive off one or two.'

'But surely the dogs would give us warning if any strangers came near?' Colin asked.

'Aye, they'd bark, but there are ower many paths among these hills where thieves could escape. Besides, other droves than ours may come this way. This is the meeting place for droves from Glen Etive as well as from Glen Coe. I thought we should have met with some of them here,' Angus explained to his young brother.

'How will you divide the watches now?' Donald asked.

'Colin can take the first watch, for it is not likely that there will be much stirring early in the night,' Angus decided. 'When you feel sleepy, Colin, you can wake me and I will take the middle turn. That leaves you the few hours before daybreak, Donald.'

'That suits me well,' Donald agreed with satisfaction. 'I am always awake long before daylight.'

'Before we wrap ourselves in our plaids to sleep I want to go to the King's House Inn,' Angus said. 'My father told me to ask the landlord there for news of a drover named Kennedy. He might be returning from the south and he could give us news of the roads.'

'Aye, Kennedy is a good man. I think I will go with you to the inn, Angus, and talk with him too. We might pick up some news from him and from the other travellers from the south what kind of roads to expect, and whether the rivers can be forded, for there has been a good deal of rain, or whether we must go by the bridges and pay the tolls.'

'Then we will take the pony, Donald, and you can ride him. That way we'll get there and back quicker. You will be all right, Colin, to be left alone with the herd for an hour?'

'Why, yes, I have the dogs, and the moon rises early,' Colin replied, quite unafraid at the prospect.

'Very well, we will get on the way at once. It is not far. All the same, tether Black Torcull close beside you. There are often mists that rise suddenly over the moor on a hot day.'

'I will keep good watch, Angus,' Colin promised.

'Here is the lantern. Keep the flint and tinder handy to light it and do not go to sleep till we come back.'

Colin nodded easily, and the two of them set off, Donald riding the pony and Angus hanging on to the stirrup and running alongside. As they went along Colin caught snatches of their conversation from time to time, till the road topped a low bank and dropped behind it and they were out of sight. Colin stirred the peat a little and added to the fire some dried heather roots he had gathered. Then he sat down beside it, still keeping the rope by which he had led the bull in his hands. The animal cropped the grass close by him. Colin began to talk to him for company as the dusk grew greyer.

'Well, now, Torcull the Black, it seems we must keep each other awake, and the dogs too. Are you awake, Sim?' he called softly and he was answered by a whine from the dog. 'Good lad!' Colin called back to him. 'Are you there, Rob?' Rob gave a short sharp bark. It was comforting to Colin to know the dogs were watching with him. He drew his plaid closer about his shoulders and looked around him as the dark gathered.

'It is very quiet here, much quieter than at the farm,' he said aloud to himself. 'And the mist is coming down off the hill above Glen Etive. I'll sing a bit for company and to pass the time, I think.'

Colin sang softly in a clear tuneful voice one of the plaintive Highland songs, and then another. The dogs crept closer to him.

Colin fed the fire with some dried stems of heather, but the blaze only seemed to make the night darker. 'Perhaps it might be as well if I lighted the lantern now,' he said to himself, and he lifted a smouldering twig from the fire, blew on it, and lighted the lantern. The mist swirled about him and blotted the lights of the inn from his sight and the dark seemed to creep in nearer to the fire. Colin looked anxiously about him. 'I cannot see the animals well now. I hope Angus will not be at the inn too long.'

Rob, the collie, lifted his head from the ground near Colin's foot and gave an uneasy whine.

'What is it, Rob?' Colin asked quickly. 'Did you think you heard something?' The dog rose from the ground and stood stiff-legged, his nose pointing to the moor. Suddenly the bull bellowed.

'Torcull's uneasy too,' Colin muttered, a little fearful himself. 'How thick the mist has grown!'

Sim, too, gave a short sharp bark. Suddenly, from a distance, there came a faint cry. Colin stood perfectly still, listening. The two dogs at his feet watched him, never taking their eyes from his face, waiting the word of command.

'There was someone calling for help,' Colin whispered in a tense voice, and listened again.

Again the cry came: 'Help! Help!' It was a girl's voice.

'It is a girl calling!' Colin exclaimed. 'Where is she? I cannot tell, for the mist curls round like smoke. Oh, if only she would call again!'

As if in answer again there came a cry of terror. 'Help! Oh, help me!'

Colin snatched up the lantern and ran through the wool-like mist shouting as he ran: 'Where are you? I'm coming.' The dog Rob ran alongside him. 'Stay you there, Sim!' Colin cried to the other dog. 'Now, help me to find her, Rob.' Obediently the dog ran from one side to the other in wide circles as though rounding up a stray bullock.

'Here! Oh, help quickly!' The girl's voice sounded near at hand and the dog barked sharply and looked to Colin for direction. Colin took hold of him by the collar. The mist hid the girl from him. 'What is it? What's the matter?' he called.

'Oh, help me! I'm fast in the bog. I'm sinking!'

'In the bog?' Colin exclaimed, terrified. Well he knew of the black peat bogs of the Moor of Rannoch where a man or a beast could sink and be sucked under the dark ooze.

'I'm up to my knees and I can't get my feet out. Every time I try I only sink deeper.' She began to sob. 'Oh, the black bog is pulling me down into it!'

Colin took a few cautious steps forward, feeling his way with his feet, testing his weight on the ground as he went, still holding on to Rob.

The girl heard him and called in alarm. 'Oh, mind you don't fall in too! But try to get me out! Oh, do get me out!'

Colin held his lantern aloft. There she was, just a few paces away from him, in one of the saucer-like hollows made by the bog.

'I dare not come nearer. The ground is getting soft and spongy,' he said. 'Keep still. Don't struggle. You'll only sink deeper. I'll throw the end of my plaid towards you. Try to catch it.'

He unwound the plaid from his shoulders and threw the end of it towards her. She reached out to catch it, but could not stretch far enough and the end of it fell short.

'Oh, I can't!' she sobbed desperately.

'Try again!' Colin said, making a cast with the plaid as if it were a fishing line.

Again the girl snatched at it; she just missed it as it swung by her, but this time her fingers caught the fringe.

'Oh! Oh, I almost had it then!'

Colin threw it towards her again, this time with a better aim.

'There! Have you got it now?'

'Yes, yes, just the end of it!'

'Then hold tight and I'll pull.'

Colin laid hold of the plaid and pulled his hardest. From the bog came gasping, slithering sounds as the girl struggled to free herself.

'I can't get a strong enough grip,' Colin said desperately. 'Can you wrap any of the plaid round your arm?'

'No, no! It isn't long enough. I can only just clutch an end of it with my hand!' She sounded frenzied.

Colin made another mighty effort but still the girl was held by the bog. 'Oh, I'm not strong enough to pull you out,' Colin exclaimed, panting, and pulling his hardest. There was a rending tearing sound and the girl sank back into the ooze with a handful of torn plaid in her fist. Colin staggered backwards with the rest of the plaid.

'Oh, what shall we do?' he cried, in an agony himself.

The girl began to sob and moan aloud. Colin took a grip on his fear.

'Listen to me,' he said sternly. 'Stop weeping like that. It won't help us. Keep very still and don't thrash about or kick. Keep your arms out of the bog. I'm going to get a rope. I'll leave the dog on this firm bit of ground beside you so I can easily find you again.' He touched the dog. 'Stay here, Rob,' he said. The dog crouched obediently upon the ground and Colin snatched up the lantern and ran back to the herd.

'The rope that tethers Torcull! That's the thing!' he said to himself as he ran. He called to the bull: 'Torcull! Torcull! Where are you in this mist?'

As if in answer there came a sharp bark from Sim,

the dog which had been left to guard the bull, and a bellow from Torcull himself.

'There you are!' Colin exclaimed in relief and ran forward to loosen the tethering rope from the boulder to which it had been tied. 'If only Angus had left the pony! I could have used the pony to drag her out,' he said desperately. Suddenly he had an idea. At Drumbeg they often used cattle to draw the plough.

'I've got it!' he cried aloud. 'I'll take Torcull. He's strong. Come on, Torcull, come on! There's work for you to do.' He began to pull the bull forward by the rope. Slowly the animal began to move at his own unhurried pace.

'Oh, Torcull, come quicker! Come quicker!' Colin urged him, tugging harder. 'At his heels, Sim! Snap at his heels!'

The dog dashed forward and barked sharply behind the bull, running close to his hind legs. Torcull gave a bellow and began to head forward at a kind of gallop. This time Colin felt himself dragged forward by the rope. He pulled back with his weight on it.

'Now, steady, steady, Torcull! I mustn't have you in the bog too. Where's Rob? Stop, Torcull! Oh this thick mist! Rob! Rob!'

The other dog appeared out of the murky darkness with a bark.

'Head the bull off, Rob! Head him off!' Colin cried.

Neatly the dog halted the bull in his headlong dash towards the bog.

'Where are you? Are you all right, lass?' Colin cried anxiously peering with the lantern to see if he could find the girl again. She answered him from a few yards away.

'Yes, I'm here. A bit deeper, but not so far as my waist yet. I've kept my arms out.'

'Good! Now can you catch the noose at the end of this rope?' Colin asked, setting the lantern on the ground again and swinging the rope towards her.

'Yes, yes, I'll try.'

She peered towards him where she could just see his figure dimly by the light of the lantern, and waited for the swing of the rope. At the second try she managed to grab hold of it.

'I've got it!' she cried.

'Good! Now, can you open the noose and put the rope round your waist under the armpits?' Colin asked.

The girl struggled with the noose and opened it wider and slipped it over her head, and then first one arm through and over it and then the other.

'I've done it. It's round my chest!' she cried.

'I'm going to pull the noose tight,' Colin warned her. 'There! Is that all right?'

'It's tight about my ribs but I'll bear it,' the girl said.

'Now, try to help yourself out of the bog when the pull comes. I am tying the other end of the rope round my bull's horns.' Quickly Colin slipped the noose at the other end over Torcull's wide horns. 'Now, forward, Torcull!' he said, giving the beast a light blow on its flanks. The bull took a pace forward, then stopped. 'On, Torcull! Move on!' Colin urged him, but the bull seemed to turn obstinate and set his legs firmly on the ground. 'Oh, pull, Torcull, pull!' Colin cried in a frenzy. 'At his heels, Rob and Sim! Send him on!'

Both dogs barked and snarled about the hind legs

of Torcull. The bull gave a bellow and made a leap forward away from the bog. The rope tightened between him and the girl.

'Oh, it hurts, it hurts, but I'll bear it!' the girl cried as the rope galled her sides and held her so close she felt she could hardly breathe.

'Bear it for a minute. We've *got* to pull you out!' Colin shouted.

There were horrible sucking noises from the bog and another cry of pain from the girl.

'There! There! You're coming out! The rope's slackening. Again! Again, Torcull!' Colin whacked the bull on his haunches and Sim snapped at his heels. The great bull started forward at a run. There were stumbling dragging sounds from the bog.

'Oh, I'm out, I'm out!' the girl cried. 'I've got my feet out now. The bull's pulled me out. Oh, I'm on firmer ground now.'

Colin hung with all his weight on the rope between the bull and the girl. 'Ease off, now, Torcull, ease off!' he commanded. 'Head him off, Rob!'

The dog ran about to the bull's head and danced about on the ground before him. The bull stood stock still, bewildered, with one dog at his heels and the other before him. Colin took a short hold of the rope near his head.

'Stop, Torcull! Stand still.' The bull, trembling a little, obeyed him.

'There, lass, give me your hand,' Colin said, assisting the girl to her feet. 'Let me help you to pull the rope off.'

Once the rope was off the girl heaved a great sigh of relief and began to chafe her bruised sides.

'Well, now you're safe and sound.'

Suddenly the girl began to weep aloud. 'Oh, thank you, thank you, lad! I was near death then. Oh, what if you had not heard me call? Oh, oh! I cannot stop weeping.' Her whole body shook with convulsive sobs. Colin stared at her in confusion, hardly knowing how to deal with such terror-stricken tears.

'Stop, now,' he said awkwardly, taking her by the arm. 'You're shaking with the cold. That's what it is. Come to the camp-fire and dry yourself.'

The girl took control of herself with an effort. 'I — I am sorry,' she said. 'I do not know what makes me weep when it is all over.'

'It is because you were too frightened to give way before,' Colin said wisely. 'I was frightened too. Now, Torcull, you lead us both back to the herd.' He urged the beast on, and Torcull moved quietly forward as Colin led him by the rope.

'Why, it is as though the bull understood you!' the girl exclaimed in surprise, forgetting her tears.

'Sometimes I think he does. I talk to him a lot,' Colin said simply.

'Do you, now? I have never known such a tame bull before,' she answered.

'Och, he is not so tame with strangers, I promise you,' Colin said with a laugh. 'Ah, there is our camp-fire still shining through the mist,' he cried with relief.

'Never have I been so glad to see a camp-fire before!' the girl exclaimed thankfully as she sank down beside it.

Colin stirred the embers and put on more dried heather and soon had the fire blazing cheerfully. He turned to the girl. 'Here! Your gown is all wet from the bog. Wrap my plaid about you.'

Thankfully the shivering girl swathed it about her shoulders and stretched out her feet towards the warmth of the fire.

'Wait now, while I tether Torcull again before he strays,' Colin said, and he caught the bull by the rope end and fastened it securely to a stone. Then he set Sim to guard the animal and returned to the fire again.

'There! Do you feel better now?' he asked the girl.

'This good fire and your plaid keep the mist and cold from biting into my bones,' she told him. Then she remarked in surprise: 'But surely you are not driving a big herd all alone?'

'Oh, no! My brother and a herdsman are with me,' Colin told her. 'They've gone to the King's House Inn to have a crack with whoever is there and to learn what news they can of the drove roads. But what are you doing alone, too, on the Moor of Rannoch?' he asked her with curiosity in his turn. 'It is a strange thing for a lass to be here all alone in this wild place at night, surely?'

'I have been at the King's House Inn too,' the girl told him. 'I — I was going back to my folk.'

'Are you a shepherd's lass, then, maybe?'

'No, I am not that,' the girl said, but it was as though she was reluctant to tell him what she was.

'Perhaps you work then at the King's House Inn,' Colin hazarded. 'There will be a great cooking of broth there and setting of meals before strangers, I have no doubt.'

'No, I am not a serving maid,' the girl told him

with a little toss of the head. She stared into the fire a minute, and then, as though she had made up her mind to say more, she began to speak in a hesitating fashion, looking at Colin to see how he would take it. 'I — I — had been there to sell my pots and pans and — well — perhaps to earn a little money by telling fortunes.'

'Telling fortunes?'

'Yes. I am — well — you may as well be knowing. I am a tinker's lass.'

'A gipsy?' Colin asked.

'Yes, if you like to call me that,' the girl said a trifle shortly.

'I have seen them sometimes at the farm door asking my mother if they could mend our pots or sell her some pegs or baskets,' Colin remarked.

'I'll be bound your mother turned them away sharply then,' the girl said with a sourish kind of smile.

'I would not say that she did not,' Colin answered honestly, and added: 'She thinks, you see —' He broke off in some confusion.

'Go on! She thinks we are rogues and thieves. Well, maybe some of us are, but it is a hard life, a tinker's. You folk sleeping soft in good homes do not understand it,' she said a little scornfully.

'I am very sorry,' Colin replied simply. 'See. I have here in my pocket some oat-bread. Could you be eating a piece of it, now?'

'Could I? Oh, it's hungry that I am!' the girl said ravenously, stretching out her hand at once.

Colin gave her the bread. She took a mouthful, then paused, and looked at him and said gravely: 'I thank you — boy.'

'My name is Colin Cameron,' he told her.

'Then I thank you, Mr Colin Cameron.' The girl laughed a little.

'And your name?'

'Bethia,' the girl replied. 'It means wisdom,' she told him solemnly.

'But do you not have a second name?'

'Oh, yes, all my people are called McFie,' the girl said carelessly. 'But it does not matter, my second name.'

'Where is your family now, Bethia?'

'Their tents are a mile away round a shoulder of yon hill.'

'What did you do with your pots and pans? Did you sell them all at the inn?'

The girl gave a start. 'Oh, dear! I lost them all in the bog. Oh, it's the wicked beating I'll get from my uncle when I get back! I was taking a short cut across the moor to our camp when the mist came down and then I lost my way indeed, and the next I knew I was plunged up to the knees in the bog, pots, pans and all.'

'But maybe you did well at the fortune telling and your uncle will not be angry.'

Bethia shrugged her shoulders. 'Och, there were few to cross the gipsy's palm with silver at the King's House Inn.'

'I would like to know how you tell fortunes,' Colin remarked with some curiosity.

'Shall I tell yours?'

'Yes,' Colin replied eagerly. 'But I have no silver to cross your hand,' he added, rather crestfallen.

'I take no silver from you, Colin Cameron!' the girl replied proudly. 'And I shall not need to look at your hand either. I shall not tell *you* the foolish stories I make up for silly women at their doors. Listen to me,' she said urgently, 'for there are times when I have the sight, truly. Do you believe me?'

Colin did not laugh. 'Go on! Tell me!' he said simply.

Bethia stared into the red embers of the fire and began speaking slowly. 'A man will ask you to take a long journey,' she said. 'Go, and do not be afraid. For you there will always be the long road — many long roads, but they will lead you in the end to success, yes, and wealth, but the wealth will not matter so much to you as your own honest name among men. Are you laughing at me?' she asked fiercely.

Colin shook his head gravely. 'No. What else do you see?'

'There is sharp fear in your heart, but do not despair. What you will lose will be restored to you again, if you have courage.'

'I will remember it.'

'You will meet many strangers soon,' the girl went on. 'One will seem your friend, yet is your enemy; but one who seems an enemy will be your friend.'

'That seems a riddle to me.' Colin shook his head.

Bethia got to her feet suddenly. 'That is all. I cannot see more. I am tired. I must go now to find my people.'

'Can you find your way?' Colin asked doubtfully.

'Yes. Look now. The mist is lifting and the moon is rising. Good-bye, Colin. I shall not forget what you and Torcull have done for me this night. Perhaps it may be that some day I shall help you too.'

'Good-bye, Bethia. I shall remember what you have told me,' Colin said gently.

'Good-bye,' she called over her shoulder, dropping his plaid to the ground. 'Look for me at Falkirk, Colin.'

So Bethia vanished into the night and Colin huddled over the camp-fire thinking of the things she had told him, and then all at once feeling very tired and wondering how long it would be till Angus and Donald came back. He thought of his father and mother at Drumbeg and wondered if they were thinking of him under the stars. Torcull cropped now and again at the short grass beside Colin, who took hold of the rope that tethered the bull and was comforted to have the animal near him. Gently he hummed a little tune to keep himself awake till Angus and Donald should return. The dog Sim crouched down beside him and every now and again his ears would give a flick as he listened for strange sounds on the Moor of Rannoch.

Half an hour later, when Colin was almost dozing, the dog gave a low growl. Colin sat up immediately.

'What is it, Sim? Do you hear Angus and Donald coming back?'

The dog growled again, his hackles rising.

'Surely it must be Angus and Donald, but that's the growl you give when you hear a stranger approaching. Thank goodness the mist has cleared.' Just then he saw a bobbing lantern coming across the moor towards him and he heard the dull thud of the pony's hoofs on the grassy road.

'That's Angus and Donald right enough,' he said with some relief. 'But I think there is another man with them too. I can see three figures, and the third is either a hunchback or he carries something heavy on his back. Well, we shall soon see.'

Sim's growl rose to a sharp bark. 'Quiet, Sim! Lie down,' Colin ordered.

Angus's voice called to him across the moor. 'It's all right, Colin. We have got a friend with us, so hold the dogs back.'

'Back, Sim! Down, Rob!' Colin commanded as the three men approached.

'Well, here is our camp, and this is my brother Colin, Mr McQuaid,' Angus announced to the stranger.

'A good evening to you, sir,' Colin replied politely.

'Mr McQuaid is a packman. He is on his way to the Tryst at Falkirk to sell his goods at the fair there,' Angus explained. 'He would like to travel in our company.'

''Deed, aye,' the packman nodded. 'The more of us there are, the better protection from thieves for both packman and drover. Besides, it's company on the road and I aye like company. It makes the way seem shorter.'

Colin eyed the talkative little man with reserve. Something made him ask: 'But shall we not go too slowly for you, Mr McQuaid? We can only go at the pace of our cattle. We cannot hurry them or they will not bring such a good price at Falkirk.'

The packman patted his shoulder in a rather familiar fashion. 'Ah, I see you have the makings of a good drover, my laddie. But a slow pace suits me weel enough. It gives me time to call at the farms as we pass by them and to show the good wives my pack. There's aye a bit of business done along the roadside, ye ken.'

Even Donald was looking a little puzzled and

"A good evening to you, young gentleman," Mr. McQuaid said

as though he was not very sure if he wanted Mr McQuaid's company either.

'We shall not be passing a great many farms,' he remarked. 'The drove roads wind ower the moors.'

'Enough for the day's business for me,' McQuaid said easily. 'I can make my way to the farms and rejoin ye at night. It's the night when the wee bit company is a good thing.'

Colin considered him gravely. 'You do not speak like a Highlander, Mr McQuaid.'

McQuaid laughed. 'Ye're the one for noticing things now, my laddie, are ye no'? 'Deed, I'm no' a Highlander. My hame's in Edinburgh.'

'You are a far cry from your home then, Mr McQuaid.'

'Och, we packmen get around, ye ken. We do a bit of buying as weel as selling. Would ye like to take a look at my pack, now, my laddie?'

'I am sorry. I have no silver to spend,' Colin replied with stiff politeness.

'Oh, I'm not after selling you anything,' the man told him. 'It's just to let you see what I'm carrying. For interest, ye ken?'

'Well, for interest, then,' Colin agreed, hesitating.

The packman spread out his pack beside the fire and set the lantern by it. 'Look now, here are stockings hand-knit that I bought in Skye. They'll sell weel to the English cattle buyers. They like our Scottish hand-knit goods. Aye, and here's a length of hand-made tweed from Harris.'

'So you have been in the islands, then?' Donald commented.

'I have so, Donald. And here are ribbons that I

sell for fairings, and silk, too, for the farmers to take to their wives from the Falkirk Tryst. And pins and needles and threads, aye, and scissors and sharp razors too. There's a bead necklace as weel. It's a two-way trade, ye ken. I both buy and sell at the farms.'

'Aye, but I'll take my word ye get a profit from both,' old Donald chuckled.

The packman slapped him on the back and let out a roar of laughter. 'Aye, ye're right there, man, ye're right, or how else would poor men like me live?'

Colin stared at the pack. 'It is a marvel to me that you carry so much and yet you pack up everything so neatly.'

'Och, that is one of the tricks of the trade, my lad. Look now. Here is an English knife that folds up. Would ye no' like to have that?' The packman picked it up and held it out to him.

'I cannot be buying things when I have no money,' Colin said sharply.

'Ah, but when ye get to Falkirk the siller will roll in when ye sell the cattle. I'll give you credit till then.'

'The buying and selling of the herd is with my brother and not with me. I shall not be handling the money. I only look after our bull.'

'Oh, so you're the one who looks after the fine bull?' the packman asked sharply.

'How do you know that he is a fine bull?' Colin retorted equally sharply. 'You have not seen him by daylight.'

'Oh, it is a byword in the inns that fine bulls come from Drumbeg,' McQuaid replied hastily. 'I suppose this one will be as good as the rest.'

'He is better than any we ever had,' Colin said with pride.

"Deed, now, is he? You must be the clever one with him to have the care of him like that,' the man said in an oily tone, as though he was anxious to win Colin's good opinion. 'But this knife, now, look! I have made a good profit today. I will *give* you the knife, if you would like it, for I have taken a fancy to you.'

Colin drew back, putting his hands behind him and shaking his head. 'Oh, no! I could not be taking it like that. I cannot pay for the knife and I have done nothing to earn it.'

'Aye, ye have your pride, I see. Nane like the Highlanders for pride!' The packman shook his head. 'Weel, it's no' a bad thing when it's joined to honesty in a young lad,' he agreed. 'But maybe when we reach Falkirk ye'll ken me better and change your mind. By then we'll be better acquent, and you can surely take a gift from a friend.'

'I will wait till I get to Falkirk, if you please,' Colin replied.

Angus put in a question. 'Have ye heard any word now, in your travels, Mr McQuaid, whether the rivers are low enough for us to cross with the cattle at the fords, or must we go by the bridges? There was a deal of heavy rain earlier in the week.'

'Aye. So there was,' McQuaid agreed. 'I did hear most of the drovers had taken their cattle across the bridges, but that would cost them a lot in toll money, ye ken.'

'Yes, my father said we were to use the fords where we could, so we would not have to pay the bridge tolls on the beasts.'

'Aye, it costs a lot at twopence the beast when ye've to go by the bridges,' the packman nodded. 'I'll tell ye what I'll do. I'll go ahead o' ye and ask at the farms what the rivers are like, and meet ye again afore ye reach them.'

'That's very obliging of you,' Angus said.

'Och, it's a downright shame we should have to pay such heavy toll at the bridges. Folk on the road do what they can for each other. Besides, a packman likes the company of honest men when there are so many thieves about.'

'I think we should wrap ourselves in our plaids and get some sleep,' Angus suggested. 'We must be early astir in the morning. I'll keep watch for a while, Colin looks sleepy.'

It was in Colin's mind to tell Angus and Donald about finding Bethia in the bog and rescuing her, but the presence of the stranger kept him silent. Perhaps it was something about McQuaid's glib tongue that put him off, but he felt he did not want the packman to know of his strange adventure. Instead he turned away.

'I will tether Black Torcull to this upstanding stone,' he said. 'I shall keep my hand on the rope all night. That way I'll know if the bull grows restless and tries to stray.'

'Is that the way ye do it, lad?' McQuaid asked with ill-disguised interest. 'Ye've a great conscience about looking after yon beast.'

'My father trusted me with him,' Colin said simply.

Donald yawned. 'Well, I'm for sleep. Wake me when it's my turn to watch, Angus.'

'I will, Donald.'

'I'll take a turn at the watching too, if ye like,' the packman offered.

'No, Mr McQuaid, thank you,' Angus answered politely. 'It is our duty to be watching our own beasts. My father would have it so.'

'Then I'll be saying good night to ye all,' McQuaid said, rolling his own plaid about him and putting his head on his pack for a pillow. There was a chorus of 'Good nights', then all was silence. Colin lay awake for a time looking at the stars above him and the moon sailing above the heights of Achruach. He took a firm hold on Torcull's rope. 'Good night, Black Torcull,' he whispered to the bull.

The Stranger at the Ford of Frew

Over the grassy roads by Inveroran and Tyndrum,
Glen Dochart and Glen Ogle, Lubnaig and Callander
came the herd. Behind the beasts, Angus and Colin
plodded, Colin leading the bull by his halter, taking care not to hurry the animals. Old Donald
brought up the rear, sometimes riding the pony,
and McQuaid, the packman, kept alongside them.
Now and again he would leave them and go to
find customers at the farms, but would always
rejoin them further along the road before sunset.
He seemed to know his way well about the countryside. Angus and Donald enjoyed his company for
he had many a merry tale to tell by the camp-fire
at night. Even the dogs grew to know him and no
longer growled when he came near, though always
Colin had a queer feeling of uncertainty about the
packman. Perhaps it was because he found McQuaid
a thought too friendly and flattering to him, though
Colin agreed with Angus that the packman was
useful to them in finding places where the rivers
could be forded, so helping them to avoid bridges.
This saved them a great deal of money in paying
the bridge tolls.

As they wound their way down the hillsides they
saw other herds on the drove roads before them,

Over the grassy roads came the herd

all heading for Falkirk Tryst. In this unhurried way they came in nine days' time to the winding river of the Forth among the green flat lands of Flanders Moss and Blair Drummond, and saw, rising before them on a great rock, the grim fortress of Stirling Castle hanging above the smoke of the many chimneys in the town. Colin stood still on the little hill and stared across the river almost unable to believe his eyes.

Angus laughed aloud at him. 'Come on, Colin! How long are you going to stand on the hillside staring? Bring Black Torcull along, now.'

Colin, astonished, continued to stare. 'Angus, Angus, is that a *town*, that place in the distance?'

'Aye, that's Stirling town right enough, built round the foot of the castle.'

Colin drew a deep breath. 'I never thought there would be so many houses in all the world!' he declared. It was all so new and strange to this boy who had lived among the mountains all his life.

''Deed, you've seen nothing yet, Colin!' Angus laughed. 'Stirling is not a very big town really, not so big as the English towns.'

'I cannot believe there is a bigger place,' Colin said, shaking his head. 'And the houses! They look so — so *tall*, as though there are houses built on top of houses, and more after that, if you look at the rows of windows. They are not like our low thatched houses at Drumbeg.'

'Indeed they are not!' Angus agreed. 'But wait till you have seen these fine houses closer. We shall have to cross the river Forth by Stirling Bridge.'

Donald was gazing towards the bridge shading his

eyes with his hand. He was looking rather troubled. 'To me it looks as if we shall be a long time before we get across the bridge,' he said. 'Look at the road leading to the bridge, Angus. Why, it's thick with cattle, at least three miles before Stirling.'

Angus shaded his eyes in his turn and looked. 'The beasts do not seem to be moving at all,' he agreed. 'I wonder if we shall get our herd across before nightfall?' The ground here is not so good for pasture. It is too close to the river if they stray.'

Donald pointed along the road. 'Look ye there! Here comes Mr McQuaid along the road carrying his pack.'

The packman had sighted them on the low hill and was waving his arm to them and signing them to stay where they were. As he approached within hailing distance he called out to them: 'Wait, Angus! Do not come down on to the road. Stay on the hillside.'

'What is happening along there?' Angus shouted back to him.

'The road is blocked with cattle. The droves can neither get forward nor go back.'

'Are they not going across the bridge, then?' Angus asked, puzzled.

''Deed they are not! The bridge-keeper will not let any more across,' the packman informed him.

'How is that?' Angus demanded.

'Wait till I come up with you, lad. I'll tell you then,' the packman said, puffing a little. Angus waited patiently, halting the herd till McQuaid should mount the hill and come up with them.

'There is an argument between the bridge-keeper

and the drover about the tax to be paid to cross the bridge,' he told them.

'But surely the bridge-keeper is not holding up all the cattle droves going to the Tryst because of that?'

'Och, aye! It seems that the drover stampeded his cattle across the bridge so fast that the bridge-keeper could not count them. He says there were eight score beasts, and the drover swears there were but six, and the bridge-keeper is counting the drove ahead of him. The drover will not pay the extra three shillings that the bridge-keeper demands.'

'But what can the bridge-keeper be doing about it when the cattle have already crossed?' Donald asked.

McQuaid laughed heartily. 'Why, man, he will not let the drover cross after them! It looks as if his beasts will have to market themselves at the Tryst if the argument does not end soon.'

Angus looked disgusted and anxious. 'And the bridge-keeper is holding up all the droves behind him just for three shillings?'

'Aye, that's the way o' it,' the packman nodded his head. 'Says the bridge-keeper, "That's a fine rascally trick to send the cattle across the bridge so fast that I could not be counting them. There were eight score at least." Says the drover, "How could ye tell if ye could not count them?" "There were eight score," says the bridge-man. "Six score," says the drover. "I'll thank ye for thirteen shillings and fourpence," says the bridge-keeper. Says the drover, "Ye may whistle till ye get it." "Then ye will not cross after your cattle, not till ye've paid," the bridge-man told him.'

Angus listened to the packman's story with growing anxiety.

'And is the drover going to pay and let us all get across?' he asked.

The packman shook his head. 'The drover will not pay and there they both stand glowering at each other with the cattle piling up behind them on the high road to the bridge, and neither of them will budge a foot. Och, it's a sight to split your sides laughing!' McQuaid shook with laughter.

Angus, however, was looking very sober and disturbed about the whole affair. 'And for three shillings the droves are packed tight on the road for three miles back? It is not so funny for us who are following after! The cattle will get hot and sweat and lose flesh. They will hurt each other with their horns, too, and they push into each other.'

McQuaid stopped laughing. 'Dinna fash yourself, laddie,' he said. 'I know a trick or two more than some of the drovers, it seems. We'll no' let you get packed in tight among the other droves. We'll go back on the road a bit.'

'But what good will that do us?' Angus wanted to know.

'We'll take a side road through the fields and cross the moss,' the packman said.

The moss was the soft marshy land along the banks of the great winding river.

'Across the moss? But there'll still be the river to cross,' Angus pointed out. 'Is it safe?'

'The road I'll take you, it is safe,' the packman promised him. 'It leads to the Ford o' Frew. The water at the ford is not so deep as it was a few days back, I hear, and the animals can easily swim and wade the river there. It'll come no higher than your shoulders, lad.'

'I'll try it!' Angus said with sudden decision. 'It's better than keeping the herd tight packed in yon heat on the road without any water. They'd only lose flesh.'

'Once we're across the river I can find ye a decent pasture for the night on the hill slopes above Bannock-burn. It's not too far a journey for the kye next day to the Tryst ground at Stenhousemuir near Falkirk.'

'I am very grateful to you, Mr McQuaid,' Angus replied. 'Why, you know the country better than the drovers do.'

'Say nothing, my laddie, say nothing!' the packman said with a large gesture of his hand. 'Knowing the country is my business, and maybe in serving you I serve myself as well. Who knows?' He gave a peculiar chuckle as though at some private joke which amused him.

'Come on, then, Donald,' Angus said. 'Let us push on with the beasts to the Ford of Frew and you follow after us with the bull, Colin.'

He whistled up the dogs and they turned the herd and went back a mile or two along the road by which they had just come, till they turned aside again down a narrow road which led among the bushes and marshy ground at a lower level. As Colin followed, leading Black Torcull patiently by his rope, little did he know what strange adventure was to befall him at the Ford of Frew, and how it was to bring him into many dangers and to change all his life.

McQuaid was as good as his word and he brought

them by a winding twisty road across the moss to the river Forth. Here the banks were clothed in woodland and thick bushes on either side, and though the river was still wide it ran over a bed of gravel and boulders. Though a strong flow of water was coming down, it was not too deep to prevent men and beasts passing across. When they reached the ford McQuaid nodded at the water and lifted his eyebrows and said: 'Well, Angus?'

Angus surveyed the water a little doubtfully but in the end he agreed. 'Aye, I think we can cross here all right, Mr McQuaid, but we shall need to take the beasts across a few at a time, for they may have to swim part of it.'

Old Donald nodded his head in vigorous agreement.

'Colin, I think it would be as well if you waited till the last with Black Torcull. If we swim him across with the herd he might get some injury from their horns or even be lamed.'

'I will hold back with him then to the last, Angus,' Colin agreed.

'You go across on the back of the pony, Donald,' Angus directed. 'I am young and better able to stand a drooking than you.'

'Aye, I will,' Donald answered gratefully. 'I'd like to live to make old bones.'

'Across with the first batch then, Donald! Drive them down into the water! Up, Rob! Up, Sim! At their heels! On! On!'

Lowing in frightened excitement the shaggy animals were driven into the water. Tossing their great horns they tried to back away from the rushing stream but the dogs forced them on and the weight of those pressing behind pushed the foremost into the water, willy-nilly. Once the current began to take them downstream they began to strike out awkwardly with their forelegs, wallowing in the deep pools. Angus watched them anxiously.

'It's a bit deeper than I thought, but they'll make it all right,' McQuaid assured him.

Angus waited till Donald had safely reached the other side and the herd were staggering up the far bank, shaking the water from their coats, then he rounded up the remainder of his herd ready to cross.

'Are ye coming with the bull now, Colin?' he said.

Black Torcull was bellowing madly, tossing his head and shaking with fear at the sight of the water.

'Torcull is terrible excited,' Colin said, struggling to control the strong animal. 'He's trembling a lot, too, and rolling his eyes. It's the sight of all the other beasts struggling in the water. I think I'll walk him up and down the bank a bit till he's calmer and used to the sight of the water.'

Angus nodded. 'Can you manage to bring him across alone? I can see Donald is having trouble with the herd on the other side.'

'Surely! He'll be all right with me. Once he sees the cattle moving along the road again on the other side of the river, he'll want to follow them. Just leave him to me.'

'All right, then, I'll go and help Donald. Come on, Mr McQuaid,' Angus said. The packman bent and rolled back his breeches. He had already sent his pack across on the back of the pony with old Donald in case it should get wet. He followed Angus, wading and stepping from boulder to boulder. Colin watched them go, talking all the while in a soothing voice to Torcull.

'Quiet now, Torcull, my dear. Be easy now,' he said to the bull. 'Do not toss your horns like that. It will be all right, now. What is there in the sight of running water to scare a fine bull like you? Walk round a little now, on the bank. That's better. In a minute or two we will go across the water, but we will wait till you stop trembling.' As he walked the animal up and down, Colin hummed a gentle Highland tune. Little by little the bull became calmer.

'There, now are you ready?' Colin said to him at last, as he saw the herd on the other side beginning to disappear round a bend in the road. 'Aye, you'll do now. Do not be afraid. See, I will keep the loop of your rope round my arm. Down to the water, then!'

Colin led the great beast down gently to the water's edge, but as soon as he tried to urge him into the water, the bull began to bellow and thrash about in a panic. Colin became impatient and slightly exasperated. He tugged at Torcull, and got him down into the water at last.

'Come now, you *must* go across, Torcull! Do not pull back now!' he cried.

When the animal felt the swirl of the water about his legs, however, he took fright again, and made a mad swerve towards the bank; but Colin headed him off. Again he forced the bull further out into the water. Then the current took the bull off his short legs and began to sweep him downstream. Desperately Colin held on to the rope and tried to pull the beast round and head him over to the opposite bank. He shouted

to Angus for help, but already the remainder of the
herd was dashing along the road on the other side in
a frightened stampede, and above the noise of their
bellowing Angus never heard his brother call. Indeed,
he was too busy rounding up the herd to pay attention
to what was happening on Colin's side of the river.

'I *must* turn Torcull! I must! I must!' Colin said
desperately to himself, and tried to get downstream
from Torcull and head him to the opposite bank. This
made the rope slack between them. All of a sudden
Colin felt a tug at his leg and found that a loop of
the rope had got entangled round it. With a bellow
the bull set off downstream again, pulling Colin off
his feet and after him through the water.

'Help! Help!' Colin cried. 'The rope's round my leg!
Help!' He was forced under the water for a moment
and when he rose out of it again he shouted: 'Help!
I'm drowning! Help!'

Suddenly from the bushes on the near bank came
a call: 'Hold on to the rope! I'm coming!' There
was a rush of running feet and a man flung himself
through the water towards Colin. As he pushed his
way through the foaming stream he pulled a knife
from his belt. He seized Colin by the collar of his
jacket, and with a quick stroke he severed the rope
between him and Torcull.

'There! You're all right! I've cut the rope,' he said
as he helped Colin to his feet and supported him
against the strong rush of the water. In a moment
Colin had regained his wits.

'Quick! Quick! Catch hold of the end of the rope!'
he cried. 'Don't let the bull go!'

Torcull had been brought up for a moment against

a huge boulder and this enabled Colin and his rescuer to wade after him. Colin snatched at the end of the rope which dangled from the bull's neck into the water.

'Help me to keep hold of the bull!' he cried.

The man laid hold of the rope and hauled too. 'I have him!' he exclaimed. 'Are you all right, boy?'

'Yes, yes, I can stand on my feet now,' Colin gasped. An eddy had taken them and the bull out of the main force of the current and its swirl had brought them nearer the bank. 'Give me a hand to pull the bull up the bank, will you? Come on, Torcull! Come on!'

Luckily they were near the far bank that Colin wanted to reach, and the bull was only too glad to escape from the water. He struggled with the two of them to get out of the river and up the bank.

'Come on, Torcull! Up with you!' Colin cried, heaving and pulling at the bull with the stranger's help. One more mad scramble and a wild thudding of hoofs and Torcull was out of the stream and mire and standing beside them on the rushy bank. Colin tightened his grip on the rope and brought him to a standstill.

'Thank goodness we're out!' he cried. He turned to the stranger. 'My sakes, but it's a mercy you came along when you did, sir, or I'd have been drowned now and the bull lost too.'

'I am glad indeed that I was on the river bank,' the man replied in a voice that sounded slightly foreign.

'Not so glad as I am!' Colin exclaimed fervently. 'I owe you my life. But now you're wet through, too, and your clothes all soaked and muddy and — and — oh — er —' He broke off in an embarrassed voice as he stared at the stranger.

'Well, what is the matter with my clothes, besides being wet, that you stare at them so?'

'Well, it is that — that they are different —' Colin stammered. 'They are not like any I have ever seen before,' he added lamely.

'Have you not? You mean that my jacket and trousers are bright yellow?' the man asked calmly. 'Or they would be if they were not muddy. And my shirt is striped blue and white?'

'Yes,' Colin agreed, a little confused.

'And you have truly never seen any clothes like these before?' the man questioned him closely.

'No, never!' Colin declared. 'They — they are like a kind of uniform.'

'Yes, they are a kind of uniform,' the man replied grimly. 'They are the uniform of a prisoner of war.' He looked hard at Colin.

Colin felt confused and in a kind of way abashed. He did not know quite what to say. 'Oh! You — you are not *English*, are you, sir?' he brought out at last.

This remark made the stranger throw his head back and laugh aloud. It was as though the grimness suddenly fell from him and he became gay all at once.

'English indeed! No!' he exclaimed. 'I told you I was a prisoner of war, lad! I am not aware that the Scots are at war with the English.'

Colin considered this statement gravely, a little puzzled, and all the fragments of history he had ever learned chased each other through his brain. 'I have not heard so either, *lately*, sir,' he commented gravely. 'But you see, I have only seen one or two Englishmen — cattle buyers who have been to our farm. The English are a strange people to me too!'

The last remark set the stranger chuckling indeed, but he suddenly stopped and asked: 'Here, what kind of a boy are you?'

'I am from the west Highlands, not far from Appin, sir,' Colin told him. 'I have come down with my brother to drive our cattle to the Falkirk Tryst. It is a great cattle fair.'

'So?' the man remarked thoughtfully, and then he glanced quickly and fearfully about him. 'It is foolish to be standing here. There might be other people coming to the ford,' he said. 'I do not wish to be seen, so we had better be moving along. Let us keep behind these bushes as we go.'

Colin pulled on Black Torcull's rope, and he came along docilely enough this time.

'Is that what you were doing by the river? Hiding?' he asked the man.

'Yes, but I did not know that anyone had seen me.'

'I saw Rob, our herd dog, go sniffing among the bushes, and then I saw you curled up behind a fallen tree trunk. My brother called Rob to help him with the cattle just then.'

'And you did not tell anyone about me?'

Colin shook his head. 'No, it was not my business. Besides, Mr McQuaid was there too, and I do not always care to be speaking before him.' Colin pursed up his mouth.

'Where are your friends going with the herd?' the stranger asked.

'They are pushing on to the high land above Bannockburn where they can find pasture for the night.'

'I suppose, if we meet any soldiers, you will give me up to them?'

'Why should I?' Colin lifted his eyebrows in aston-ishment.

'Because I am a Frenchman, an escaped prisoner of war,' the man confessed.

'I see.' Colin nodded gravely, turning the matter over in his mind, then he added: 'But I do not think I shall give you up to the soldiers.'

'Why not?' the Frenchman asked, but his eyes glowed suddenly with new hope.

'Have you not saved my life and our bull?' Colin demanded staunchly. 'Besides, I do not think I want to see you cast into prison.'

'You could be cast into prison yourself for sheltering me,' the prisoner told him frankly. 'Have you thought of that?'

'*You* did not think of being captured again when you plunged into the river to save my life,' Colin reminded him. 'It would have been easy for you to stay still among the bushes and to leave me to drown.'

'Before long I shall be missed and men will come to look for me,' the Frenchman informed him. 'It is not likely that I shall get far in these bright yellow clothes.'

'Where have you escaped from? A prison?' Colin asked.

The man shook his head. 'No. I was one of a number of prisoners sent from Edinburgh to help to dig drains across the Moss of Flanders and Drummond Moss. They are trying to make the land into good farming land by draining away the water on it. Today I decided to escape, and when no one was looking my way I managed to creep away along a trench we had dug.'

'But where were you going?'

'I hoped to lie low among the bushes till nightfall and then to cross the river under cover of darkness and make my way to Grangemouth.'

'Grangemouth?' Colin repeated, puzzled, for the name was new to him.

'It is a port on the Firth of Forth not far from here,' the Frenchman told him. 'At Grangemouth I thought I might find a friend who would help me to stow away in a boat going to Holland, maybe. There is a sea-captain there with whom I did business as a merchant before the war.'

'Perhaps we might help you to get to Grangemouth,' Colin said thoughtfully.

' "We"?' the man repeated, wrinkling his brows. 'Who is "we"?'

'My brother and I and old Donald the herd. Angus will be grateful to you indeed when he hears how you saved my life *and* our bull. Now, I have been thinking — if you could go along with us as if you were helping with the herd . . .' Colin began.

'That is an idea,' the Frenchman agreed, but then his face fell and he pointed to his clothes. 'But in these clothes? Whoever saw a drover in a mustard-coloured coat?'

'Yes, we must be finding you some other clothes indeed. I will speak to my brother. He has another plaid in the pony's saddle-bags and also his best breeches for when he reaches the Tryst, so that he will not be ashamed of his appearance before the English buyers. I will ask him to put them on and to lend you his kilt. That will make you look like a Highland drover indeed, and though your speech is a little foreign, it could be taken for a Highland tongue.'

'It might work . . . if it could be done,' the prisoner said eagerly.

'I think it could, if I can get Angus alone for a few minutes to talk to him first,' Colin declared. 'But it would not do for you to come up to the herd wearing those clothes. For one thing, Mr McQuaid is with us.'

'Ah, yes, the packman.' The Frenchman nodded understanding.

'Look over yonder.' Colin pointed. 'There is a strip of woodland just ahead of us, on the slopes of yon hill that rises steeply from the moss.'

'Yes, I see it.'

'The trees are very thick there,' Colin observed. 'I think you could hide there well. When it is dark I will come to the wood, to the east end of it, over there, where you see yon tall fir trees, and I will bring Angus's clothes. I will hoot three times like an owl and when you hear it, give a whistle like this.' Colin gave a low whistle on two notes.

'Yes, I will do that.'

'And now we had better part or Angus will be looking for us to see why I have not caught up with them, and whether I am having any trouble with the bull. But what is your name, sir, before I go?'

The Frenchman hesitated at first as though he did not wish to tell it. At once Colin said: 'No, do not tell me if you would rather keep it a secret.'

The man made up his mind at once. 'But I will,' he said. 'I can trust you, I think. It is Simon de Conceau.'

'Simon,' Colin said thoughtfully, pronouncing it in the French fashion as he had heard it, so that it sounded like 'Seemon'. 'That is like our name *Simon*.

We had better call you Simon, I think. We must have
another name for you too. I have it! Chisholm! We
will call you Simon Chisholm.'

'Simon Chisholm! Yes, that will do. I will remember
it,' the Frenchman said with a laugh.

'My name is Colin Cameron,' Colin told him in
return.

'Thank you, Colin.'

Colin gave a slap to Torcull's haunches to urge
him on his way and took up the slack of his halter
rope and tugged. 'Till nightfall then,' he called over
his shoulder to Simon.

'Till nightfall, adieu!' Simon replied in a low voice,
lifting his hand in a gesture of farewell.

'Come away, Torcull! Come away!' Colin cried.
'On with you!'

Slowly the black bull made his way along the
muddy lane of the moss. Simon stood watching them
for a minute, a kindly smile on his face, then once
more he dropped to his knees and crawled out of
sight among the bushes.

Colin plodded along behind Torcull till they were
almost clear of the flat marshy land and beginning
the gentle ascent of the foothills to the higher land
beyond. Here the moors rose steeply from the bed
of the river, almost in a cliff-like wall. Just then
Angus came round the bend of the lane, looking
very anxious indeed. As soon as he saw Colin he
began to run towards him.

'Hi, there, Colin! What a time you've been!' he
cried. 'Was the bull awkward at the ford? I had to go
after the cattle for they were beginning to stampede
and Donald could not hold them himself. As soon

as we got them going easily towards the hill I came back to find you.

'We're both all right, Angus.'

Just then Angus noticed Colin's garments, from which the water still dripped. 'Why, you're soaked to the skin, lad! Plaid and all!' he cried. 'Surely that was not just with crossing the river?'

'No, it was not. I tripped over a boulder and Torcull dragged me through the water,' Colin informed him.

'Sakes, laddie, you might have been drowned!' Angus exclaimed with consternation.

'I would have been but for a friend who helped me, for the rope was twisted round my leg,' Colin told him candidly. 'There was a man who dashed into the water to rescue me.'

'That was a brave-like thing, now. Was he a farmer or another drover?' Angus asked.

'He was neither.' Colin lowered his voice and spoke abruptly. 'Listen to me, Angus, please, and promise me you will not be saying anything before Mr McQuaid.'

'Mr McQuaid is away to visit a farm over by Bannockburn where he says he can get us a night's stance for the cattle at very little cost. Well, why do you look about over your shoulders?' Angus asked Colin impatiently. 'What have you to tell me?'

'Angus, the man who saved my life was a Frenchman, a prisoner of war,' Colin confessed all in a breath.

Angus stood stock still. 'My sakes!' he exclaimed, looking troubled.

'He was one of the prisoners set to dig trenches to drain Flanders Moss,' Colin explained further.

'He has escaped and he is trying to get out of the country. Angus, I would like fine to help him.' Colin's voice took on a soft coaxing tone that few folk could withstand, but Angus was plucking at his lower lip in a rather scared fashion.

'Mercy on us, laddie, d'ye ken ye might be imprisoned or put to death for helping an escaped prisoner of war?'

'I do not care!' Colin stuck out his chin obstinately. 'He saved my life. He may be a Frenchman, but he is a fine man for all that.'

'But how can *we* be any use, Colin? We have nowhere to hide him.'

'He could go with us behind the cattle as if he were a drover,' Colin suggested.

'But does he speak English? What if anyone heard him speak with a foreign tongue?' Angus demurred.

'He speaks English almost as well as we do. He has been a merchant trading with England, aye, and with Scotland too, so he told me. He speaks English almost like a Highlander does. You know there are many of us who have little more than the Gaelic and speak English as if it is a strange tongue.'

Angus turned Colin's words over in his mind for a few moments without speaking, then he agreed: 'That is true enough.'

Having disposed of the first difficulty with Angus, Colin went on to deal with the second. 'It is his clothes which are the trouble. They are *yellow*!'

'Yellow! Mercy on us! He couldn't follow the drove far in a yellow coat without someone knowing him for a prisoner of war,' Angus declared, as though that was the end of the subject.

'That is where I would like *you* to help him, Angus,' Colin said quietly.

'I? What can I do?'

'You could put on your breeks and your best shirt and your other plaid, and lend Simon your kilt and shirt and this old faded plaid.'

'But my breeks are my father's — the ones he wears to the kirk,' Angus protested. 'He has lent them to me only for the market when I go to speak with Mr Barlow at the Tryst.'

'I think he would not say "No" if you were to wear the breeks a day or two before the Tryst and lend your kilt to the Frenchman, when Father hears how he saved our bull.'

'Well — now —' Angus began to hesitate.

'Could you not do it now, Angus? It would let the Frenchman get to Grangemouth, perhaps, and so on to ship,' Colin said persuasively.

'What? Wearing my kilt?' Angus cried. 'How would I get it back?'

Colin's face fell. 'Oh! I had not thought of that!' he cried in a crestfallen voice. 'Perhaps he might be able to buy some other clothes while he is wearing your kilt. It is an old kilt, now, faded and mended,' he cajoled Angus. 'Is it not a small thing, now, to set beside our bull and my life? Will you not lend it to him, Angus?'

Angus began to smile. 'You have the coaxing tongue, Colin. Oh, well then, if it means so much to you —'

'It does! It does! Oh, thank you, Angus!' Colin almost jumped for joy.

'But wait! How are you to get the clothes to him?'

'Simon will be hiding in that long wood at the foot of the hill behind us. I said I would take the clothes to him at nightfall.'

'Oh, you did, did you?' Angus said, half-laughing, half-scolding. 'You were pretty sure I would lend you the clothes, eh?'

'Oh, please, Angus! I cannot fail Simon now,' Colin begged, fearful lest Angus should change his mind. 'I gave him my word. His name is Simon de Conceau, but we decided he should be called Simon Chisholm.'

'Och, so you decided that too? Well, that beats all!' Angus said, vexed but having to laugh.

'You are not angry with me, are you, Angus?'

'N-no!' Angus was not quite sure. 'I think, all the same, that when you go to keep your appointment with Mr Simon Chisholm tonight I will come too. There are a few questions I would like to ask him before I agree to take him on as a drover.'

'Yes, Angus, but will you keep it a secret? Donald will have to know, of course, but please do not be saying anything before Mr McQuaid,' Colin implored his brother.

'Why not? He is a good man, McQuaid, and he has helped us a lot,' Angus said.

'Still, he is not one of *us*,' Colin insisted. 'Besides, the fewer people who know that Simon is a Frenchman, the better!'

Angus nodded his head. 'Yes, maybe you are right. I will say nothing then to Mr McQuaid, and I will change into my breeks in the barn at the farm when he is not there. But we must hurry Torcull a little now and try to come up with the herd.'

That night the herd was pastured at a farm on the

hill slopes above Bannockburn, at a short distance from the farm itself, on the edge of the Gargunnock Hills. Below them the land sloped to the level plains of the Forth with its many windings, and the stretches of woodland tucked into the little valleys of the streams among the cultivated lands.

McQuaid had disappeared on some business of his own at the farms in the lower lands, and Colin was glad, somehow, that he had not returned when the darkness fell and it was time for them to seek out Simon in the long wood. Angus had changed into his father's breeks and rolled his kilt and plaid up under his arm. They took old Donald into their confidence and warned him not to say a word to anyone that Simon was a Frenchman, especially to McQuaid, if he returned before them.

"Deed, and am I not knowing how to hold my tongue?' the old man asked. 'If there is one thing the droving teaches a man, it is when to hold his tongue and when to speak. You will find that for yourselves when you come to sell the beasts at the Tryst,' he chuckled wisely.

With some misgiving about the wisdom of helping Simon, Angus set off with Colin under cover of darkness, leaving Donald to look after the herd as he sat by the watch-fire with the two dogs at his feet, and Torcull the Black tethered to a tree close beside him.

When they reached the wood Colin plunged into it without hesitation, and as soon as they were concealed by the trees and bushes, he hooted three times like an owl. There was silence for a moment or two as the boys waited tensely, then from some bushes close at hand there came the sound of a low whistle on two notes. A moment's pause and it was repeated again.

Colin called softly: 'Are you there, Simon?'

A figure rose from behind the bushes. 'I am here, Colin, but there are two of you. Who is with you?'

'It is my brother Angus. We have brought you his clothes.'

Angus came forward with hand outstretched. 'I am indeed grateful to you for saving my brother's life,' he said, 'but I should like the favour of a few words with you, sir, before I hand over my clothes.'

'Willingly, monsieur.'

'Colin has told me you are an escaped prisoner of war,' Angus began without further beating about the bush.

'That is true. I escaped from a party of prisoners who were digging trenches to drain Flanders Moss, down by the river,' Simon replied equally frankly.

'You give me your word of honour you are not a French spy, sir?'

'Indeed I am not! I will swear to that.'

'You speak English very well indeed for a Frenchman,' Angus commented candidly.

'I am a merchant, monsieur. I traded in silks and laces and French perfumes with Edinburgh merchants through the port of Leith. That was, of course, before the war.'

'How then did you come to be a soldier in the French army?' Angus asked, rather puzzled.

Simon shook his head slowly. 'I was never a soldier in the French army,' he declared. 'It so happened that when war broke out I was in Edinburgh on my business as a merchant. I booked a berth in a

French ship that was to sail from Leith in a day's time, but the captain foolishly delayed his sailing. When we did sail and we were less than a day out from Leith and still in the Forth, the ship was taken by a British man-of-war. All those aboard her, most of them sailors, were taken prisoner, and I was taken among them. At first I was imprisoned in Edinburgh Castle, but after eight dreary years there, I was sent with other prisoners to work on the land.'

'I see,' Angus said, turning this information over in his mind before answering. 'Then you have never really taken up arms against this country?'

'No, I have not. I am sorry our countries are at war, for I am a peaceful man, and I have many friends in England and Scotland, but war takes no account of friendships, alas!'

'Why did you want to escape? Were you ill treated?' Angus asked.

'No. My gaolers were not unkind, but I had word through another prisoner that my wife had been very ill, and that my brother who had been looking after my business for me had died, and that my business was falling into ruin. I felt that I *must* try to reach my home again. Ten years is a very long time to be a prisoner.'

Angus nodded with some sympathy. 'Yes, I understand. Very well, then, if you will give me your word that you do not intend any harm to my country, I will help you.'

'I give you my word, truly,' Simon promised, offering Angus his hand.

Angus grasped it warmly and said: 'Then you can go along with us as if you were driving the herd. Here are the clothes for you to wear. You can put them on and go with us now.' He handed over the bundle to Simon.

'I thank you with all my heart, monsieur!'

Angus gave a short laugh. 'It might be as well if you did not call me *monsieur*. That might give us all away. You must give me my name, Angus, and I will call you Simon.'

'Very well, Angus,' Simon agreed, and he went behind the bushes to change into the kilt and shirt and plaid that Angus had brought for him. When he reappeared Colin exclaimed with delight: 'Why, Simon, you look the very picture of a wild Highlander! You would take in anyone!'

'Anyone save a Highlander!' Angus warned him soberly. 'It would be as well for you not to talk too much to the men in kilts, Simon, or they will soon know that you have not the Gaelic.'

'I will remember that,' Simon promised him.

'Donald, our herd man, we have already told about you. He will keep silence, but trust no one else. And now we must be getting back to the herd, for old Donald is looking after Torcull, the bull, and all the beasts, alone.'

After they had concealed Simon's yellow clothes under a big stone in the wood, they set off to join the herd, and Simon strode along beside Colin in the new freedom of his kilt, feeling a new freedom too in his heart as his spirit rose within him.

The Falkirk Tryst

It was as well that Angus and Colin had taken Donald
into their confidence and told him about the Frenchman hiding in the woods and their plan to help
him, for McQuaid returned to the camp before they
had returned with Simon. The packman sat down
beside Donald and appeared surprised to find him
all alone.

'That's strange, now, for both Colin and Angus to
go off and leave you to guard the cattle alone, surely?'
he asked with a lift of his eyebrows.

Donald gave a careless shrug. ''Deed, now, it was
only for a short time. Angus had a friend to meet —
another drover.'

McQuaid still seemed to find something strange in
the matter. 'But why did he not leave Colin behind?'
he asked. 'I thought Colin always had charge of the
bull?'

Donald took time to consider his answer and when
he did, it was not a direct one to the question asked.

'This man helped Colin when he fell into the river,'
he said slowly. 'Colin brought word to Angus, and
when Angus was hearing who the man was, he wished
to see him and thank him for saving Colin.'

'What was the man's name?'

'Och, I cannot be minding,' Donald said with some

show of forgetfulness. 'It is stupid of me now, but I have forgotten. He is a drover that Angus was knowing about.'

'Is he from your part of the world?' McQuaid asked with curiosity.

'I do not think so,' Donald replied cautiously, not wishing to commit himself too much, for he did not know what tale Angus and Colin might make up about the Frenchman. 'It could be that Angus met him before at the droving, last year, maybe, when he came down with the master, Mr Cameron.'

'I see,' McQuaid said, stroking his chin, then he jerked his head up quickly. 'Listen! I can hear someone coming up the farm lane.'

Donald listened too. 'Aye, that is Colin's voice.'

They heard Colin's excited voice as he talked to Simon. He was evidently speaking about the bull.

'Aye, he's the fine bull, is Torcull — the best that ever came out of Drumbeg, aye, or out of Lochaber or Appin either!'

Angus laughed aloud. 'Don't boast now, Colin.'

'You should get a good price for the bull at the Falkirk Tryst, then?' Simon asked with interest.

'That is what we hope,' Colin rattled on. 'Well, here we are at the camp-fire. Old Donald has got a good blaze. I hope he has made the oatmeal for our supper. I'm hungry.'

'McQuaid is back. I can see him sitting beside Donald,' Angus announced.

Colin dropped his voice to a whisper. 'Be careful then, Simon.'

Angus hailed McQuaid as they drew close to the

fire. 'Well, did ye find the friends ye had gone to seek at Bannockburn, Mr McQuaid?'

'I did so,' McQuaid said with a kind of secret satisfaction. 'I hear from Donald that you have been finding an old friend too?' He could not suppress the curiosity in his voice.

'An old friend?' Donald made a quick gesture with his hand that could have been a warning, and Angus was quick to recover. 'Oh, yes! Here is our friend, Simon Chisholm. Simon, this is Mr McQuaid, the packman, who has journeyed with us and been mighty obliging.'

McQuaid and the Frenchman exchanged quick glances.

'Good evening to you, Mr Chisholm,' McQuaid said with courtesy.

'Good evening, sir,' Simon replied with a half-bow which stopped midway.

'I see by your dress you are from the Highlands. What part might ye be from now, Mr Chisholm?' the packman inquired.

The question caught Simon totally unprepared. 'I — oh — I have lived in the neighbourhood of Doune.'

'Have ye now?' said McQuaid with much interest. 'That's very interesting, now, very interesting. Ye'll ken the grand cotton-mill that has been built at Doune, maybe?'

'I — I have heard of it,' Simon replied cautiously.

'Ye've only *heard* o' it!' McQuaid exclaimed in surprise. 'Och, man, ye'll surely ken Mr James Smith who is the manager of it?'

'It is a familiar name, Smith!' Simon replied, the

corners of his mouth twitching a little in a smile he could not help.

'Why, everybody about Doune kens Mr James Smith,' the packman cried. 'I've often bought table-cloths and towels from his mill to sell on my rounds. Are ye on your way to the Tryst, Mr Chisholm?'

Simon hesitated, but Angus came quickly to his rescue.

'Simon has offered to help us to take the drove to market before he goes back home,' he informed McQuaid. 'We can always be doing with an extra pair of hands to keep our drove separated from the others. But I see the oatmeal is ready for our supper, and I for one am ready for it.' Angus hoped to put McQuaid off his inquisitive questioning by eating. Quietly he handed an extra bowl to Donald, who filled it without a word and gave it to Simon. Even supper, however, did not silence McQuaid.

'And have you no drove of your own, then, Mr Chisholm?' the packman asked.

'Er — not now, Mr McQuaid, not now.'

'You've surely not sold your beasts *before* the Tryst, man?'

'No doubt Simon knew his buyers,' Angus put in quickly. 'He is not the one to make a bad bargain. But it will be wise now for us all to get what sleep we can. I want to be early on the road tomorrow to get a good stance on Stenhousemuir for the cat-tle.'

'Aye, I see you're dressed for the market, Angus,' the packman remarked. 'Ye've got your good breeks on. A braw figure ye cut, too, my lad,' he added in flattering tones. 'But before ye roll yourself in your plaid, bide a minute. I have a bottle here in my pocket.'

Angus looked rather shocked and waved the proffered bottle away hastily. 'No, no, Mr McQuaid! I promised my father I would not take any strong drink. I have the charge of the cattle, you know, and besides I am not used to it.'

McQuaid laughed at him. 'Who says this is strong drink? I would not be offering it to you if it were. No, this is a home-made herb drink, made from nettles, so Mistress Forsyth at the farm told me. She brewed it herself, and it is mighty refreshing after a hot day, I can tell you. She sent it along that ye might try it. Come now, bring out your drinking horns. This is not the kind of beer to make anyone drunk.'

'Well, now —' Angus hesitated.

'Mistress Forsyth will take it ill if you do not try her brewing of herbs, and she obliged us by letting the pasture for the cattle at a low rate, too. One and sixpence the score of beasts was all her price,' McQuaid said persuasively.

'That is very reasonable for a night's pasture,' Angus said, pleased. 'I had thought to pay two shillings the score.'

'Aye, and she threw in the herb beer as well. Come on! Hand me your drinking horns.'

Angus and the other two passed their smooth polished drinking horns, made from the horns of a bullock, to McQuaid. He poured the herb beer into them and turned to Simon.

'Have you no horn nor cup, Mr Chisholm?' he asked sharply.

'I — I left my cup behind at my last lodging.'

'What? You a drover and ye've no horn!' McQuaid expressed great surprise. 'Ah, well, I will pass you the bottle. Now, a health to Mistress Forsyth and our thanks to her.'

Donald, Angus and Colin lifted their horns and drank. Colin slipped a quick glance at the packman. 'But you are not drinking any of the nettle beer yourself, Mr McQuaid,' he remarked.

'Och, I have had some already,' the packman replied with an assumed heartiness. 'Maybe there'll be a drop left in the bottle when Mr Chisholm has finished with it.'

'Have you heard how prices are likely to go at the Tryst?' Angus asked, again diverting McQuaid's attention from Simon.

McQuaid was rather flattered to have his opinion asked. 'Well, my lads, stirks will fetch eight pounds apiece, easy, and maybe more. The Navy has placed big orders with the London butchers, so the news goes round, and the butchers are buying all the meat they can. Folk may say what they like, but a war brings money to the farmers and drovers, and we're out to beat Napoleon this year. You'll have no difficulty in selling your cattle well.'

'That's good news. That will please my father,' Angus said with satisfaction.

'What's this I hear from Donald about you taking a tumble in the river, Colin?' McQuaid asked.

'Oh, it was just that Black Torcull bolted, but luckily Simon was at hand to help me out and to catch the bull.'

'That was a mighty piece of luck that Mr Chisholm

should chance to be so near by,' the packman commented, looking sideways at Simon. 'Where did you spring from, Mr Chisholm?'

Simon did not understand the last question and looked puzzled. 'I beg your pardon. What do you mean?' he asked politely.

'Oh, Simon had been at a farm close by,' Colin answered quickly for him.

'Had he now!' the packman said with interest. 'Folk tell me they're using prisoners of war to work on some of the farms by the river. Is that true, sir?' He looked narrowly at Simon.

'I believe so,' Simon tried to reply carelessly, but he could not help a slight uneasiness creeping into his voice.

Before McQuaid could ask any more difficult questions, Angus interrupted. 'Look! There's old Donald nodding his head already, and I can scarcely keep my eyes open either. Will you take the first turn at watching, Colin?'

'Aye, I'll do that, Angus,' Colin agreed.

Angus yawned a little. 'Keep a good watch then, laddie, for the closer we get to the Tryst, the more cattle thieves there are likely to be about.'

'Man, you're right there!' McQuaid agreed heartily.

'I will watch well,' Colin promised. 'I will loop Torcull's rope round this stone against which I am leaning, and I will keep an end of the rope in my hand.'

'Good! Call me when you are ready to sleep yourself, Colin,' Angus directed him.

There was a chorus of 'Good nights' from everyone, and the others wrapped their plaids around them and lay upon the grass. Only Colin remained sitting upright, his back against the big boulder, and the end of Torcull's rope looped round his wrist, keeping watch over the sleeping beasts and men.

When all was silent save for the occasional lowing of an ox, and the crackle of wood in the fire, Colin found himself beginning to yawn too, and to wonder how long he must wait before it would be his turn to waken Angus. A sleepy shudder crept down between his shoulders and he shook himself impatiently and yawned again.

'I think my dip in the river has made me sleepy too,' he said to himself. 'Why, Angus is fast asleep already! So are the others, even Mr McQuaid, though he had so much to say such a short time ago! And Simon too!' He leaned towards Simon and looked with friendliness into the thin dark face. Simon stirred a little, then settled off to sleep again.

'He has a fine strong face, Simon, an *honest* face,' Colin said to himself. Again he could not hold back a mighty yawn. 'Even Torcull has stopped cropping the grass and seems asleep. Oh, I wish the time would pass for Angus to take his watch!' he sighed. 'I am so sleepy — so sleepy — so — sleepy —' His whispering voice trailed away into silence.

Now entire sleep reigned over herd and men alike and there was no one to keep watch against the perils of the night.

It was some hours later when the dawn was pale in the sky and the sun peeping over the shoulder of the hill that Angus stirred and wakened. He rubbed his eyes sleepily, and stared about him, still dazed.

'What time is it?' he said to himself. 'The sun's

up already. The beasts are beginning to stir. Has Donald fallen asleep at his watch?' He turned about him. There was Donald still lying on the ground by the ashes of the camp-fire, his head pillowed on his arm and his plaid hugged about his old shoulders.

'Why! There he lies, still snoring!' Angus exclaimed, vexed. He leaped up and shook the old man hard by the shoulder. 'Hi, Donald! Wake up! Wake up!' he cried.

'What's wrong? What is it?' Donald muttered, stirring sleepily.

Angus shook him harder still. 'You've fallen asleep at your watch, man!' he cried.

Donald was awake in an instant at this accusation, and sat up at once. 'Fallen asleep? Never!' he cried indignantly. 'Never have I been known to fall asleep on my watch once I have been wakened!'

'But you *were* sleeping!'

'Then you could not have wakened me!' Donald declared. 'I do not remember now that you ever did waken me. It is you who have fallen asleep on *your* watch, Angus. You have failed to waken *me*!'

'Surely not?' Angus exclaimed, bewildered. 'That is not a thing I have ever done, either. But it is true, now, I do not remember waking you, Donald. What has happened to me? Colin!' But Colin was fast asleep and did not answer.

'Why, the lad's asleep yet! Colin!' Angus cried again, then he opened his eyes wide at a sudden thought. 'Come to think, Donald, did Colin wake me at all, now?' He went over and shook the sleeping boy.

'Oh, all right! Stop shaking me!' Colin said, sitting

up at last. 'I'm awake now. Oh, but I'm stiff and heavy.'

'You must have been asleep on the ground all night,' Angus scolded. 'Did you waken me to take my watch? Did you?'

Colin shook his head in a confused fashion. 'I cannot think — I — I do not know. I remember feeling very sleepy by the red fire and wishing my watch was over and then — then — I think I must have fallen asleep,' he finished guiltily.

'Oh, Colin! Why did you not tell me if you were too tired to watch?' Angus asked in vexation.

Colin did not reply, however. He was staring at the end of the rope still looped about his wrist.

'What's this, Angus?' he cried in sudden dismay.

'What, Colin?' Angus cried, not understanding at first.

'This loose end of rope in my hand!' Colin cried wildly, jumping to his feet. He stared about him, his mouth open, the blood draining away from his face. 'Where's Torcull? He was tethered to this stone and I was holding the end of his rope!'

'Maybe he is with the herd,' Donald said.

'No, no, he is not! There is no sign of him anywhere,' Angus exclaimed frantically.

'He's gone! He's gone!' Colin shouted, white to his lips.

'Perhaps he broke his rope and wandered away,' Donald suggested.

'No, if he had broken it I should have felt the pull of the rope in my hand,' Colin declared. 'He's been stolen! He's been stolen!'

His lamentations aroused the packman, who was

still sleeping by the black remains of the fire. He stirred sleepily, sat up, and asked: 'What's to do? What's to do? It's never time to move on yet before we've eaten our porridge, surely?'

'Oh, Mr McQuaid, the bull has been stolen!' Angus told him. 'Torcull the Black has been stolen!'

The packman sat up at once, shocked. 'Surely no'?' he exclaimed. 'Not with all of you keeping your watch in turn?'

'Colin fell asleep and did not waken me. We all slept through the night,' Angus confessed.

'But didn't Colin tether the bull to a stone and keep the slack of the rope looped round his arm as well?' McQuaid asked. 'Surely he felt a jerk when the rope was loosened?'

'It wasn't loosened. Look! It's been cut!' Colin showed the end of the rope, cleanly severed.

'Aye, and it was a right sharp knife did that too,' Donald commented. 'It's not even frayed at all. I'm feared a clever cattle thief has taken our bull, Angus.'

The tears started in Colin's eyes, though he did his best to keep them back. 'My father trusted me,' he said unhappily. 'He trusted me with the bull and I fell asleep on my watch. Oh, Angus!'

'Where's your friend Mr Chisholm?' McQuaid demanded suddenly.

'Chisholm?' Angus cried, startled. In the upset he had forgotten all about the escaped Frenchman.

'Aye, the fellow who came back with you last night. Where's he gone?'

'Simon? Why, where is he?' Colin said staring about him. 'He was sleeping by the fire last night. Why, I remember watching him stir a little in his sleep —'

The packman gave a coarse laugh. 'It seems to me he's stirred a lot, lad. He must have waited till you fell asleep and then he stirred himself and the bull clean away, I'm thinking!'

'Oh, no, no! I'm sure he would never do that!' Colin exclaimed in great distress, though he could not help the poisoned arrow of doubt entering his mind.

'Well, he's gone, anyway, and so has the bull!' McQuaid replied with a snort. 'But ye were well acquainted with him, were ye no', Angus?' he added slyly.

'Not well enough acquainted, it seems!' Angus declared bitterly. 'I should have known better than to trust him.'

Donald was looking puzzled. 'Simon did not seem a man to be a thief now,' he said in his slow Highland voice. 'I would not have thought it. But to creep away in the night like that, that is queer.'

'Aye, and with the bull creeping after him too,' the packman jeered.

Colin stood up straight and turned upon him. 'We do not *know* that Simon took the bull,' he defended his friend. 'It might well have been some other thief.'

'What other thief could it be?' the packman asked impatiently. 'Yon fellow Chisholm hasn't waited to bid you farewell, anyway.'

'It was my fault that I fell asleep,' Colin said in sorrow. 'I am not fit for my father to trust me. I am not fit to be a drover.'

Even Angus, miserable as he was at the loss of the bull, felt some compassion for Colin. 'Now, Colin, I am to blame too. I asked Simon to come back with us. *I* should have taken the watch first after you had been half-drowned in yon river. You were tried past your strength, laddie.'

His brother's kindness made Colin weep indeed. 'But Torcull is gone! Torcull the Black! Whatever shall we tell my father?'

'The truth!' Angus said soberly, with a grimace of distaste. 'We must tell him that we were all found wanting and that the thief was quicker-witted than we were. Well, there is nothing for it but to push on to the Tryst and try to sell the rest of the cattle.'

'Aye, lad, that's all you can do,' McQuaid agreed. 'I'll see if I can get word of the bull anywhere. Whiles I hear a thing or two as I go among the drovers at the fair and somebody must have seen him.'

'You might see if you can hear tell of Simon Chisholm too!' Angus declared angrily. 'It might help if you asked if anyone knew of an escaped French prisoner!'

Hardly were the words out of his mouth and he saw Colin's stricken face, than Angus could have wished them unspoken. The packman looked from one to another, his eyes glinting.

'Oh, so that's the way of it, is it?' he said. 'Ah, well, I will keep a good look-out for him, the black-hearted scoundrel!'

'Oh, Angus!' was all Colin could say.

'Come on, Colin! It's done now,' Angus said roughly. 'Help me to get the cattle herded and on the move. I shall have to find Mr Barlow at the Tryst too and let him know what has happened. That will be a sore thing to have to tell. Come, let us get on to Stenhousemuir.'

Sorrowfully Colin followed the herd along the road to the Tryst, and he did not know which was the greatest sorrow in his heart, that he had failed in his trust to his father and that Torcull had gone, or that he had been deceived by Simon, or that Angus had betrayed the Frenchman to McQuaid. When a man has saved your life at the risk of his own, there is something which tugs at the heart. From time to time Colin had to blink back the tears which came to his eyes, tears both for his splendid Torcull and for Simon.

As they plodded along the road they encountered many other droves till it was like a river of cattle rolling towards Stenhousemuir. The air was noisy with the shouts of the drovers, the whacks of their sticks, the barking of their dogs, and the lowing of the cattle. It was hard hot work running hither and thither to keep the herd together, and Colin took off his Highland bonnet to fan himself with it. Of a sudden, out of it there floated a scrap of paper with writing in pencil upon it. Hurriedly Colin picked it up, and looked over his shoulder to make sure that McQuaid had not seen it. Then he slipped it into his sporran and hurried after the beasts.

Unhappy as Colin was, the sight of Falkirk Tryst almost took his breath away. In the centre of the ground the drovers stood with their cattle, all trying to keep their herds separate from each other. Two men who each claimed to be the owner of a stray stirk were threatening each other with cudgels. Around the field tents and booths were set up and over open fires huge cauldrons of meat-broth simmered, that the drovers were buying at threepence the bowl. In the tents men were selling whisky and ale. Along the fringes of the crowd packmen were showing ribbons and laces, beads and brooches, and all kinds of fairings. A fiddler wandered up and down, playing and begging from the folk. There were two men wrestling for a prize of five shillings and a crowd stood gaping at them.

A number of gipsies were selling baskets and clothes-pegs and telling fortunes. Colin watched one or two sly fellows who pushed their way among the crowd and whom he would not have trusted within reach of his pocket. A man standing on a box was crying his pills which he said would cure anything from a headache to a broken leg.

Among the herds the English and Lowland buyers wandered, poking this beast and feeling the sides of that one. Never had Colin heard so many different voices before! There was the soft slow speech of the Highlander, the gruff Yorkshire dialect, the burr of the Cumberland tongue, the sharper Cockney voices of the men from the London markets. Over all these tongues was the babel of hucksters calling their wares, the sound of music played on a fiddle competing with the drone of the bagpipes, the barking of dogs, the shouts of the drovers, the plaintive cries of the sheep, and the constant lowing of the cattle. Colin was bewildered and fascinated and in the strange new excitement of the Tryst he almost forgot his sorrow at the loss of Black Torcull.

Angus was looking anxiously from right to left as they drove the cattle into the great field where the selling pens were.

'Here's a space big enough for our herd. Drive the beasts in here, Colin,' he directed.

It was a tough hard task to get the excited animals safely into the space allotted to them and to keep the stray stirks from mixing with other herds, but with Donald's wise guidance it was accomplished at last. Angus wiped the perspiration from his brow and heaved a long sigh.

'Will you and Colin look after the beasts, Donald, while I go to pay the market taxes?' he said. 'I want to go and make inquiries at yon wooden shed over there for Mr Barlow. It is the banking booth. My father told me Mr Barlow would leave a message there for us.'

'Aye, Angus.' Old Donald nodded.

McQuaid picked up his pedlar's pack. 'I'll be taking my leave of you now, Angus. I am going to spread out my pack between those tents on the other side of the field. I wish you all the luck of the Tryst and good prices for your cattle.'

'Thank you, Mr McQuaid,' Angus said, shaking hands with him. 'I hope you will be doing well too.'

McQuaid chuckled to himself. 'Oh, I'll do well, never fear! I'll be staying here for a two-three days to the end of the Tryst. Good-bye, then, and a good road home for ye, too.'

He went off chuckling to himself as though something amused him vastly. For his part, Colin was not sorry to see him go.

'I must go and find Mr Barlow,' Angus said. 'Keep your eyes open, Colin, and watch the herds, now.'

Donald and Colin watched Angus striding across

the field, and Colin shook his head sadly. 'If only we had Black Torcull to show Mr Barlow!'

'Aye, it is a pity about the bull.'

'You know, Donald, I cannot think how it is that I did not feel the jerk of the rope in my hand when the thief cut it,' Colin said, knitting his brows in a troubled frown.

'You were hard asleep, no doubt.'

'But it is not easy to cut through a thick rope like that and not waken the person who is holding the end of it, even though it was looped round a stone. There is another thing, too, Donald. The ends were not frayed as they would be if a knife hacked them. They were clean cut,' Colin pointed out.

'Aye, I noticed that myself,' Donald said.

'Did you now, Donald?' Colin exclaimed, a little excited. 'Did you not think it was done with a sharp thing — like a *razor*?'

Donald stroked his chin. ''Deed, yes, it could be. Had the Frenchman a razor, now?'

'No, not the Frenchman, not Simon! He had a beard. But someone else had a razor. The packman, McQuaid! He had razors in his pack to sell.'

The old drover looked puzzled. 'Aye, but McQuaid was still sleeping beside us when we all woke up in the morning. How could he have stolen the bull and still be with us?'

'That I do not know,' Colin admitted. 'We must have been asleep a long time.'

'Aye, but where is the bull, then?' Donald asked. 'McQuaid is yonder selling his goods. He has not got the bull tied up in his pack, my laddie!'

'No, but the bull must be somewhere, and not far

away at that.'

'Ah, well, McQuaid had been with us more than a week and we found him honest enough,' Donald pointed out. 'The other man we did not know at all.'

Colin, however, took no notice of this remark for he was still busy reasoning things out in his own mind. 'There is another thing puzzles me too. Why was it that the dogs never barked last night when a thief came to take Torcull? You know what a noise they make if a stranger comes near.'

Donald scratched his head. 'Aye, you're right there. That has puzzled me too,' he admitted.

'Could it be because it was someone they *knew* who took the bull away?' Colin asked sharply.

'Maybe, Colin, maybe, but I canna work it out.' The old man shook his head, looking troubled.

'Listen, Donald.' Colin suddenly decided to take him into his confidence. 'Simon left a note tucked inside my bonnet. Here it is.' Colin took it from the inside of his woollen Highland bonnet, like a Tam o' Shanter. 'How glad I am now that my father sent us to the minister to learn how to read and write,' he said with satisfaction. 'It is a leaf torn from a notebook and the writing is in pencil.' He began to read the note aloud.

'If I stay with you, I only put your lives in danger. The packman asks too many questions and I think he is suspicious. I shall hide in a place I know and leave the country tomorrow night. Farewell and a million thanks.

Always your friend,

Simon.'

'Well, that is a strange thing now,' Donald commented when Colin had finished reading. 'Why should he write you a letter like that if he was stealing the bull? A thief would be anxious to get away while we were all asleep.'

'That's what I think. It makes me more sure than ever that Simon did not steal our bull,' Colin declared.

'I am not quick at thinking a thing out,' Donald said. 'It would be well for you to be speaking to Angus about it.'

'I will, when I can get him alone,' Colin decided.

'Here he comes now with Mr Barlow,' Donald said, pointing them out moving through the crowd. Angus was approaching, followed by a thick-set man with a slight limp. He had a rosy cheerful face set off by his thick grey hair. He came forward in genial fashion to shake hands with Donald.

'Good day to you, Donald,' he said in a broad Cumberland accent. 'Angus here has been telling me about the accident to his father. A nasty business that, and I'm sorry to hear it.'

''Deed, aye, Mr Barlow. The master was very vexed to miss the Tryst,' Donald said.

Angus brought Colin forward. 'This is my young brother Colin who came to help us with the droving.'

'You're learning the droving early, my lad,' Barlow said with a nod of approval. 'Well, it's a grand life if you can make your mind up to it. So you've got a bunch of stirks for me to look at, eh?' he added in brisk businesslike fashion.

'Aye, here they are,' Angus said.

Mr Barlow looked over all the animals very

carefully, going among the herd with Angus. As he returned to the front of the cattle pen again, he appeared satisfied.

'Aye, they're a likely lot of beasts and they've not been over-driven. Well, Angus, I'm willing to buy them if we can strike a bargain. Name your price, my boy.'

Angus eyed him cautiously. 'It would be a better thing if you would name your price first, Mr Barlow,' he said respectfully but firmly.

Barlow gave a chuckle. 'I see your father has taught you a thing or two about cattle selling. Yon's a man I've a great respect for, James Cameron! Well, now, what about seven pounds a beast for a quick sale?'

'Oh, I'm in no hurry to sell quickly,' Angus assured him. 'The Tryst will last three days yet. I could be getting twelve pounds a head for those stirks, I have no doubt.'

Barlow grinned at him good-humouredly. 'Maybe, but not from me, my lad! Well, Angus, I'll come to eight pounds.'

The serious business of bargaining was begun and Angus was quick to take it up.

'Eight pounds is not enough, but I will take eleven pounds from a good old customer like yourself,' he offered.

'Nay, lad, I'm too old a customer to fall for flattery,' Barlow laughed, but he advanced his price all the same. 'Shall we say nine pounds, then?'

'I will not haggle for a pound,' Angus said in very generous tones. 'I will accept ten pounds.'

Again the chuckle from Barlow. 'Well, now, we're

getting within sight of striking a bargain. I'll split the difference with you, Angus. Nine pounds ten shillings a head, shall we say, if you'll drive the herd to my farm at Penrith for me?'

Angus was very pleased at having struck so satisfactory a bargain, for he had not expected to get more than nine pounds a head for his animals, even though prices were high because of the war with Napoleon, but he was not going to give in too easily.

'Yes, I will agree to your price if you will pay the three of us drovers' wages of a shilling a day each,' he bargained further.

Barlow appeared satisfied. 'Done, then!' He placed a penny in Angus's hand as a token that the bargain was concluded. This was known as 'the penny of arles', and it was customary between buyer and seller in the cattle markets of Scotland. Once a seller had taken the penny in his hand, he could not in honesty go back upon his bargain. It was one of the laws of the market.

'Well, that's the bargain sealed,' Barlow said, looking pleased. 'And I might tell you, Angus lad, you're as keen a blade at driving a bargain as your father. Well, I don't mind giving good money for good meat. But there was a bull ye were to bring with ye, too. Where is it?'

Angus and Colin exchanged glances and Colin hung his head in shame.

'We have not got it now,' Angus stated baldly.

Mr Barlow looked slightly annoyed. 'Nay, you don't mean to tell me you've parted with it already, before you've seen me first? Your father made me a promise that he'd give me the first chance to make an offer for it.'

Angus saw that the only thing was to tell the truth to Mr Barlow. 'Last night the bull was stolen from us while we rested the cattle at a farm pasture above Bannockburn,' he explained.

'Stolen! Never!' Barlow exclaimed in surprise.

'It was all my fault, Mr Barlow,' Colin admitted in a shamed voice. 'I fell asleep at my watch. I am very sorry, for my father wanted us to sell the bull to you. When we woke, the bull was gone.'

'Well, that's a right disappointment for I was fairly interested in yon bull when I saw him last year,' Barlow said. 'Have ye no idea who stole him?'

'Well, we have,' Angus began. 'There was a man whom we trusted, to whom we had done a good turn, but he proved a rascal —'

'Aye, there are plenty of rascals to choose from at the Tryst,' Mr Barlow put in. 'It is a pity you lost the bull, but there are some things only learned by experience and ye're both young lads yet. Now, ye'd greatly oblige me if ye'd drive these beasts to my farm, Catterlen, near Penrith. But I'd like you to wait till tomorrow as there's another small lot I fancy that will be for sale then, and you could drive them for me with your own herd, if you would?'

'Yes, we will do that,' Angus agreed.

'Good! Then we will go to the bank and I will settle the account with you. Will you take half the money now and half when you deliver the herd at Penrith? That is the usual custom.'

'Yes, I will agree to that.'

'Come back with me to the bank, then,' Barlow said.

'You watch the cattle with Donald, Colin. I shall not be long,' Angus directed.

Angus departed with Mr Barlow and Donald strolled round to the back of the herd to see that all was well there, and Colin was left standing at the front of the cattle-pen. He was whistling a tune to himself and gazing about him when someone touched his elbow. It was a gipsy lass.

'Will you have your fortune told, young sir? If you would cross my palm with silver, I would tell you the best fortune in the world,' she begged in a whining flattering voice. 'A shilling, now? Just a shilling for a fine fortune I'll whisper to you.'

Colin shook her impatiently from his elbow. 'I have no shilling. I do not wish my fortune told,' he said curtly without looking at her. She gripped his arm again, however.

'Nay, do not turn away, young gentleman. If you have not a shilling, surely you have a sixpence in your pocket?'

'Go away. I have no money,' Colin said roughly, shaking her off.

'Colin Cameron, will you not turn and look at me?' the gipsy hissed in his ear. 'I've something to say to you.'

Colin turned sharply. 'Bethia!' he exclaimed. It was the young gipsy whose life he had saved on the Moor of Rannoch.

'Ssh!' she said, putting a finger to her lip. 'You do not know who may be near. Do not show you know me, but pretend to let me tell your fortune.'

Colin turned sharply. "Bethia!" he exclaimed

Her voice was so urgent that Colin fell in with her wishes. He gave her his hand, palm upwards, and said: 'All right, then. I will hear my fortune,' in a loud voice that anyone might hear.

'Cross my palm with a sixpence then,' Bethia said equally loudly. 'Thank you, sir. Now listen to me.' In a lower voice she said: 'Bend your head near to me, Colin, so that no one else can hear.'

Colin obeyed her.

'You have lost Torcull the bull,' Bethia told him.

Colin was considerably startled. 'How did *you* know?' he gasped.

'Listen! He was brought to our camp in the Torwood by my uncle, Peter the Gipsy, last night. He had got him from McQuaid, the packman, during the night when you were all asleep. He crept up within a couple of hundred yards of your camp and McQuaid severed the rope and led the bull to him,' Bethia informed Colin.

'*Now* I understand it all!' Colin exclaimed.'It was McQuaid, the black-hearted rogue, after all!'

'Quiet!' Bethia warned him. 'I heard the men talking round our camp-fire. They thought I was asleep, but I was in my tent close by with the other women, listening all the time. I heard the older women talking among themselves today, too. The men will guard the bull all day in the woods and tonight, when it is dark, they mean to take him to Grangemouth.'

'Grangemouth?' Colin exclaimed, surprised.

'Ssh! Not so loud! There they will take the bull aboard a boat. They have a customer for him at Queensferry. They will land the bull there while it is still night.'

'I shall go to the Torwood and find Torcull and take him back!' Colin determined.

'No! no!' Bethia said in terror. 'At Torwood your life would be in danger. There are too many of the gipsies there. Go to Grangemouth instead, but take your brother with you. At Grangemouth there will only be two people with the bull, McQuaid and Laidlaw.'

'Laidlaw? Why, he's the man who came pretending to buy our bull!' Colin exclaimed in astonishment.

'He is a wicked man indeed. You must beware of him, Colin. He and McQuaid have followed you all the way from the farm to steal the bull. They said they might as well let you have the trouble of driving him down to Falkirk for them.'

'The rogues!' Colin cried.

'Yes, they are all of that, and so is my uncle, Peter the Gipsy. But listen! Look for a little wooden jetty down by the Carron shore. The boat is to be waiting there to take the bull.'

'I will remember what you say,' Colin promised. 'I am grateful to you, indeed, Bethia, but why have you told me this against your own people, the gipsies?'

'I have a debt to pay you,' Bethia replied seriously. 'You and Torcull saved my life. Besides, I am not liking all the things the gipsies do. My uncle is not kind to me. I have no father nor mother. Sometimes I think I shall run away.' There was a hint of desperation in the girl's voice. 'Be careful though. I can see McQuaid looking our way across the field. Laugh as if the fortune amuses you.'

Colin threw back his head and laughed. 'You're telling me that, now?'

Bethia raised her voice. 'Aye, you will go a long way, young sir, and make many journeys, but great wealth will come to you out of them.'

'I will believe that when I see it!'

'It will come by your own hard work and honesty! And that at least is true,' she added in a lower voice. 'That is all, kind sir,' she said loudly, as one of her own folk passed by them. 'Thank ye, and may good luck go with the fortune!' In a whisper she added: 'Keep out of McQuaid's way, Colin. Farewell.' In a second she had vanished from Colin's side and was mingling with the crowd again, begging shamelessly like the rest of the gipsies.

Donald returned from the back of the herd. 'Aye, everything is all right there,' he reported. 'Rob is crouched at the back of the animals, watching them. He will stay there till I whistle him up. Here comes Angus back again. Mr Barlow is still with him.'

Angus approached them quickly. 'Donald, will you and Colin take the herd over to yon pasture on that low hill to the south? Wait for me there. Mr Barlow wants me to go and look at some other cattle with him.'

Colin stepped forward eagerly, very excited at the news he had learnt from Bethia. 'Angus, I have something to say to you. I have seen someone at the fair —'

Angus cut him short. 'I have no time now. Mr Barlow is waiting. It must keep till I come back again, Colin.'

'Oh, very well,' Colin said in a disappointed tone, though he thought there was little could be done about the bull till nightfall. Besides, it was plain that Angus was in a great hurry.

'I have some distance to go,' Angus told Donald. 'It is to see some cattle that are still pastured across the river at Sherriffmuir that Mr Barlow thinks of buying. I will take the pony. You will be all right, now?'

'Aye, we shall do fine. I know yon farm well where we are to pasture the beasts. The folk are honest enough. You can be taking your time, Angus. We will move off now with the herd. Come on, Colin. Whistle the dogs.'

Soon they were moving with the herd away from the Tryst while Angus was riding alongside Mr Barlow in the opposite direction. Colin hoped with all his heart that Angus would soon be back again and he could tell him Bethia's news.

The Return of Simon

At last Donald and Colin got the herd safely out of Falkirk and a few miles to the south where they pastured them at a farm that Donald knew well, where Mr Cameron usually stayed on his droving journeys into England. Donald looked about him at the green hillside with satisfaction, then placed a stone comfortably by the camp-fire for a seat.

'Quiet it is up here after all the noises of the Tryst,' he said. 'Though I am enjoying the Tryst while I am at it, for it is a change, mark you, from Drumbeg, yet I shall be glad, too, when we leave it behind.'

Colin, slightly excited, thought of the journey which lay before them. 'Tomorrow we take the road to *England*, Donald!' he said with elation.

'Aye,' Donald replied in a matter-of-fact voice.

Colin took a deep breath. 'It is the first time I have ever been out of Scotland to a foreign-like country. You have been to England before, though, have you not, Donald?'

'Aye, many a time with the droves.'

'What is it like? Tell me, Donald?' Colin asked eagerly.

'Och, one drove road is much like another, laddie. It goes over the hillsides and down across the rivers in England just as it does in Scotland. Maybe our hills are higher and wilder, and it is not easy to find free pastures in England,' the old man said.

'But the people? They are different, are they not?'

Donald considered the question gravely before he gave his answer. 'The older I grow, the more I am thinking that people are much alike too. True, their words and their voices are different, but their thoughts are much the same. There are good and bad men, honest men and thieves, in England as well as in Scotland. Their oatmeal is not so good in England, and the farmers' wives do not make oat-bread so much as wheaten bread. I have noticed that. Oh, and they have more ploughlands to their farms.'

Colin looked at him crestfallen and disappointed. 'I had thought it would be so different,' he said.

'Ah, well, in the big towns it might well be,' Donald agreed, 'but I always kept well away from the towns. The herd is my life and it is as easy to be contented on one grassy hillside as another, in England or in Scotland, if there is enough to eat and the weather is good.' That was Donald's philosophy of life.

Colin looked anxiously towards the north and the road leading to the Forth. 'Angus is a long time coming back. The shadows are growing long on the hills,' he said.

'Aye, but he will be having a lot of business to talk over with Mr Barlow, no doubt, and it is a good way to Sherriffmuir too.'

Colin hesitated for a minute and then he said: 'There is something I wanted to tell Angus before it grew dark, Donald. There is a thing I must do. It is about Torcull the bull. I *must* get him back.'

'It is no use fretting about the bull now, Colin.

Nothing can be done,' Donald said kindly. 'Where would you find him among the many thousands of cattle that will be coming and going from the Tryst? No, the bull is gone and there is no more to be said.'

'But I know *where* to find him,' Colin put in quickly. 'Someone I met at the fair, someone I am sure can be trusted, told me where the thieves had hidden him. He is to be taken by a boat out of Grangemouth tonight when it is full dark.'

'You are sure of that?' Donald asked.

'Yes. I wanted Angus to go with me, but he will not be back in time to go all the way to Grangemouth, and if once Torcull is taken in that boat we shall never see him again.'

'There is no doubt you are right there,' Donald agreed, looking perplexed. 'Oh, if only Angus would come, he would know what to do.'

'I must go myself, Donald,' Colin said with determination.

'No, no, Colin! Your life might be in danger. It would never do!' Donald protested. 'I would go myself, but I cannot be leaving the herd. There are too many cattle thieves about.'

'I am the one who can best be spared. We lost the bull because I fell asleep on my watch, so *I* must be the one to bring him back again. Never fear, Donald, I shall be all right,' Colin said boldly, with an assurance he was far from feeling.

'If only Angus would come back!' Donald sighed, looking more troubled than ever.

'Do not be distressed, Donald. I might meet Angus on the way. There is a plan in my head too.'

'Will you take one of the dogs with you then? I can manage with the other.'

'Yes, that is a good thought, Donald. I will take Rob. He is obedient and keeps silence when he is told. I had better go now, for I must reach Grangemouth by the time darkness falls.'

'Be careful, then,' Donald warned him.

'I will. Tell Angus where I have gone and that I shall be coming back with Torcull,' Colin said with an assumed confidence that did not deceive Donald. He whistled up the dog. 'Come on, Rob!'

With the black-and-white collie dog at his heels Colin set off down the hill towards Grangemouth at a good pace. He took a side road to the east that cut out Falkirk and the Tryst ground, and made his way towards the shore of the Firth of Forth. Soon he found himself walking by the Carron river and he knew he was heading in the right direction for the little port. The land was flat and swampy and so different from his Highland home or the country they had traversed on the drove roads. He felt strange and ill at ease, and as he went his thoughts dwelt on Simon and he wondered if Simon had made his way to Grangemouth too, as he had said that he would.

'If he leaves this country, it must be by boat, and he knows a sea captain at Grangemouth,' Colin reasoned with himself, and as he went along he became more and more convinced that if Simon had made for any port at all, it would be Grangemouth. He crossed the wide street that was Grangemouth's market place, and found himself among a maze of little streets that ran along the riverside down to the new canal and the harbour. He reached the stone pier which jutted

out into the firth and the warehouse that stood at
the landward end of it. There was also a shed in
which a couple of boats were drawn up out of the
water. At one side of the pier a two-masted vessel
was moored, but all was silent and there appeared
to be no one aboard her, for no lights were showing.
Colin hesitated, at a loss to know quite what he should
do next. There was no one about the little harbour at
all. Colin whistled up the dog.

'To heel, Rob! Not a sound!' he said, and taking the
dog by the collar he led him into the open boat-shed
and crouched down behind the boat nearest to the
stone pier.

'Quiet now, Rob. We will wait here where we can
see all the boats and who comes to them.'

For a time they heard nothing but the beating of
the waves against the stone pier and the cries of the
seagulls as they wheeled overhead.

While Colin and Rob were waiting to see what
would happen, hiding in the old boat-shed, Simon,
the Frenchman, was making his way to Grangemouth
too. All that day he had waited among the Gargunnock
Hills, in the shelter of a quarry overgrown with bushes,
and when dusk fell he walked boldly along the road
in his borrowed kilt, looking as if he were some
shepherd or herdsman. Like Colin he skirted the
town of Falkirk and made his way towards the
port of Grangemouth. No one spoke to him or
challenged him, for there were many Highland
drovers on the roads at the Tryst time, and those
men who were looking for an escaped prisoner of
war were certainly not looking for him in a kilt of
the Cameron tartan!

'Well, here I am at Grangemouth and so far no one has stopped me,' Simon said to himself with satisfaction. 'So far, so good! And now to find Captain John Aitken.' Like Colin he now found himself at a loss. He was not even sure whether the captain was at sea or ashore, nor where he lived in the little port. He found himself just outside the Three Fishers Inn. From within came the buzz of many voices.

'I shall have to take a chance and ask someone, if I am not to stand in the main street all night,' Simon told himself. 'They will know at the inn where the captain is to be found, no doubt, and a stranger asking there will not attract too much attention in all that crowd.'

Making up his mind, he opened the door cautiously and thrust his head inside. The room was filled with iron-workers from the Carron iron-works just across the canal, and with seafaring men from the Forth, and one or two who looked like farmers and drovers. Behind the counter a stout landlord was filling a tankard with ale from a barrel. Simon decided to be bold and walked straight up to the counter.

'Good evening to you, landlord,' he said politely.

The landlord looked up and took him for a Highland drover. 'Weel, Highlander, what is your pleasure?' he asked.

'I am looking for a Captain John Aitken. I understand his ship is in the harbour,' Simon said, drawing a bow at a venture.

'Aye, that's right. The *Bonnie Nancy* arrived with

a cargo from Norway yesterday,' the landlord told him.

Simon's heart jumped with relief. 'Will the captain be aboard the *Bonnie Nancy* now, do you think?' he asked.

The landlord scratched his head and looked doubtful. 'Wait while I ask the wife,' he said. 'She'll ken. She served the captain with his dinner the day.'

He disappeared into some premises behind the inn parlour and Simon rested his hand on the counter and waited, taking a look at the crowded room as he did so. Two men were seated in a corner of the room drinking. One of them saw Simon, and gave a start. It was the packman McQuaid! He tapped his companion lightly on the hand and leaned forward across the table, keeping his head down so that his face could not be easily seen.

'Listen, Laidlaw!' he whispered. 'Take a look round at yon man leaning against the counter — the one who has just finished speaking with the landlord.'

Laidlaw stared hard at Simon.

'He was with Cameron's herd last night,' McQuaid informed him.

Laidlaw gave a start and looked alarmed. 'Mercy on us!' he exclaimed.

McQuaid gave a low laugh. 'Dinna fash yourself,' he said with something like contempt in his voice. 'The man canna see us in this corner. Besides, he knows nothing about the taking of the bull. He was away before I cut the bull loose. He knows nothing about what happened after he'd gone, but I have reason to think he's no' the drover he makes himself out to be.'

'What do you mean?'

'I think he is an escaped prisoner of war, a Frenchman,' McQuaid hissed into Laidlaw's ear.

Laidlaw looked up quickly. 'But, man, if he is, then there'll be a price on his head.'

McQuaid nodded. 'I know that well. If we hand him over to a magistrate we can claim a reward. What do you say we follow him when he leaves the inn?'

Laidlaw looked rather doubtful. 'Will there be time before we take the bull aboard the boat?'

'Oh, aye, plenty!' McQuaid said with confidence and spat on the floor. 'Peter the Gipsy is to meet me with the bull by Bothkennar Churchyard in an hour's time. The boat is lying down at the creek already. There'll be time to account for yon Frenchman in the bargain and put a little gold in our pockets.'

'I'm with ye, then,' Laidlaw agreed.

Just then the kitchen door behind the counter was opened again and the landlord came back into the room.

'I'm sorry to be so long, man, but the wife was at her mother's next door,' he explained to Simon. 'She says Captain Aitken has gone to Falkirk, but he'll likely be back in a two-three hours as he wants to sail with the tide tomorrow morn early.'

'Thank you for your trouble, landlord,' Simon said, laying a shilling upon the counter. 'I'll go down to the harbour and leave a message aboard his ship if there is anyone there. Good night to you.'

'Good night, sir, good night,' the landlord returned, full of sudden respect at the unexpected sight of the shilling. All the same he said to himself as he pocketed the coin: 'That's no' very like a Highland drover. They're usually ower careful with their money.'

Simon closed the door behind him, but hardly had he gone when McQuaid and Laidlaw rose, leaving their tankards half-empty, and followed him through the door. They saw him striding down the street ahead of them towards the harbour.

'Steal after him,' McQuaid said in a low voice. 'Keep to the shadows. He's making for the harbour.' He took Laidlaw by the arm. 'Quick! Down this close! It's a short cut that brings us out on the harbour side. We'll get there before him.'

Once in the close the men started to run. When they reached the end of it, McQuaid stopped abruptly and peeped round the corner at the quayside. Simon's quick footsteps echoed along the road to the stone pier.

'Wait! He's coming along now,' McQuaid said a little breathlessly. 'When he draws level with us, leap on him out of the shadow. I've got a scarf to bind him when we've knocked him down.'

The men waited tensely, not daring to move a muscle as the approaching footsteps came nearer. In the boat-shed Colin waited too, his hand over Rob's mouth. He too had heard the footsteps.

'Quiet, Rob!' he whispered in the dog's ear. 'There's someone coming. Keep still. It's a man by himself. Suppose it could be Simon? We'll wait till we're sure.' The dog stayed crouched by him obediently, but the short hairs at the back of his neck rose as he listened too.

Nearer came the footsteps. All at once, with a sudden shout, McQuaid and Laidlaw leaped out from their hiding-place and fell upon Simon with blows as he passed the mouth of the close.

'At him! Get the hold of him!' McQuaid shouted.

For a moment Simon staggered, then he lifted his fists and hit out right and left at the two men.

'You thieves and rascals! Take that! And take that!' he cried.

McQuaid had expected Simon to drop to the ground with the shock of their first assault, but he had never thought he would turn upon them and give them as good as he got. He reeled back from Simon, clutching at his stomach and groaning. 'Oh! Oh! He's winded me!' he gasped. 'Get hold of him, Laidlaw! Don't let him go!'

Laidlaw made a grab at Simon, but Simon stepped back quickly, then came in again and gave Laidlaw a hard blow that made him sit down suddenly.

'That'll teach you to meddle with me!' Simon cried, and turned and made for the pier.

The fight was over before Colin had time hardly to realize what had happened. Then, all at once he saw Simon fleeing down the pier with the two rogues after him. He knew that at the end of the stone quay, Simon would have to turn and fight the two of them again. He loosed his hold on Rob's collar.

'After them, Rob! At their heels! Snap at their heels!'

The dog needed no second bidding. He raced down the quayside after Laidlaw, who was not aware of the pursuing terror. Rob seized him just above the ankle. Laidlaw let out a sharp yell of pain.

'There's a dog at my legs!' Laidlaw cried, dancing

round madly in a kind of circle and trying to beat the dog off. 'Off with ye, ye savage brute!'

McQuaid had paused for a moment in his chase after Simon, but now he shouted: 'Catch the Frenchman first!' and continued his pursuit. There was a sudden loud splash in the water below the stone pier and Simon disappeared from sight. McQuaid pulled himself up sharply.

'There he goes! Clean off the pier into the firth!' he shouted. 'He's leaped into the water.'

Colin, from the darkness of the shed, had seen Simon jump over the edge of the quay too, and fearful lest Rob should fall into the water he gave a low whistle, which the dog heard and instantly obeyed. Colin grabbed him as he returned to the shed and thrust him under the boat, keeping a firm hold of his muzzle lest the dog should bark and betray him.

'Quiet now, Rob!' he whispered.

McQuaid turned upon Laidlaw. 'Losh, man, you had the fellow in your hand and you let him go! Why did ye no' keep a grip on him?'

'How could I when yon dog took the hold of my leg?' Laidlaw asked hotly. 'You should have kept a grip on the Fenchman yourself!'

'And me winded with his elbow in my ribs and his fist in my eye!' McQuaid cried indignantly. 'Talk sense, man!'

'I didna ken the Frenchie had a dog with him or I would have thought twice of attacking him,' Laidlaw said in a surly tone.

'Neither did I think he had a dog.'

'Where's the brute gone?' Laidlaw demanded, looking about him uneasily.

'Och, far enough away likely!' McQuaid declared impatiently. 'Where's the man? That's more important. Come to the end of the harbour wall and look.'

They peered out over the breastwork into the darkness of the firth beyond, but it was impossible to see anything other than the white edge of the waves as they curled over against the stonework.

'I canna see anything,' Laidlaw said shortly.

'The Frenchie must be somewhere down there in the water,' McQuaid insisted.

'Then, if he is, he's a half-drowned man already,' Laidlaw said callously.

'There'll be a boat up yonder in yon shed. We might get it launched and ply round in the water a while with it.'

Laidlaw shook his head with determination. 'No' me!' he exclaimed. 'I'm no swimmer. Besides, there's no time to go rowing if we're to get back in time to fetch the bull from Bothkennar.'

McQuaid looked backward towards the firth with reluctance. 'I'm vexed to let the Frenchie go,' he said.

Laidlaw gave a tug at his arm to fetch him along. 'Och, the tide will account for him, never fear!' he said brutally. 'Come on back to the inn. I wish I had the hold of that dog, though!'

As they passed the boat-shed McQuaid hesitated for a moment. 'I wonder if the dog went in there,' he said.

Laidlaw did not seem very anxious to look for the dog once the opportunity was offered him, however. 'Och, come along! There's no time now,' he said impatiently.

Crouched in the shed Colin hardly dared to breathe lest the dog should bark and betray them both. He kept his hand firmly over Rob's muzzle, and the dog kept obediently still. Not till the sound of the men's footsteps died away up the close did Colin dare to stir, and then he rushed out on to the stone pier with the dog at his heels.

'Simon! Simon!' he half-called, half-whispered. 'Oh, I fear he'll be drowned! Oh, Simon, are you down there in the water? Simon? Simon?' he called cautiously, keeping his voice low. Then, all at once he remembered their signal in the wood, and he hooted three times like an owl. It was the last call of despair. In the silence that followed he was about to turn away when he heard a low whistle on two notes from the other side of the stone pier. Quickly he faced about. Up out of the greyness at the edge of the stone quay loomed a dark figure climbing up on to the pier. Colin's heart jumped. The figure hesitated.

'Hello! Is that you, Colin?' came in a low voice.

Colin ran towards him. 'Simon! Save us, but you gave me a start, coming up like that out of the water! I thought you were drowned!'

Simon laughed. 'Drowned? Not I! Why, there's less than a couple of feet of water down there. The tide's out! I was more spattered with mud than drowned.'

'Thank goodness for that!'

'Yes, thank goodness for a dark moonless night and a low tide!' Simon echoed. 'Once I was in the water I flattened myself against the stone pier and held my breath. The men couldn't see me there unless they put their head over and peered right down below them. They could hear the lap of the waves against the stone-work and they thought I was drowned. All I had to do was to wait till they were gone and to walk round the pier to the other side where there was a ladder out of the water.' Simon laughed again at the success of his trick. 'Was it you who set the dog at them?'

Colin nodded. 'Yes. I was just going to leap on them myself when I heard you jump into the water. It was no use showing myself then, so I stayed in the boat-shed where I was hiding. But your clothes? Aren't they wet?' he asked.

Simon shrugged his shoulders. 'The kilt is a bit splashed and the hem of it is wet, that is all. It will dry as we walk along. But what were *you* doing at Grangemouth, Colin?'

'For one thing, I was looking for you.'

'For me?' Simon exclaimed, amazed.

'Yes. You had told me you would try to get a boat from Grangemouth,' Colin reminded him.

'So I did. I had forgotten.'

'I wanted to tell you, too, that I knew you would never steal our bull, Simon, and to ask your help to get him back,' Colin said, forgetting in his turn that Simon did not know about the theft of the bull.

'Steal the bull? Get him back?' Simon repeated, mystified.

'Torcull the Black was stolen the night you left us.'

Simon stared at Colin. 'Stolen!' Light began to dawn upon him. 'And you thought because I had disappeared that *I* had taken your bull?'

'*I* never thought so,' Colin replied staunchly. 'It was that rascal McQuaid said it, and all the time he was the thief. A gipsy girl told me so today. There must have been some sleeping draught in that herb beer that he gave us to make us all sleep through our watches the way we did. Perhaps it was some draught of herbs that the gipsies made up.'

Simon gave a laugh. 'That could be true. I never drank mine, but poured it quietly out of the bottle into the ground because I thought it was too bitter. But McQuaid? The packman? Colin, one of those two men just now —'

'Yes, one was McQuaid,' Colin broke in. 'I'm sure of it. The other was Laidlaw who tried to steal our bull from the farm and shot at my father. Listen, Simon! He has a plan to smuggle Torcull the bull out of Grangemouth tonight in a boat. But I will tell you about it as we go along.'

'Yes, it would not do to hang round the harbour here too long lest those two ruffians come back,' Simon agreed.

Colin called Rob to heel, and as they went along he told Simon the whole story of how McQuaid had handed over the bull to the gipsies.

When Simon heard the tale he promised to help Colin to try to recover the bull when the two men should try to embark him. They followed the river down to the little creek by the Carron shore. The sky in the east was growing bright and the moon beginning to rise.

'The rogues will need moonlight to get the bull aboard the boat,' Colin remarked. 'Torcull will not be easy to handle where there is water.'

Simon caught him by the arm. 'Look down there at the mouth of the little creek. There's a boat there and there's someone in it,' he whispered. 'Stoop down behind these bushes and watch. Will the dog keep silence?'

'Aye, Rob is well trained.'

'We will wriggle along on our hands and knees till we reach the place where the bushes are thickest near the boat. Then we'll wait.'

Colin took Rob by the collar. 'Quiet, Rob! Not a sound!'

As if the dog understood him, he sank down on his stomach and dragged himself silently along the ground as though stalking an escaped animal.

'Stop here!' Simon whispered when they reached the thick shadow cast by the bushes. 'We are quite near to the boat and the edge of the river here. Keep your hand on the dog's mouth. You know what to do, Colin?'

'Yes, I'm ready.'

They peered through the bushes at the silent black figure on the boat. It was Laidlaw right enough, outlined in the moonlight. Just then Colin lifted his head sharply.

'Listen! Is that McQuaid coming with the bull?' he hissed in Simon's ear.

They both crouched stock still, listening, and Colin kept his hand round Rob's muzzle. They could plainly hear the sound of a man and a four-footed beast coming along the narrow lane that wound by the side of the river. Then they heard the man urging the animal on and striking at it with his stick.

'On with you, ye brute! Get along there!' The stick

fell with a thud and there was a frightened bellow
from the bull. Colin clenched his teeth and vowed
vengeance on McQuaid for ill-treating Torcull.

From the boat Laidlaw hailed the packman. 'Is that
you with the bull, McQuaid?'

'Aye. Is everything all right?'

'Yes. I'm ready to hoist the sail. There's not a soul
stirring along the shore. All's been quiet.'

McQuaid struck Torcull again. 'Come on up, ye
beast! Pull back, would ye? Come on!' The stick
descended again and Colin gritted his teeth to prevent
himself from crying out: 'Stop, you wicked brute!'
The bull bellowed in pain.

'Quiet, ye beast!' McQuaid exclaimed. 'If it was
not that I wanted to sell you well, I'd lay my stick
about your back, ye obstinate creature!'

Just as the stick was raised again, it was suddenly
snatched from the packman's grasp and the blow fell
on his own shoulders.

'Take that, you villain!' Simon cried, leaping out
upon him from behind the bushes.

Colin sprang from his hiding-place too with the
dog. 'Out, Rob! Turn the bull! Turn the bull! At his
heels!' he shouted.

In a moment Rob had faced the bull about and
was snapping at his heels. The frightened bull tossed
his horns and stampeded along the path by which he
had come, almost knocking McQuaid down. Rob and
Colin followed hard after him.

'What's to do, McQuaid? What's to do?' Laidlaw
shouted from the boat.

'Save us! It's the black fiend himself after me!'
McQuaid yelled.

Laidlaw thought that McQuaid must have been attacked by half a dozen men at least. 'Mercy on us! Let me get the boat off!' he cried, more anxious to save his own skin than help his accomplice.

He cast off the mooring rope from the stump and pushed the boat off the bank with the aid of his oar. McQuaid, rushing in the direction of the boat, saw the gap of water widening between the boat and the shore and yelled in a panic: 'Wait for me, Laidlaw! Wait for me! Don't push off till I'm aboard. Help! Help! Mercy!'

'No mercy for you, you scoundrel!' Simon cried, clutching at McQuaid's jacket.

McQuaid gave a terrific twist and wrenched himself from Simon's grasp, and leaped after the boat. The gap between was too wide, however, and with a mighty splash he dropped into the water and disappeared from sight. A moment afterwards his head appeared above the water.

'I'm drowning! Help me out, Laidlaw! Come back, man! I've fallen in the water,' he cried.

Laidlaw, however, was rowing for dear life. 'No, I'm no' staying!' he shouted back. 'No' me!'

'Get me out or I'll drown!'

'You'll not drown in four feet of water, man!' Simon told him scornfully. 'A mud bath will cool you down a bit. There goes your friend down the creek as fast as he can row. You'd better go after him and wade the creek to the other side. If you dare to pull yourself up this bank again, I'm waiting for you with your own stick.'

McQuaid stood up to his waist in the water and shook his fist at Simon. 'You dirty French rogue!' he cried, recognizing him at last. 'I'll get even with you for this, you villain! I'll be revenged, you'll see.'

Simon laughed scornfully and waited till he had seen McQuaid pull himself up, a mud-bedaubed spectacle, at the other side of the river.

'He'll be too busy drying his clothes to come in search of me tonight,' Simon chuckled to himself, and then he turned and ran as fast as he could after Colin and the bull.

He caught up with them a good quarter of a mile further along the lane.

'Is the bull all right, Colin?' he cried as he came up with them.

'He's a bit frightened, that's all, but he knows my voice. He's calming down,' Colin assured him. 'Are *you* all right, Simon?'

'Never have I so enjoyed myself for a long time,' Simon said with relish. 'But now we must move along faster before McQuaid recovers his wits and Laidlaw his courage. Can you hurry the bull a bit more?'

'I'll do my best,' Colin said, giving Torcull a light slap on his flanks. 'Come up, Torcull! On with you! The quicker we can reach Angus and the herd, the better it will be for all of us.'

So, by way of field and woodland, along narrow paths and over grassy hills, they drove Torcull the Black with Rob padding at his heels, and before the moon had reached its height in the heavens they came to the place where Donald and Angus were camped with the herd.

Angus came running down the hill in the moonlight and with fierce joy and pride, Colin urged Torcull towards him. To Simon, striding beside him, Colin's heart surged in such a flood of friendship as he had never known for anyone before, and when Angus came forward and clasped Simon warmly by the hand, Colin could scarcely speak for the fullness of his heart.

That night, round the camp-fire, Simon and Colin told of the way they had taken back Torcull the Black from McQuaid. Old Donald chuckled for sheer joy at the thought of the way the thieves had been outwitted, but though he smiled, Angus stared rather unhappily into the fire. At last he turned and spoke to Simon.

'Simon, it was I who betrayed you for an escaped prisoner of war to McQuaid,' he confessed. 'I should have guarded my tongue better, but at the time I was sore because I thought you had stolen our bull. Now I know how wrong I was and I ask you to forgive me.'

Simon took his outstretched hand. 'We can all make mistakes. I agree that things must have looked very black against me at the time, Angus.'

'If you will travel the roads with us again, I will do my best to make amends,' Angus promised humbly, while Colin looked from one to the other with great joy.

'Tomorrow we will go and seek out Mr Barlow again, Colin, and show Torcull to him, while you, Donald and Simon, stay here with the herd,' Angus decided. 'That is unless you have other plans, Simon? You will not go to Grangemouth again, will you?'

Simon shook his head. 'No. Those ruffians will be looking for me there, that is pretty certain. McQuaid will not let me alone easily now.'

'Have you any plans, then?' Angus asked.

Simon knit his brows. 'Perhaps if I might get to the

coast, I might take ship to a foreign port. I have some
money. If you will help me, I could pay you —'

'Say no more about that.' Angus said. 'We are
debtors.'

'I am grateful,' Simon told him. 'Some day when
times are kinder I shall show my gratitude.'

'You would be safer with the herd than alone,'
Angus gave his opinion. 'When I have seen Mr Barlow
in the morn, we shall be taking the animals south to
Penrith for him. Once you are across the Solway, you
might make your way to Whitehaven. From there you
can easily get a ship to Ireland, and the rest of the
journey to France should be easy after that.'

'That is a good plan indeed,' Simon agreed. 'But if
I come with you, that might put your lives in danger
too. You could be cast into prison for helping me,
you know.'

'We will risk it,' Angus said with a smile. 'Once
we reach England, I do not think anyone would take
you for other than than a Highland drover, dressed
as you are.'

'Oh, Angus, I am so glad Simon is coming with
us,' Colin said gratefully.

'It will be a help to us, too, having Simon, for we
can do with an extra herdsman when we take the
other beasts Mr Barlow has bought. And now, I will
take the watch, while the rest of you get what sleep
you can, for it will soon be dawn.'

Angus and Donald made sure the herd was well
guarded that night, especially Torcull the Black, but
no one came near them and there was no cause for
alarm. Slowly the moon went down in the west and
the brightness of day appeared in the east.

Colin Strikes a Bargain

As soon as it was daylight Angus and Colin took the bull and made their way back to the Trysting ground at Stenhousemuir, leaving Donald and Simon with the herd. When Angus reached the cattle stances, he said: 'Stand you here, Colin, while I go and look for Mr Barlow. Be sure to keep a tight grip on the bull.'

Colin took an even firmer hold of the bull's halter. 'You may be sure I will this time,' he said grimly.

Angus looked from him to the bull, hesitating. 'It is time you learned something of buying and selling too,' he made up his mind. 'I think I shall leave you to do the bargaining with Mr Barlow for the bull.'

Colin looked horrified at the suggestion. 'Oh, Angus, would it not be much better for you to speak with him?' he asked.

'No. You have saved the bull for us and so it is only right that you should have the honour of selling him too. You know the price our father thought the bull ought to fetch?'

Colin nodded. 'Yes. A hundred and twenty guineas.'

'Then you must try to strike the bargain at that, so ask a little more, so as to leave you room to bring your price down to the one Father named,' Angus

counselled him. 'I shall only interfere if I think you
are not doing very well.'

'Very well. I will do my best, but I am very afraid,'
Colin said doubtfully.

'Look! There goes Mr Barlow pushing his way
through the crowds,' Angus cried, and ran after him
and caught him by the arm. 'A word with you, please,
Mr Barlow.'

Mr Barlow turned. 'Oh, Angus! I was just looking
for you about the other cattle you promised to drive
for me —' He caught sight of the bull and broke off
abruptly: 'But what's this?' He strode back to where
Colin was standing holding the bull.

'It is Torcull the Black, sir. We have got him back
again!' Colin said proudly.

'Colin heard a thing yesterday at the fair. Someone
told him where the bull was to be found and so he
went after it himself,' Angus explained.

'That was surely a risky thing to do?' Barlow
remarked.

'It was indeed, but a friend helped him and they
put up a good fight to win the bull back,' Angus
explained, rather proud of Colin.

'Well, ye're a lad after my own heart, Colin, a lad
that's not easily beaten,' Mr Barlow said, and Colin
glowed at these words of praise. 'Well, now, let's have
a look at this bull,' the Cumberland farmer went on,
his keen eye taking in the bull's good points. 'Aye,
aye, he's a well-built fellow. I'll not deny he's a good
animal,' he agreed. 'Well, name your price for him,
Angus.'

Angus waved a hand towards Colin. 'This time it
is Colin who is doing the selling.'

Thomas Barlow turned to Colin, smiling at the lad's eager flushed face. 'So that's the way of it? Well, Colin, how much for your bull?'

Colin remembered his father's words and replied very precisely: 'I would rather you made me an offer for the bull, Mr Barlow.'

Barlow laughed. 'Oh, you're the clever lad right enough! I can see your father has taught you something about selling cattle as well as he has Angus. By the way, what did your father say was a fair price for the bull?'

He rapped out his question so sharply that Colin, unused to ways of buyers, had not time to think, and before he realized what he was saying, he blurted out: 'A hundred and twenty guineas.' Then he gasped and his hand went to his mouth. 'Oh, what have I said!' he cried.

Angus looked dismayed. 'Oh, Colin, you should have bargained with Mr Barlow for the bull, not told him the price straight out like that!'

Colin looked vexed too. 'Well, it is done now,' he replied in a sullen tone. 'That was the price my father named, anyway. What is the use of all this bargaining if a fair price is asked to start with?'

'You might have got more than the price Father named,' Angus pointed out to him.

'I wish now you had done the bargaining yourself, seeing that you are the clever one, Angus,' Colin exclaimed angrily.

'Nay, now, Colin, keep your temper lad,' Mr Barlow advised him in friendly fashion. 'A good drover always keeps his temper. And, Angus, you hold off the lad a bit. He's new to the job, and I'm not so sure that I

hold with all this argy-bargying of bargaining myself.'
He turned to Colin again. 'Well, Colin, your father
named a fair price *for last year*.'

Colin looked bewildered. 'I do not understand.'

'This war with Napoleon has sent prices up a lot
since last year, my lad. The government wants all the
beef it can lay its hands on to salt down for the Navy.
The more beef we can raise, the better for everyone,
and it helps the war too. Good bulls like yon are
worth a lot of money,' Mr Barlow informed him.

Colin stared at the farmer. 'Do you mean that
Torcull is worth more than the price I said?'

'I do, lad.' Thomas Barlow nodded his head in
emphasis.

'But it is not to your advantage to be telling me
this, Mr Barlow,' Colin said, utterly surprised. Angus
opened his eyes wide too.

'Maybe not. Maybe not, Colin,' Mr Barlow said in
a whimsical voice. 'Well, now, will you name your
price for the bull again in the light of what I have
just told you?' He looked keenly at the lad.

Colin looked him straight in the face. 'A hundred
and twenty guineas,' he repeated doggedly.

'Colin! Are ye daft?' Angus cried.

'That was the price my father said, and that was
the price I named to Mr Barlow, and I will not now
go back on my word,' Colin replied obstinately.

'Bravo, Colin! I see you are an honest man,' Mr
Barlow said, shaking him warmly by the hand. 'You're
a man of your word. Well, lad, so am I. I'll be straight
with you as you have been straight with me. Listen
now! I'll make you an offer of a hundred and fifty
guineas for your bull.'

Colin's mouth dropped open, and Angus gave an exclamation of astonishment.

'Mr Barlow, are you joking?' Colin asked.

'No, I am not. I'll not hide it from you that I'll very likely sell the bull again at a profit. That's my business as a cattle buyer and seller. I know a customer who'll be at the Tryst today and will give me a better price still than the one I am offering you. He is a Lowland breeder who wants a good bull. Well, will my price suit ye?' he asked briskly.

'It will indeed,' Colin replied.

'And are you satisfied, Angus?'

'Yes, I am.'

'Then here's the penny to mark the deal, Colin.' Mr Barlow took out his purse and put a penny in Colin's hand, the token of acceptance of a bargain. 'And now, Angus, I'll say a word to ye, why I gave Colin a better price than the one he asked. It was for my own good name. Listen now! We none of us like a man who plays us a smart trick, do we?'

'That is very true, sir.'

'And we take care not to deal with him again?' Mr Barlow spoke sternly.

'Y-yes, that is right, too.'

'Well, now, if your father heard that I had got the better of him by a mean trick on his sons, he would not sell me any more bulls, eh?' the farmer asked, lifting one eyebrow.

'No, he would not, Mr Barlow.'

'There are good bulls come out of Drumbeg. I have bought them from your father and sold them again at a profit, as your father knows, for these many years,' the farmer told them. 'I have got a name for straightforward dealing that means more to me than gold, lads, for it is my living. Now, Colin, you lay that to heart, and you'll make a grand honest name for yourself as a drover, and it'll bring success and wealth with it too. Believe me, lad, the only wealth worth having is what is come by honestly.'

'I'll carry that in mind, Mr Barlow,' Colin said respectfully.

'Aye, and you can tell James Cameron from me that he has reason to be proud of his lads. Now, Angus, I'll go with Colin to the bank to pay over the money and *you* can hold the bull,' Mr Barlow proposed with something of a twinkle in his eye.

'Very well, Mr Barlow. Look well after the money, Colin,' Angus added with some anxiety.

'Oh, he'll do that, never fear!' Mr Barlow assured Angus with an amused smile. 'Then, when that is paid over, I'll take you along to my topsman and you can hand over the bull to him, and collect the herd that I want you to drive to Penrith with your own.'

Colin stroked the shaggy sides of the black bull. 'Good-bye, Torcull the Black,' he murmured in the bull's ear. 'You were the best bull that ever came out of Drumbeg. Good-bye, dear friend Torcull.' The beast looked at him out of melancholy brown eyes, and it was with much ado that Colin prevented the tears starting to his own at parting with the animal which he had cared for for so long. He hurried after Mr Barlow towards the shed at one side of the field.

'This is the booth of the Falkirk bank, Colin,' Mr Barlow informed him.

Colin looked at it with some disappointment. 'It is just a wooden shed. I thought banks were grand places, now.'

'Oh, there's a handsome building in Falkirk town if you want one. This is just a shed they put up for the drovers and buyers at the Tryst for our banking affairs,' Mr Barlow said as they entered. 'Well, now, the money for the bull? I take it you will want it paid into your father's account?'

'No, sir. My father has no bank account,' Colin replied promptly, much to Mr Barlow's surprise. 'He does not like banks. Besides, at Drumbeg there is no bank nearer to us than Fort William, and that is not handy.'

Mr Barlow looked troubled. 'But you can't go travelling round the country with all that money in your sporran, my boy. It wouldn't be safe.'

'It was my father's instruction, sir, that we should take the money with us,' Colin said firmly.

'Not a wise notion at all, to my mind.' Mr Barlow shook his head. 'You couldn't carry all that in gold, anyway. It would weigh too much.'

'Are there not such things as bank notes, sir?' Colin asked.

'Well, there are, I suppose,' Mr Barlow hesitated.

'Are there bank notes for fifty pounds, maybe?' Colin inquired.

'Mm. Yes. But —'

'Then I will take three bank notes for fifty pounds each, and the rest of the money in gold,' Colin informed him.

'Well, you know what you want all right,' Mr Barlow said with a grudging admiration. 'But suppose you lose the notes, Colin? They're only bits of paper, you know.'

'I shall not lose them,' Colin said. 'I have thought of a place where I can hide them.'

'Well, it's your business, but get them safe home to your father,' Thomas Barlow cautioned him. He drew the money from the bank teller and handed it over to Colin, who stowed it safely away in his sporran, the large purse he carried in the front of his kilt, before he left the bank.

'Thank you, Mr Barlow. I hope some day I shall have the honour of doing business again with you,' Colin told him with old-fashioned courtesy.

'Well spoken, youngster! On your own account, maybe, *sir*!' Mr Barlow replied with becoming gravity, repressing a smile.

'Maybe, Mr Barlow. A stranger thing could happen,' Colin answered him.

'Well, good luck to you, Colin. I shall be seeing you at Penrith with the herd, for I shall travel by the coach when the Tryst is ended and get to Cumberland before ye.' He shook Colin warmly by the hand in farewell.

Colin returned to Angus who greeted him eagerly. 'Did you get the money all right, Colin?'

'I did. It is in bank notes for fifty pounds each and the rest is in gold.'

'Good! Then perhaps you had better give me the notes for safety.'

Colin stared at him. 'What? In the middle of all this crowd?'

'Well, no, perhaps not just now,' Angus said, reddening a little. 'Later on when we reach the fields. But look that you take care of it meanwhile.'

Colin faced Angus. 'See, Angus, if I am to be trusted with the bull, I am to be trusted with the money too. You are only four years older than I am.'

'It is just that I am responsible to my father,' Angus told him with just a little importance.

'So am I,' Colin pointed out. 'You already hold half the money for the herd. If we each keep part of the money is it not a better thing? Then it cannot all be lost or stolen from us at the same time.'

'Yes, there is something in what you say,' Angus agreed grudgingly. 'But you have no safe pocket.'

'I am going to make a safe place. Will you give me a shilling, please?' Colin asked.

'What for?' Angus demanded.

'To buy needles and black thread. I am going to sew the notes separately into the pleats of my kilt, inside, near the belt. That way they will lie snug against my stomach, all the time, day and night, seeing that I sleep in my kilt too.'

Angus was forced to approve this plan. 'Take the shilling then, Colin,' he said. 'There is a packman selling threads just over there.'

'Not Mr McQuaid, I hope?' Colin said with a start.

'No, indeed!' Angus laughed. 'I hope we have seen the last of him. There is no sign of him at the Tryst this morning. I expect he is still waiting for his clothes to dry.' They both laughed, and Angus gave Colin an affectionate push. 'Hurry, buying your threads, so that we can get back to the herd and on the road again. The sooner we leave Falkirk, the better for us and Simon. I will deliver the bull to Mr Barlow's man, and we will collect the other cattle we are to drive, and then let us be off.'

When they reached the camping ground and the herd again, Colin went to a lonely sheep-pen on the hill where no one could see him, and he sewed the notes to the inside of his kilt, making pockets of the pleats near the waist-band. Then he felt the money was safe at last.

They drove the herd by way of Bathgate and the Cauldstane Slap over the Pentlands, and came across the brown moors, bright with the tawny bracken, to the gentle green hills of the south. Below them a dozen little burns foamed downwards like threads of silver to join and widen in the lovely river Tweed. Though these hills were not grand and forbidding mountains like those of the north, there was a sweetness and freshness about them that made Colin take great breaths in his lungs and look across the rolling lands with joy.

They came to the Devil's Beeftub, and Colin peered fearfully over the screes into the great gloomy hollow. Old Donald told them tales of the bad old times when every Border chieftain's hand was against his neighbour, and the Johnstones of Annandale drove their stolen cattle into the hollow of the Devil's Beeftub and hid them there.

Simon took his share in the droving and soon learned to whistle the dogs and bring up the stragglers of the herd. As they went along he told them many tales of France, of his home at Le Havre, of his warehouse and merchandise. The others were never weary of listening to him. So, untroubled, they brought the herds to the quiet lanes about Gretna Green and the

Scottish Border. When they came close to Gretna, however, Donald advised them to turn aside and to take another road to Carlisle.

'If you follow this road through Gretna, you'll have to cross two muckle great bridges,' he told them, 'and pay a tax on your beasts that will fair ruin ye, Angus.'

Angus was anxious to save as much expense on the road as he could and impress Mr Barlow with his good qualities as a drover, but he did not see how they could avoid crossing the bridges over the Solway and the river Eden.

'Aye, I know that,' he said to Donald. 'But we've got to get across the Solway somehow to get to Carlisle and Penrith.'

'There is a way I could be telling you if you would go a little out of your road to the west,' Donald informed him.

'Yes?'

'You must take the road that winds by the low pastures along Solway side. The shore there is low and sandy. You'll come too a village called Dornock, with a church and a square tower.'

'Go on, I'm listening,' Angus told him.

'There the Solway is less than two miles wide. There is a narrow channel called the Dornock Wath, then a great sandbank in the middle of the firth, then another narrow channel ye could almost leap, and there ye are at Bowness on the Cumberland side.'

'But the sea comes up the firth,' Angus objected.

'Aye, but at low tide there's but a trickle of water in the channels, that would not come above a man's ankles, and there are good sands the rest of the way. It's easy on the beasts' feet, a short two-mile of firm sand, and you're in Cumberland without paying bridge tolls and taxes, lad.'

'Have you ever been this way before, Donald?' Angus asked.

''Deed have I! Three times, no less!'

Angus made up his mind. 'Then we'll try it. Turn the beasts along the road, Colin.'

They took the herd along the pleasant lane that wound by the north side of the Solway Firth, a mossy road, never far from the sea itself and the salt pools among the stretches of spongy turf, where the sea-pinks blew in the light wind. At last they came to a tiny village with the church and its square tower, and then the lane plunged abruptly down to the sandy shore. They found themselves among the saltings with the channel of the Dornock Wath before them.

'This is the place where we must cross,' Donald told them. He pointed across the firth. 'See, yonder is Bowness on the Cumberland shore.'

Angus looked across the wide sandy flats of the Solway to the huddle of house-tops.

'It looks a long way across yon waste of sands,' he said with some doubt. 'There is a mist hanging above the far shore, too.'

'It is not so far as it looks,' Donald reassured him. 'Come, man, let us be going if we are to get across before the tide turns.'

'All right!' Angus agreed suddenly. 'Drive the cattle down into the firth.'

To the shouts of the drovers, the barking of the dogs, and the whistles which directed them the herd stampeded down with a great thunder of hoofs into the channel of water, almost falling head over heels down its clean-cut sides of firm sand. Colin was relieved to find when they got down on to the water that Donald was quite right and it was a mere trickle of three or four inches, very easy to wade.

'Up the other bank with them!' Angus urged them on. 'Quicker, Colin! Do not let the beasts stray,' he shouted sharply.

Colin was having some difficulty in preventing the cattle from heading downstream instead of climbing the opposite bank.

'Och, they are frightened at the water and stubborn,' he called back to Angus. 'On with you, now! On to the sand-bank!'

It took longer than they thought to get the herd across the Dornock Wath. Without Simon's additional help it would have been more difficult still. He mopped his brow when they had the herd safe on the firm sand again.

'Be easy. It is behind us now and the sand will be good going for the animals,' old Donald reassured them. 'All we have to do now is to make straight for yon low point on the opposite shore.'

Angus cast an anxious glance at the distance they still had to cover. 'A little quicker, if you can urge the cattle on, Colin,' he directed. 'Somehow I am not liking this place very much.'

'We must not be driving the beasts too fast or they will lose flesh,' Donald reminded him.

'Look! There goes Brown Sandy back to the water again and half the herd after him!' Colin exclaimed in exasperation. 'Was there ever such a stupid beast!'

'After them, Rob! After them, Sim!' Angus shouted.

'Simon, will you bring up the animals that have got to the far side of the channel again?'

There was again the tricky work of rounding up the nervous beasts. At last, once more the herd was assembled in a cluster on the firm sand-bank.

'Oh, this scatter of the animals causes delay,' Angus fretted impatiently. 'How long does the tide stay low, Donald?'

Donald himself was beginning to look a little anxious. 'I am not knowing exactly,' he confessed. 'But the water is still running *down* the channel, so the tide has not yet turned and there is no need for alarm.'

Colin called to Angus from the far side of the herd. 'We've got them all rounded up again, Angus.'

'Good! Try to keep the animals close together. Now we must make quickly for the rocky point on the other side.' He looked across the firth in the direction of Bowness, and then he gave a cry of alarm. 'Oh, where has the town gone?'

It was as though Bowness had been wiped out by a white blanket.

'It's the mist,' said Colin. 'It's thicker on the far shore.'

'Had we better turn back, Donald?' Angus asked anxiously.

'Why, we must be more than half-way across and the cattle are going well now and no bother. It would take longer to turn them about now, than to go on,' he pointed out.

'That's true. We'll go on, only keep the herd together at the back and push them hard, Colin and Simon,' Angus directed.

Once more the herd plodded on over the sands in

the direction they thought Bowness and the southern shore should lie.

'Look, Simon! The mist is drifting across the sand towards us,' Colin said uneasily.

'Yes, I do not like it either.'

'I cannot see the far shore at all. I hope Donald is certain of the way,' Colin remarked as they struggled along over the hard sand behind the herd.

From the front where he was leading the herd Angus shouted over his shoulder: 'Keep the herd together behind there, Colin. The mist is coming down on us.'

'I will try to keep at your heels with the animals, Angus.'

'Oh, how the mist blows round us like smoke! I wish it would clear. I can't even tell if we are driving the cattle straight across the firth,' Angus cried in trepidation.

'I am wishing too that we had gone the other way by the bridge,' Donald admitted, looking uneasily about him. 'Does it seem to you that your feet sink a little, Angus, as though the sand is softer than at first?' The old man lifted one foot wearily after the other over the sodden sands.

'Aye, it does,' Angus confirmed his observation. 'Here, Donald, you mount the pony. That way we might get along quicker.' He whistled to the dog. 'Fetch them up, Rob.'

Colin watched the sea mist swirling around them with fear too. 'I can see nothing but the beasts just in front of us. In this fog they look twice their size,' he told Simon. They were keeping within speaking distance of each other, for fear they lost sight of each other in the white dampness that blotted out the sand around them.

'I hope we are not going round in circles,' Simon said anxiously. 'Look! There are the marks of the feet of cattle to our right. Up with you, Big Jock! After him, Sim!' He cleverly rounded up a beast that was straying from the herd.

Colin stopped dead in his tracks. 'See there! Here's Donald on the pony coming back towards us. Stop, Donald, stop! Which way are you going?' he cried.

'Och, it's turning the beasts round in a circle on themselves, we are!' Donald lamented. 'We've lost our way. We cannot see the Cumberland shore.'

Angus ran up to take control. 'Stop! Hold your part of the herd back, Colin. We must try to find out where we are. For all we know we may be heading straight down the firth and out to sea! It's no use pushing on till we have found our bearings.'

'Oh, that *I* should have brought you this way,' Donald almost wailed. 'If only I could see the channel on the far side, the Bowness Wath!'

'The sand seems to be getting wetter,' Simon observed.

Angus suddenly felt the breath of a light wind on his cheek. 'Wait! There's a breeze coming up! The mist is clearing again. I can see the far shore now,' he cried, as the wind tore the mist apart and began to clear it from the sands in wraith-like shapes.

'Aye, I can see the shore too, but we're heading the cattle away from it,' Donald cried.

'Get the herd turned, Colin! This way, Simon! Round behind them, Rob! Fetch them round, Sim!' Running and shouting they brought the herd round at last, though at first all was chaos with the cattle heading in every direction, and milling around. But Colin used the two dogs cleverly behind the herd, and with them barking and snapping at the cattle, the men got the animals on the move in the right direction at last.

'I think we are nearly three-quarters of the way across now,' Angus estimated with some relief.

'Then we should soon be at the Bowness Channel. Watch for it closely for we drop steeply into it,' Donald warned them.

Simon stopped suddenly and stood still. 'Listen! What is that strange roaring sound?' he cried.

The roaring rushing sound of many waters advanced quickly upon them. They stared round about them, terror-struck.

Colin pointed in sudden fear. 'Oh, look! Look! There's the channel right ahead of us, and a wall of water four feet high rushing up it!'

'It's the Solway Bore! It's the wave that rushes up the channel when the tide turns!' Donald cried in horror.

Angus collected his wits first. 'Quick! Simon and Colin, each of you get astride a bullock and hold tight to its horns!' he shouted. 'We are going to have to swim the cattle across.'

Colin held on to the horns of Brown Sandy, and pulled himself up on to the animal's back, then he looked round fearfully for Simon.

'Are you all right, Simon? Are you all right?' he yelled.

Simon appeared at his elbow astride Big Jock, and holding on to the shaggy hair of his hide. 'Aye, the stirk's swimming bravely,' he called back.

"Are you all right, Simon?" he yelled

The herd all began swimming through the piled-up swirling waters in the channel. Their instinct led them towards the shore and they could smell the green turf ahead on the edge of the beach.

'Another few yards and we shall be safe ashore,' Donald said, urging on his pony. 'Hold tight, Angus!'

'Oh, look! There's a young stirk rolled over by the backwash!' Colin cried. 'He's been carried down the channel.' He made as if to leap from his own beast and go to rescue the stirk, but Angus perceived what he was going to do, and shouted: 'Keep hold of Brown Sandy, Colin. Don't let go! You cannot save the stirk now.'

Two waves had already driven up the channel, two solid walls of water that carried all before them. The animals were carried upstream by the force and sucked down channel again with the undersurge of the backwash. Yet a third wave came rushing up the channel. This time it had not quite the same driving force, as it was checked by the backward flow of the first two waves, but its swirl took the animals nearer in to the Bowness shore of the firth.

'This time it's helping us!' Donald cried. 'It is washing the animals up the creek towards the shore.'

'I touched the bottom with my feet then!' Angus cried with thankfulness. 'I touched sand. We are going up the far bank.'

The herd followed Donald on his pony and one and all began to struggle out of the water and on to the sand-bank beyond, over which the edge of the wave purled, spreading out in a fan-like flood to a depth of several inches. The water receded to Angus's waist and then to his knees, and then, in just a step or two, to his ankles. The first of the herd began to struggle ashore. As soon as they reached the dry sand they made a stampede for the soft green turf that bordered it, as though that gave them relief from fear, and confidence again.

'They've made the crossing!' Angus cried with great thankfulness. 'I am thinking we did well to come out of it with the loss of only one beast.'

'It's sorry I am, Angus, that I brought you this way and risked the beasts and all your lives,' Donald said.

'We must be thankful indeed that we were spared. Do not blame yourself, Donald,' Angus said kindly. 'You did your best. You were not to know the mist would come on us. We shall know better than to ford the firth again at the turn of the tide. We will rest the herd awhile here where there is good sweet grass, and we will make a fire of driftwood to dry our clothes. There are some dead twigs among those bushes there.'

'Look along the shore there! Look!' Donald cried. 'Right down there by the point of land jutting out into the sea! The lost stirk! He's coming over the short grass, munching at it as though nothing had happened.'

'Oh, that's fine, that's fine!' Angus cried, delighted. 'Now we have all the herd again and can face Mr Barlow without feeling ashamed that we have lost one of his beasts.'

'There is a stretch of common land behind us. How would it be if we rested the cattle here for the night where they can feed, Angus?' Donald suggested.

'Yes, we will do that,' Angus agreed at once. 'It will help the cattle to recover from their swim and let us rest too. We will take to the road again tomorrow.'

Simon looked rather thoughtful. 'Tomorrow I would like to visit Carlisle, if we pass anywhere near the town,' he said.

'We shall not be taking the herd through the town but we shall be going very near it, eh, Donald?' Angus asked.

'Aye, there is a farm three miles south of Carlisle where the farmer will let us pasture the herd for the night at a low price,' Donald replied.

'Is Carlisle bigger than Falkirk?' Colin asked with sudden curiosity.

''Deed, yes, it is a city. There is a great castle there,' Donald told him.

'How I would like to see a city!' Colin sighed.

'Would you like to come with me tomorrow evening, Colin?' Simon asked him.

'Oh, yes, I would! Indeed I would!'

'After we have pastured the herd tomorrow, can you spare Colin to go with me, Angus?'

'Yes, Simon. Donald and I will stay with the herd.'

'Oh, thank you, Angus! Thank you!' Colin cried gratefully.

'I want to buy trousers and a jacket there suitable for a seafaring man, so I can return your kilt to you, Angus,' Simon told him. 'The day after tomorrow I must make my way to Whitehaven to see if I can get a ship there for Ireland. Though I am indeed grateful to you for your kilt, it is not the kind of garb for a man who pretends to be a sailor.' Simon laughed a little self-consciously. 'The time has come for me to say farewell, I fear.'

'Oh, Simon, I wish you had not to leave us!' Colin cried in sorrow at the thought of losing his friend.

'I am sorry too, Colin, but I must go home to look after my family and my business,' Simon pointed out. 'But be cheerful! When the war is over, I shall come again to Scotland and seek you out at Drumbeg. I promise you that.'

Though Colin was sore at heart at the thought that Simon was to leave them, yet he knew it was not safe for him to stay. It was better for him to go to Whitehaven and to take ship there. As they sat round the camp-fire drying their clothes, they all fell very silent, and that night there was not the same cheerful song and merry tale among them as there had been at other camp-fires on the drove road.

Pursuit in Carlisle

The next evening the cattle were pastured on a rising green hill above the little village of Orton, a couple of miles from Carlisle. From there Colin could see the roofs of the town with their smoking chimneys, and sad as he was because of the coming parting with Simon, his spirits began to rise at the thought of seeing a city for the first time in Simon's company. When the herd was all safely rounded up, he and Simon set out together in the late afternoon for Carlisle. As they came up Scotch Street and into English Street, the Highland lad stared with wonder at the shop windows. He had no idea there could be shops that sold so many things.

'Simon! Look there!' he cried. 'A shop with women's dresses in it! Do the women of Carlisle buy their dresses in *shops*?'

'I expect they do,' Simon laughed. 'That is a dressmaker's shop. See the sign, "Mistress Park, gown and mantle maker".'

'My!' Colin said, taking a deep breath. 'I wish my mother could see yon shop. She would never believe her eyes.'

'Why? Does she never buy a dress in a shop?' Simon asked.

''Deed, no!' Colin looked astonished at the idea.

'She spins wool from our sheep and weaves it herself into cloth. Then she takes the cloth to Mistress Euphemia Macdonald at Glencoe village, who is handy with her needle, and she makes it into a dress for my mother. But it is not a dress like that in the window, all shining and with little sprigs of flowers in the pattern,' Colin added rather regretfully.

'That is a silk brocade, perhaps a French brocade, very like the ones I used to sell from my warehouses in Paris and Le Havre,' Simon told him.

'Do you sell cloth like yon?' Colin asked in a voice of awe.

'Why, yes.'

''Deed, now, I cannot believe it. But I would like fine to see my mother in a grand dress such as that one, or in yon fine silk shawl that's in the window. Och, she'd look handsome in that!' Colin sighed a little, then his attention was caught by something at the shop next door. 'But look! What's that strange black curly head sticking out above that shop door there?'

'That's a blackamoor's head from Africa. That means you can buy tobacco and snuff at that shop.'

'And are the people of Africa really black like that?'

'Yes, they are.'

'Think of that, now!' Colin said in wonderment.

'Here is a saddler's shop where you can buy saddles and reins and stirrups — anything for a horse, and anything made of leather,' Simon said.

'I like the smell of that shop,' Colin remarked. 'Oh, and the smell of the one next to it, too.'

Simon laughed aloud. 'No wonder! That is a baker's shop! When we are ready to go back to the herd we will buy a great meat pie and take it to eat at the camp-fire tonight with Angus and Donald.'

'My mouth is watering already,' Colin confessed. 'But where can we find a shop where you can buy sailor's clothes? Will this one do that has fine cloaks in the window and high hats and coats with tails to them?'

Simon shook his head. 'No, I think not, Colin. I must find a quiet little shop in some back street — a shop that sells old clothes, and see if I can get dark blue breeches and a coat to go with them. I think we might turn under this archway and have a look down this narrow street behind the cathedral.'

Colin stopped and stared at the great building. 'Is yon a cathedral?' he asked.

'Yes,' Simon nodded.

'A cathedral is a kirk where people go on Sundays?' Colin questioned him further.

'Yes, it is a *kirk*, as the Scottish people call a church.'

'Losh! You could almost put our kirk into one corner of it. I would be afraid to go in there.'

'Nonsense!' Simon laughed. 'You had better come inside and take a look at it.'

They stood just outside a tavern that faced the cathedral, their backs to the small-paned, bow-fronted window, so that they did not notice two men peering cautiously at them, who drew back hastily further inside the room as they turned.

Colin made up his mind. 'All right, I will go with you inside the cathedral, Simon,' he agreed. 'Who knows? I may never see another, and it will be something to tell my mother when I get home again.'

The two men watched them cross the cobbled street and one winked at the other with satisfaction. 'I thought we should run across them in Carlisle when I heard they were driving a herd of cattle down for Thomas Barlow,' he said, 'but that was a piece of luck to see them just now.'

Colin and Simon left the cathedral by the south door and made their way round the Cathedral Green to the maze of little streets that lay behind it and to the west. They did not notice that the two men had left the tavern and followed them at a short distance, peering round corners of the narrow lanes to see where they were going. Simon paused before a small shop window, a window that seemed to shrink discreetly back from the shadowy street.

'Here we are at a quiet dark little shop,' Simon said. 'This seems to be the kind we want. We will ask if they have clothes to sell for a seafaring man.'

As they entered the door, a bell gave a 'ping' somewhere in the living-rooms behind the shop. The shop itself was lighted by an oil lamp that cast strange shadows around about and made the coats which hung on a line look like queer little hunched-up men. Neither Colin nor Simon observed the two men pass quickly by the door and turn up a side-entry that led to the back of the premises.

From some sort of kitchen behind the shop a man came forward. He peered at them uncertainly over his spectacles.

'Well, have you come to sell something?' he asked

in a querulous voice. 'I don't know that I want to buy any more old clothes now.'

'On the contrary, my friend, I want to buy something from you,' Simon said lightly. 'A coat and jacket, if you have some to fit me?'

The shopkeeper's attitude altered at once. He became instantly more polite. 'Aye, sir, certainly,' he said, coming nearer and rubbing his hands. 'You want some grand clothes to show the folk in the Highlands, maybe?' He reached to a clothes line behind him and drew down one or two garments. 'Now I have here a wine-coloured coat with brass buttons, and a lavender waistcoat, with scarce more than a grease mark or two on it — very fashionable indeed.' He displayed them.

'I am not looking for anything fashionable, sir,' Simon told him. 'I want something dark, knee breeches and stockings and jacket, such as a sailor might wear at sea.'

The shopkeeper's attitude to them altered again, and he became a shade less polite and respectful. 'You will not cut much of a dash at home in the like of yon,' he said with a sniff.

'I do not wish to cut a dash, sir. I wish to go to sea,' Simon informed him.

The shopkeeper stared at him in something approaching disgust. 'What? With a war on?' he exclaimed. 'Why, young man, you'd be better off going back to the Highlands!'

Simon shrugged his shoulders. 'Oh, I have a fancy to see the world, maybe! But have you no clothes that will meet my purpose?'

'Oh, aye, I have no doubt I can supply you with

something,' the man said in a dissatisfied tone. 'Wait a moment. I might have something in the room at the back of the shop that might do.'

He was gone quite a long time, and Colin thought he could hear the low murmur of voices in the room behind the shop. At last the man returned, carrying some garments over his arm.

'Here is this dark blue pair of breeches, now,' he said. 'And I have the hose that will go with them. How's that?' He held them out to Simon, looking at him closely.

Simon turned the breeches over with a slight look of distaste at their dusty greasy condition. 'Yes, these might do,' he said at last, bearing in mind that he was seeking a disguise and not fine clothing. 'And have you a jacket too?'

'Aye, here is the very thing,' the shopkeeper said, reaching one down. 'This is a jacket a sailor sold me when he ran away from his ship. It's not badly worn, either. A patch at the elbow, but what's that?'

'Yes, that suits me. It does not look too — new,' Simon said, half to himself.

The shopkeeper looked at him slyly. 'Aye, there's many a man comes to me that wants to get rid of his clothing and take on another kind. But there are no ships come to Carlisle, my man. It is not a port,' he added with a kind of prying curiosity.

'No, I am going to the coast to take ship,' Simon said shortly.

'Ah, Whitehaven, maybe?' the shopkeeper nodded cleverly, rather pleased at his guess, when Simon did not deny it. 'That's the nearest port of any size. That'll be where you're going. Ships to Ireland *and* America from Whitehaven,' the shopkeeper commented. He turned to Colin. 'And are you going too, my lad?'

'Oh, no! I am staying to drive the herd,' Colin replied with his naive honesty.

'And where might that be?' the shopkeeper asked.

This time Colin was not to be trapped so easily into an answer.

'We have pastured on the Solway side,' he told the man with a slight reserve in his voice.

Simon prevented any more questioning by the shopkeeper by saying quickly: 'I will buy these clothes. What price do you want for them?'

'Seven shillings for the breeches and ten for the coat,' the man replied promptly.

Simon thought it might be wise not to appear too eager to buy at the high price the man was asking.

'That is dear, surely, seeing the clothes are far from new,' he protested mildly.

'A man must pay for what he requires in a hurry,' the shopkeeper said with a crafty leer. 'There is not much choice of seafaring clothes in Carlisle, young man.'

Simon guessed there was some truth in the last assertion, so he replied quietly: 'Very well, I will take the clothes.'

'I will bundle them together and wrap them up for you in the room behind the shop while you are counting out your money,' the shopkeeper said, taking the clothes with him. He left the door to the inner room slightly ajar.

Colin tugged at Simon's arm and whispered in his ear: 'Simon, will you get out of here as quick as you

can. There is something about this shop and that man
that I do not like.'

'What is it?' Simon asked.

'There is someone else in that room there, behind
the shop. The shopkeeper keeps whispering to him
when he goes in.'

'It is his wife, maybe?'

'No, it is a man's voice answering, and there is
something I seem to know about it. Listen!'

They crept on tiptoe to the crack where the door
was ajar and listened tensely. There was a low mutter
of voices. Only one or two words could be distinguished. 'Whitehaven', someone repeated, and 'It
should be easy'. Then the shopkeeper's voice: 'Hush!'

Colin and Simon stepped back lightly into the
centre of the shop again.

'Keep a watch, Colin, while I pay the shopkeeper,'
Simon said in a low voice.

In a minute or so the man returned, bringing with
him a parcel. 'Well, have you the money?' he asked.

'Here is a guinea,' Simon said, vexed that he had
no less change to offer, so that they could get away
at once.

The shopkeeper turned the coin over and even rang
it upon the counter to make sure it was a good guinea.
'Not often drovers like you offer gold in a shop, but it
seems to ring true enough,' he remarked. Simon's face
grew black with anger. 'All the same, I'll take an extra
shilling for changing it too. That's my price,' the man
went on impudently. 'That's seventeen shillings for
the clothes, then, and the extra shilling for changing
your guinea, eighteen shillings altogether. You must
wait while I get the change. I do not leave money in

my shop. Too many shady characters about! I might have to ask a neighbour to oblige me with change, so just wait here.' He left the parcel on the counter and went back to the room behind the shop.

'Simon! Do not wait for your change,' Colin urged. 'A man in that room peeped round the door just now. I think it was Laidlaw.'

'Surely not!' Simon exclaimed.

'Yes, I'm almost certain. There are other men in there too. Let us get away quickly before they fall on us here in the shop.'

Simon snatched his parcel from the counter. 'Quick, then, Colin. Outside and run for it!'

They had counted without the ping of the door-bell. As Colin tugged the door open it sounded sharply. There was a sudden exclamation from the room behind the shop. As Colin and Simon bolted through the door, Simon pulled it to hurriedly behind him so as to impede any pursuers. They had not got to the end of the short street before they heard the bell ping again and shouts behind them: 'Stop! Stop!'

Simon dashed round a corner, then round another corner at the end of a row of cottages, Colin following at his heels. As they ran they heard the clatter of running feet behind them. Down another street they fled, and still the sounds of pursuit came after them. Simon thrust Colin into a dark entry. 'Quick! Down this alley!' he panted. The alley ran straight through a block of buildings and came out in a street parallel to the one they had just left. Simon doubled to the left. As they ran they heard the feet of their pursuers hesitate at the entrance to the alley, then trampling along it.

'They're still following!' Colin gasped.

'We should be near to English Street. Run faster yet!' Simon urged. With hearts pumping and their breath coming in great tearing gasps, the two of them ran on. Luckily, by now, it was dark and there were not many people in the streets to watch them running. Round a last corner they went, with footsteps echoing behind them. Simon pulled Colin into a shop doorway just round the corner.

'Into this shop after me, Colin, and do not look surprised,' he warned him. As they entered the shop, Colin exclaimed: 'Why, it is the gown shop!'

Simon closed the door quickly behind him, then leaned against the counter, panting. The shop was lighted by an oil lamp, and there was a screen between the shop window and the shop itself, so that anyone looking in could not see inside the shop. A lady advanced towards the counter, looking a little surprised at the sight of the man and lad in kilts.

'Good evening, sir. What can I do for you?' she asked Simon politely.

Simon bowed. 'Good evening, madam. I would like to look at some shawls, silk shawls, if you please.'

'Certainly, sir,' she said, looking even more surprised. She could not help adding: 'Why, you do sound out of breath!'

'Yes,' Simon panted. 'I was sadly afraid you might have closed your shop before I reached it, madam.'

'*La*, no, sir! Not for an hour or more yet. Now, what colour of shawl would you like, sir?'

Simon appeared rather at a loss at this question. 'Well — er — I have not thought —' he stammered.

'Is it for a young or an old lady, sir?'

Simon hesitated, his brows puckered. 'Oh, no, not very young —' he began. 'But — er — certainly not old,' he added quickly on second thoughts.

'Coming on a little in years, sir, but still looking young and active?'

'Oh, yes, very active!' Simon agreed hastily.

'Is the lady fair or dark, sir?'

Simon cast a hasty glance at Colin, still recovering his breath. 'Oh — er — it would be dark, I think, but have you a shawl that might suit both?'

'Ah, the lady is a little grey, perhaps?' the girl said tactfully, a little amused by his efforts to remember.

'Yes, that is it. A little grey!' Simon said gratefully.

The shop attendant produced some shawls from a drawer. 'Well now, here is a black shawl embroidered with red roses — a little elderly perhaps?' she asked. 'Would you like a rich brown shawl for day wear, or a pretty pink one for balls and dances?'

'No. I do not think the lady goes to many dances now,' Simon said. 'Here, Colin, *you* help me choose the shawl.'

'But I have never chosen a shawl for a lady in my life!' Colin exclaimed in surprise.

'Perhaps not, but supposing, now, your mother was buying one, which one do you think she would choose?' Simon asked.

'But my mother would never be buying a silk shawl!'

'Then pretend she is buying one, and try to be some help to me!' Simon said, slightly exasperated.

Colin looked slightly astonished, but he hastened to please Simon. 'You know more about these things than I do,' he said. 'But this shawl here is a very pretty colour, now, almost like the breast of a dove.'

The young lady applauded his choice. 'Yes, that lavender-coloured shawl is very pretty and becoming, sir,' she agreed.

'It is very beautiful,' Colin said, touching it lightly with one finger. 'She will be the lucky lady who has that one,' he added wistfully, as his thoughts flew to his mother at Drumbeg who had never had such a shawl in her life, and who was not in the least likely ever to possess one.

'I will buy that shawl,' Simon said with sudden decision.

'But you have never asked the price, sir,' the lady protested, astonished. That was not the way the folk from Carlisle generally bought their goods.

'How much is it, then?' Simon asked.

'It is one of the best I have,' the girl began rather apologetically. 'You see, it is of the purest French silk, and I cannot get any more because of the war.'

'Yes, I can see it is good French silk,' Simon agreed.

'You know that, sir?' The girl lifted her voice, surprised. 'But I thought from your dress you were Scotsmen – Highlanders come over the Border with the cattle, maybe?'

'Oh, we see French silks sometimes, even in the Highlands,' Simon said gaily. 'Your price, madam?'

'It — it is two guineas,' the lady told him doubtfully, as though she wondered if he could pay it. 'But if that is too much, perhaps I can show you another —'

'I will have that one and no other,' Simon said with determination. 'Here is the money.' He placed two guineas upon the counter.

'Oh, thank you, sir. Is there anything else that I can show you, now? Gloves, perhaps?'

'No, thank you. I have bought my fairing now,' Simon laughed. 'But I wonder, madam, if you would oblige me with a drink of water? Shopping for ladies is a thirsty business.'

'Why, certainly. Wait a minute, sir.' The girl disappeared through a door leading to the premises behind the shop.

'Peep past the window curtain into the street, Colin. Are any of the men there?' Simon asked.

Colin very gingerly lifted a corner of the window curtain and looked along the street, but he could not see anyone of a suspicious character. 'There's no sign of them,' he reported to Simon.

'It looks as if our trick has succeeded,' Simon whispered. 'The fellows never thought we would enter a ladies' gown shop. They must have run past it and be looking for us nearer Scotch Street. We must be careful they are not lingering in a doorway when we go out, though.'

The shop attendant returned with the water, and Simon drank it and thanked her while she parcelled up the shawl into a small packet. Then they bade her good night and left the shop.

'Well, Colin, there's no one about. Buying this shawl seems to have saved us from the villains,' Simon said with satisfaction.

'It was a lucky thought, that!' Colin agreed.

'Indeed, and if it had not been for you, Colin, I should never have thought of it,' Simon said with a chuckle. Before Colin could ask him what he meant, a cart came clattering along the street, driven by a farmer's lad. In the cart were some small squealing pigs. Simon stepped out into the road at once and held up his hand.

'Hi, lad, are you taking the road out of the town towards Wigton?' he asked.

'Aye,' the lad replied, briefly, pulling up his horse.

'Would you like to earn sixpence by giving us a lift on our way for two or three miles?' Simon asked.

'You'll have to ride among the pigs,' the lad said.

'We shall not mind that. We're used to animals,' Simon replied.

'Drovers, are ye?' the lad said, eyeing their dress. 'Up wi' ye, then!'

Simon and Colin scrambled into the cart alongside the little pigs, and the lad flicked his whip and the horse set off at a good spanking pace again. Simon and Colin kept well down in the cart, but they caught sight of neither Laidlaw nor the man who had been with him, whom they guessed to be McQuaid. Soon they left the town behind and took to the Wigton road. They continued along this for perhaps a couple of miles, when the farm lad drew up the cart. 'This is the lane where I turn off to my farm,' he told them.

Simon handed him his sixpence and with a cheerful 'Good night' he left them, the pigs still squealing away in the cart.

'If we bear down this lane to the west, I think we should not be far from Angus and the herd,' Colin said.

'Yes. That was a lucky lift we got in the cart,' Simon said. 'No doubt those rascals are still searching the streets of Carlisle for us.'

'Simon, I have been thinking, will it be wise for

you to go to Whitehaven now?' Colin asked. 'You remember, yon fellow in the shop dragged it out of you that you were thinking of going there.'

'So he did. Perhaps I will avoid Whitehaven and try some of the smaller ports along the coast. But we will see what tomorrow brings, Colin.'

At last they reached the herd and found all was well as they had left it. Colin told Angus of their encounter with Laidlaw in Carlisle, and he looked very serious indeed.

'I do not like it,' he said. 'I do not like it at all. Neither Laidlaw nor McQuaid will easily give up the search for us, and they will have inquired from drovers at Falkirk where we were to take the herd. It is hard to hide a whole herd of cattle.'

Old Donald nodded his head too. 'Aye, maybe it was not a bad thing at all to cross the Solway Sands instead of going by the bridges,' he said sagely. 'No doubt they would be watching for us at the bridges, and by crossing the firth we outwitted them. They will know now that Simon is with us, and there will be a reward for an escaped prisoner of war. Besides that, they will have found out that you are carrying the price of the bull with you, I am sure. The gold will be even better to them than the bull, for money is not so easily recognized. I do not think they will leave us long alone now.'

They all saw the sense of the old herdsman's reasoning, and Angus looked very worried.

'Tomorrow we must rise before the sun is up and push on as far as we can to Penrith,' he decided. 'There is this in our favour. The rogues do not know where we are pastured tonight. Another two nights and we shall have reached Catterlen where Mr Barlow lives. Once we are there, at least the cattle will be delivered safely and we shall be among friends. But we must get some sleep now if we are to rise early. I will take the first watch.'

The rest of them rolled themselves in their plaids and settled themselves for sleep. Little did they think, especially Angus, what the morrow was to bring.

The Cattle Stampede

The next day, while the dawn was still grey in the sky, Angus had them all roused and ready for the road. As they took their frugal breakfast of oatmeal porridge, Angus asked Donald: 'Do you know the road well from here to Penrith, Donald?'

Donald answered a little wearily: 'There are plenty roads you could be taking, now. Between here and Penrith there are many lanes among the farming lands. Some of the rivers are full of deep pools and great boulders, but we must cross them by the bridges, that is all.'

Angus looked a little relieved. 'Then if there are so many ways by which we can get to Penrith, it will not be so easy for Laidlaw and McQuaid to trace us.'

'If we take the high road through the village of Calston and cross the river there, then we can strike through the lanes toward the higher ground where the villages are smaller and we shall meet fewer people.'

'That is a good plan, Donald,' Angus approved.

'It is just over a mile to the bridge. We have to cross the main Wigton road,' Donald informed them.

Simon was looking very thoughtful. 'Then I will come and set you on your way as far as the main Wigton road, Angus. It would be better for you if

I left you today. I do not want you to get into trouble because you have helped me.' Simon was wearing his new seafaring clothes and he handed over his kilt to Angus. 'I owe my life to your kindness in lending that to me, Angus,' he said simply.

'It was nothing. Look what you have done for Colin and for me,' Angus replied.

Simon handed Colin the little flat packet they had brought from Carlisle. 'Here is a little packet to remind you of our adventure in Carlisle and the narrow escape we had,' he said. 'It is for your mother. Take it as your fairing to her, I beg you, Colin.'

'Simon! It is the silk shawl!' Colin cried, touched almost to tears.

'Yes, I meant it for your mother all the time,' Simon confessed with a laugh. 'When we were running away from those men, *pouf!* I thought of the shop and in we went! We owe our lives to this shawl. I would like your mother to have it very much.'

'She will never have had such a fine shawl before,' Colin said proudly. 'Will you pack it carefully for me in the saddle-bags, Donald, please?'

'Surely! The mistress will be well pleased indeed,' Donald said, well pleased himself.

Angus rose and wrapped his plaid about him. 'We had better be on our way now to cross the Wigton road before too many people are astir on it,' he said. 'It is daylight already. You take the pony, Donald.'

Donald pointed to the foot of the hill. 'Yon village is Thursby. There we cut straight across the main road and along by the side of that burn you can see over yonder. We climb along by it to Hawkesdale Common and Sebergham Common. There you can get free pasture for the beasts, and the next day it will not be more than twelve miles to Catterlen near Penrith where Mr Barlow has his farm.'

'Only two days more and we hand the herd over!' Angus said with a sigh of relief. 'It will be glad I am when they are safe with Mr Barlow indeed! I think we will drive the cattle as fast as we can across the Wigton road before too many folk see us.'

'I will help you with the herd, Angus, and into the lane you are to take beyond,' Simon offered. 'After that I will say adieu to you all, and take the road to Wigton and the coast.'

'Oh, Simon!' Colin cried in sorrow.

'It has to come, Colin, it has to come, lad,' Simon said kindly, but he too looked sad at the thought of parting with his friends.

'Are you ready, Donald?' Angus asked.

From the back of the pony Donald called 'Yes.'

'Then we will drive the beasts!' Angus said, whistling and shouting to the dogs.

Down the little hill the cattle thundered, frightened by the sudden start, and in another minute they were pouring on to the Wigton road. Instead of crossing it, however, they turned up it and began to charge in the direction of Wigton.

'Och, they're turning up the Wigton road!' Angus shouted. 'Head them off, Colin!'

With Rob, Colin did his best, but all was confusion with the animals behind pressing against those in front. The cattle galloped along the main road.

Suddenly from round a bend in the road there came a loud rumbling of wheels, and the thudding of hoofs of cantering horses. The loud notes of the post-horn among the hills.

'Look out, Angus! The coach! The stage coach!' Donald cried in agony of fear. 'It's coming round the bend. Oh, the cattle will be under the coach!'

Bravely Angus raced among the bewildered beasts, trying to drive them to the side of the road and out of the path of the stage coach. The dogs barked loudly and ran in and out among the animals.

'Oh, Angus! Angus! Take care!' Colin cried, frightened.

When the stage coach came thundering down upon them the cattle stampeded and turned and headed in a wild gallop down the road. Angus was right in their path. He had no time to get to the side of the road before the frightened animals were upon him. Like a black tide they surged round him and Angus disappeared from view.

'Angus is down! I must get to him!' Colin yelled, plunging in among the terror-stricken beasts.

'Colin! Colin! Come back! You'll be knocked down too!' Simon shouted in a frenzy, but Colin paid no heed.

'I must help Angus! I must! I must!' he cried. 'I'm coming, Angus!' Another instant he too was swallowed up by the herd.

'Head the beasts off Colin with the pony, Donald!' Simon shouted. 'Head them off! I'm going to him!' Simon, too, dashed in among the plunging hoofs and horns.

'In, Rob! In, Sim! Part the herd!' Donald gave his

"Look out, Angus! The stage coach!" Donald cried

directions to the dogs. There was a sudden shout from Colin.

'I've got to Angus! Back, ye beasts! Drive them back, Rob! Back!' he cried. 'Angus is here on the ground, Simon.'

'I'm coming, Colin! Back, you, back!' Simon thrust among the herd with his stick. 'Back with them, Sim!' Another second and he had reached Colin and Angus. Colin was down on his knees beside his brother.

'Oh, Simon, help me to lift him. He's lying so still,' Colin cried in anguish.

With the pony and the dogs Donald kept the herd back while Simon and Colin lifted Angus on to a grass bank by the side of the road. At first Angus lay so still that they feared the worst, and Simon put a hand to his heart. Just then Angus groaned a little and stirred slightly.

'Oh, he's alive, thank Heaven!' Colin cried. 'But he's sore hurt.'

'Yes, he was trampled by one bullock. I saw it myself,' Simon said, shaking his head as he tried to discover the extent of Angus's injuries. 'It looks as if he has had a kick on the head too.'

'Oh, Angus! Angus! He doesn't speak!' Colin wept.

The stage coach had pulled up among the milling herd higher up the road and the coachman had dismounted from his high seat, handing his reins to the post-boy, and come towards them. He was in a violent temper.

'What do you mean by letting your herd straggle all over the King's highway when my coach is due to pass?' he demanded.

'We were not knowing about the stage coach,' Donald replied simply.

'Why, man! Are ye daft? Could ye not hear the horn?' the coachman demanded. 'Ye might have done serious damage to my horses with these bullocks, aye, and injured my passengers too.'

'The injured one is here,' Colin cried indignantly. 'It is my brother. The herd took fright at your coach. They knocked him down and trampled on him.'

At the sight of the lad's anguish the coachman's anger died away. 'Here, let me look at him,' he said, and bent over Angus. He pressed his side gently. 'Aye, it looks as if he's got some ribs broken and he's badly stunned, but he's breathing steadily.'

Simon had wrung out his handkerchief in a little stream that ran in the ditch and he began to bathe Angus's head with it. The cold water began to bring Angus round and he opened his eyes slowly, and groaned again.

'What is it? Where am I?' he muttered.

'Look now! He's beginning to come round,' the coachman said himself, with some relief. He had no wish to be delayed by the death of this young man by the roadside.

'Oh, Angus, are you sore hurt?' Colin breathed, kneeling beside him.

'My head! My head! It hurts when I take a breath,' Angus groaned.

'Aye, that'll be his ribs right enough,' the coachman gave his opinion. 'But he's a well set-up young man and he'll soon be over it. He'll take a tossing all right. Don't fret now, young 'un, it could have been much worse,' he said to Colin with a rough kindness. 'I

must get back to my coach. We can't have the stage
coach delayed. Watch out better next time ye come
across a main road,' he advised old Donald. Once
more he took his seat on the box, and was handed
the reins by the post-boy. He cracked his whip and
shouted 'Come up, now' to his horses, and the stage
coach set off again along the road. The rumble of
the wheels and the sound of the post-horn receded
into the distance. The scattered cattle had began to
browse among the hedges and strip of green at the
side of the road.

'Are you any easier, Angus?' Simon asked anxiously. Angus struggled to sit up.

'I'm queer and dazed and my side hurts, but I'm
not so faint now,' he declared. 'Were any of the beasts
hurt?'

'No, I do not think so. We were lucky in that,'
Donald told him.

'We will move on then, as soon as I can stand. Help
me to my feet, Simon.'

'Don't be in too big a hurry to move about. Take
your time, Angus,' Simon cautioned him.

'If it had not been for Colin rushing in among the
beasts and parting them, and Simon driving them
back, so we could get ye out, ye might well have
been a dead man, Angus,' Donald told him.

'Thank you, Colin and Simon,' Angus said in a
voice that trembled a little.

'Should you not be getting on your way to the coast
now, Simon?' Colin asked anxiously.

Simon hesitated for a moment and he said quietly:
'I am not going to the coast.'

'Not going?' Colin exclaimed, astonished.

'No, I have decided instead to go with you to Penrith.'

'But Simon —?' Colin began.

'With broken ribs and an injured head, Angus will not be fit to drive the cattle,' Simon went on. 'He will have to ride on the pony. It is a big drove for you and Donald to handle alone, so I shall come with you to lend a hand.'

'Oh, Simon, how good you are!' Colin cried.

Angus recovered his senses though he was still very pale. 'But it will not be safe for you, Simon,' he said in anxiety. 'The stage coach — that coachman will be telling in Carlisle, perhaps, how he ran into a drove of cattle. Suppose it came to Laidlaw's or McQuaid's ears?'

'The better, then, that I do not go to the coast,' Simon reasoned. 'If the coachman tells anything, it will be that the cattle were on the Wigton and Whitehaven road. *There* is where McQuaid will look for me.'

'Aye, if we cut over the hills to Penrith, we shall not be so easy found in all these byways,' Donald put in.

'Whatever happens, Colin, you must get the herd to Mr Barlow at Catterlen. He has paid half the money for them. In honour bound we must deliver them.' Angus spoke with urgency.

'I will do my best, Angus,' Colin promised him.

'Help me on to the pony, then, Simon,' Angus said, but when he tried to rise, he gave a groan.

'Can you manage to mount?' Simon asked anxiously, supporting Angus with his arm.

'I *must*! We must get our beasts over the hills to Catterlen before McQuaid comes to hunt for Simon, aye, and you too, Colin.' He made a mighty effort, and with Simon's help managed to hoist himself on to the pony's back, though he winced with pain.

'Simon, will you walk beside Angus and lead the pony in case he turns faint?' Colin asked.

'Never fear, Colin, I will watch him,' Simon said, so Colin and Donald went to round up the herd again, and when they had collected the scattered animals, they crossed carefully into the leafy lane at the far side of the main road, and commenced the long drove towards the Sebergham Common.

It was a sore day indeed for them all, but most of all for Angus. Donald and Colin ran back and forth with the dogs, for Colin was determined that none of the cattle should stray again, though his limbs ached for weariness. Simon took the pony's bridle and picked his way over the tawny bracken of the common lands and along the deeply rutted lanes, watching every step for fear a sudden jolt should give Angus a stoun of pain. At times he swayed in the saddle, white to the lips with the torment of his broken ribs and aching head, but Simon was always there to catch hold of him gently until the faintness had passed.

When they came to Sebergham Common they pastured the herd on the eastern slope of it that night. They made a bed of soft bracken fronds and spread their plaids on it for Angus. Donald made the oatmeal for supper, but Angus could not take a mouthful of it. All he asked was 'Water! Water!' in a hoarse cracked voice not like his own.

That night Simon and Colin watched the herd together while old Donald slept. All night Angus moaned uneasily and when the dawn came he was flushed and hot. Luckily it was quiet on the common and there was no sign of McQuaid or the tinkers. It was with difficulty next morning that Simon and Colin managed to hoist Angus on to the pony's saddle, and it was hard for him to keep his seat, he was so dizzy with pain and fever. They were forced, however, to get him along the road, though Colin's heart was sick with fear for him, especially when they had to ford the running burns. For all that, Colin was glad to see the hills. They had a friendly look and he thought of the psalm they sang in the little church at home.

' "I to the hills will lift mine eyes, from whence doth come mine aid",' he whispered to himself and he felt strangely comforted.

Now the road was often green and softer to the feet, and at last they came down the slopes of a grassy hill and Donald gave a great cry of gladness.

'Yon's Catterlen at last! Yon great farm there!'

Before them stretched a rambling old house in grey stone, ivy bedecked, set in a gracious green parkland, and with the whitewashed farm buildings crowding behind the house. They entered the gates and drove the cattle over a wide pasture where they stopped as if they knew they were at the end of their journey, and began to browse contentedly. From the farm-house a stout figure came hurrying.

'Here comes Mr Barlow himself,' Donald cried.

'So ye're here at last wi' the cattle, Angus!' Thomas Barlow greeted them heartily. 'Had ye good roads?'

Angus began to answer him in a faint halting voice: 'Mr Barlow, I —' His voice stopped abruptly and he toppled forward. Simon sprang forward to catch him.

'I've got him! Help me to lift him off the pony, Colin!' he cried.

Mr Barlow sprang to lend a hand too. 'Why, what's wrong?' he demanded, as he helped them to steady Angus and lay him gently on the ground.

'His ribs are broken, I think, and his head is hurt too,' Simon told him.

'What happened?' Barlow asked.

'A stage coach frightened the cattle and they stampeded and they knocked Angus down and trampled on him,' Colin informed him.

'That's bad!' Barlow shook his head. 'Here, we'll take him into the house.' He lifted his voice: 'Sam! Ned!' Two of his farm hands came running from the byres. 'Lend a hand here to carry this lad into the house,' he directed.

Very gently and slowly they raised Angus and carried him towards the farm door. Just as they were entering, Mrs Barlow appeared.

'What's the matter, Thomas? What's to do?' she gasped.

'It's a drover, wife, one of James Cameron's lads. He's been injured by the cattle. Have ye a bed for him, missus?'

Mrs Barlow took charge of the situation at once. 'Lift him on to the settle in the kitchen. Let's see how he's hurt first,' she said practically.

'It's his ribs and his head, mistress,' Colin explained. He helped Mr Barlow to strip off Angus's jacket. Mr Barlow felt tenderly at Angus's side. 'Aye, aye, there are a couple of ribs gone right enough. His head?' He examined that carefully. 'I'm not sure but a bone is cracked there as well,' he said seriously. 'As near as I can tell for this great lump on it.'

Mrs Barlow pressed her cool hand on Angus's

forehead. 'It's plain the lad's fevered,' she decided. 'He wants no food, but plenty of hot drinks to bring the fever down. We must get him to bed.' She called to a small serving-maid in the back premises. 'Betty, fill the warming pan with hot coals and put it on the bed in the spare room. Set the kettle on the fire first, though. Now, where's that old linen sheet that I keep for bandages?' She opened an oak chest and pried into its depths and brought out the sheet from which she tore long broad strips.

'Help me to bind this round his chest to hold the ribs in place, Thomas,' she said to her husband. 'Turn him a little while I get the bandage round.' Careful and deft though she was, Angus gave a groan.

'That's all right, Angus. You're coming round. You're in good hands. You'll be all right now,' Thomas Barlow reassured him.

Angus stared round him with glazed eyes. 'Where am I? What is this place?'

'You're at Catterlen, Mr Barlow's farm, Angus,' Colin told him.

Recollection began to flood back upon Angus. 'Did ye — did ye bring the cattle safe?' he asked faintly.

'I did, Angus.'

'All of them?' Angus persisted.

'All of them. Not a stirk lost!' Colin told him with a faint pride.

'Now, my lad, less talking, if you please. It'll do you no good,' Mr Barlow said sternly to Angus.

'There! That's your ribs bandaged,' Mrs Barlow said. 'Now for your head.'

'Thank you indeed, mistress. I am sorry to be troubling you,' Angus said weakly.

'Quiet now!' Mrs Barlow said firmly. Betty brought the hot water in a bowl, and a clean towel. Mrs Barlow took a piece of the old clean linen sheet and very gently washed the wound in the boy's head, cleansing the dried blood from the matted hair.

'Thank you, mistress. That eases the pain of it,' Angus whispered gratefully. Mrs Barlow took another strip of linen and bandaged his head lightly.

'There, now, Thomas, if you and this other young man —' She turned to Simon.

'Simon Chisholm, madam.'

'If you, Thomas, and Mr Chisholm will help to get Angus up the stairs —' she began again, when this time she was interrupted by Angus in great consternation.

'Oh, no, mistress. I cannot be giving you such trouble,' he cried. 'A bed on the hay in your barn perhaps, for a night or two, and then I shall be ready for the road to Scotland again.'

'What? With two cracked ribs and a broken head?' Mrs Barlow demanded. 'Indeed you'll not! You will do as I tell you, young man, and stay in your bed till the fever is gone and your head healed.'

'It's no use arguing, Angus. You may as well give in. The missus is used to having her way,' Mr Barlow grinned.

Angus would have protested again but Mr Barlow said briskly: 'No more talk! Get him up the stairs and into bed before he faints again. The lad has stood enough.'

Part-carrying, part-supporting, with Angus using his legs like a man in a dream, Mr Barlow and Simon took Angus up the stairs to the spare room and saw him safely into the bed. Mrs Barlow came down the stairs again, leaving Simon and Mr Barlow to watch Angus while she prepared the supper. Colin was still standing in the kitchen, uncertain what to do.

'I've no doubt you could be doing with a meal, my lad?' Mrs Barlow remarked without beating about the bush.

'I — I thank you, mistress, but —' Colin stammered.

'No nonsense, now!' Mrs Barlow said brusquely. 'You look hungry, boy.'

Colin's natural honesty made him blurt out: 'Well — yes, I *am* hungry. I did not eat much today. I was troubled about my brother.'

'I'll be bound you were,' Mrs Barlow said with a rough sympathy. 'Then there's your friend upstairs. Is he a new drover? He's not been here before.'

'Simon? Yes, mistress.'

'He's a very well-mannered man, that one,' Mrs Barlow commented.

'Oh, yes, he has the fine manners, Simon has,' Colin agreed.

'I'll be bound he can do with some supper too. And then there's the old herdsman who has been here so many times before — old Donald, eh?'

'That is right,' Colin said.

'Set three more places at the table, Betty,' Mrs Barlow directed.

She made a hot drink of black currants for Angus and took it up to him. When she returned again to the kitchen, Thomas Barlow and Simon were with her.

'Your brother is all right now,' she told Colin. 'He

is drowsy and likely to sleep. Rest is the best thing for him.'

They all sat down at the big table covered with a spotless white linen cloth and Mr Barlow carved away at a big ham while Betty brought a great dish of steaming potatoes and greens from the fireside, and Mrs Barlow poured out tea from a gigantic teapot. Colin, desperately hungry, felt that never had he tasted a meal so good before. When the first keen edge was off his hunger, he told Mr Barlow how the cattle had come to stampede. Mr Barlow heard his story with friendly interest.

'Well, Colin, lad,' he said at the end of it. 'I'm sorry about the injury to Angus, but don't bother yourself. Mrs Barlow will soon have him right again, if anyone can.' He looked proudly at his capable wife. 'Meanwhile, you're all welcome to stay at the farm until Angus is fit to take to the road again.'

'That's very good of you, sir,' Colin said gratefully.

'I'm pleased to do it for your father's sake, Colin. I've a very great respect for him. Besides, you did very well to bring the cattle on yourself after Angus's injury. You can tell your father you haven't failed.'

'Thank you, Mr Barlow,' Colin said gratefully.

'Now, I'm sorry I haven't beds in the house for all of you, but you're welcome to a shake-down among the hay in the barn and the mistress will give you blankets.'

'The barn will do us very well indeed, sir. It'll be a better bed than we've had since we left home,' Colin told him.

'Aye, we're used to sleeping rough, you know, sir, in all winds and weather,' Donald reminded him.

'And what about you, Chisholm?' Mr Barlow asked, with a rather peculiar curiosity in his voice.

'Oh, I have not been used to the comforts of a home for a very long time now, but I have often slept in barns,' Simon told him with a humour that was lost on Mr Barlow.

'Have you been a drover long?' the farmer asked.

'Not very long,' Simon admitted. 'Before that I was engaged in er — work on the land, sir,' Simon said, parrying the question cleverly. 'While we are here I should like to earn my keep. I do not like to take my bread and meat for nothing, but I should like to stay till I know that Angus is out of danger.'

'You speak honestly, Chisholm. Well, I've no doubt I can find you a job. Can you do milking?'

'I am sorry. I have not done milking before,' Simon had to tell him.

'What? And you have worked on a farm, too?' Barlow seemed very surprised.

'My — er — work was chiefly hedging and ditching, especially ditching,' Simon told him.

Again came the keen glance from Mr Barlow. 'Was it now?' he asked in a rather curious tone. 'Well, we'll see what you can do.'

'Donald and I will give you help with the animals, sir,' Colin offered.

'Yes, I would not like to be sitting idle, either. I am good with sick cows,' Donald said simply.

'Very well. I can do with the help, for it will let us get the winter ploughing done early while the season is still open,' the farmer admitted. 'Right, then, make yourselves at home on the farm till Angus is well again.'

Escape from Catterlen

It was close on a week before Angus was out of danger. The wound in his head took longer to heal than had been expected, and for a day or two the fever ran high. Mistress Barlow was kindness itself and nursed him as if Angus had been her own son. With grateful hearts the others worked their best on the farm. Mr Barlow declared that he had never had a better ditcher than Simon, who set to work to drain a marshy pasture.

'You must have spent a lot of time at ditching, man,' he said to Simon.

'Yes, a bit too long,' Simon replied with a chuckle.

Then, one morning, there came a knock to the farm door and Mistress Barlow went herself to answer it. There was a gipsy girl standing there.

'Well, my lass?' Mrs Barlow asked sharply.

'Would you be wanting any pegs, now, mistress, or baskets?' the girl asked timidly.

'No, I have all I need of both,' Mrs Barlow said shortly and prepared to shut the door.

'It's the strong pegs they are, mistress, good for twenty years,' the girl pleaded.

'No, my lass, I don't want any,' Mrs Barlow told her firmly.

'Will you have a look then at the baskets? Close

woven they are, see?' The lass held them up for her inspection.

'I've plenty baskets,' Mrs Barlow said impatiently.

'If you would let me see your hand, mistress, it's the beautiful fortune I could be telling you.' It seemed as if the girl was anxious to keep her at the door.

'No doubt!' Mrs Barlow said dryly, 'but I've neither the time nor the silver to waste on such nonsense.'

The gipsy lass took a deep breath. 'Is this the farm called Catterlen, mistress?' she asked.

'It is, but why do you want to know?' Mrs Barlow asked sharply.

'I've heard that you have drovers staying with you from Scotland.'

'Well, what about it?' Mrs Barlow snapped at her.

'Could I be speaking to one of them, mistress, please?'

'They'll not want to buy anything either,' Mrs Barlow told her flatly.

'It is not to sell them anything. I have a message for one of them.'

'Which one?' Mrs Barlow demanded curtly.

'The young one they call Colin Cameron,' the girl said.

'Why did you keep me so long at the door, then, without telling me? I've half a mind to send you packing,' Mrs Barlow declared, much annoyed.

'Oh, mistress, I was afraid to ask you at first,' the lass said in distress. 'It is an important message to Colin. If you please —'

'Very well, then,' Mrs Barlow consented. She stepped back into the kitchen and called up the stairs to Colin who was speaking to Angus. 'Colin, there is a gipsy wench here who says she has a message for you.'

Colin came running quickly down the stairs. Mrs Barlow put out a hand to detain him. 'I think it is just a trick to sell you something,' she said in a low voice. 'Send her about her business as quick as you can. I must get back to my oven or the bread will be burnt.'

Colin strode to the door. When he saw who was there he fell back a pace. 'Bethia!' he cried.

'I must speak to you quietly, Colin,' she begged. 'Walk me towards the farm gate.'

'Yes, what is it?' Colin asked as they went along.

'Is the Frenchman still with you?'

'How did *you* know about the Frenchman?' Colin asked quickly.

'Never mind about that now. Is he still at the farm?'

'Why?' Colin asked, unwilling to give away information about his friend.

'I have a warning for him. McQuaid and Laidlaw have found out he is at Catterlen.'

Colin drew in his breath sharply. 'Where is McQuaid?' he asked.

'At a house in Penrith. He means to bring the Town Guard here to arrest the Frenchman,' Bethia told him.

'That will mean trouble for Mr Barlow — for all of us.'

'Yes. You must get the Frenchman away quickly. The captain of the guard is waiting to get a magistrate's warrant to search here for him. The magistrate will not be at home till the afternoon. You have till then.'

'I will find Simon at once. There is no time to lose. He must not be found here.'

'Tell him not to go to Whitehaven. He is watched for there too. Now I must get away from here before the tinkers find out I have given you warning. Good-bye, Colin.' Bethia lifted her baskets and pegs.

'Good-bye, Bethia. A thousand thanks!' He turned and ran towards the tool-shed where Simon was busy sharpening his ditching spade.

'Simon! Simon! There is no time to lose!' he cried, rushing into the shed. 'You must leave here at once. McQuaid has discovered where you are. He is coming with the Town Guard to arrest you.' Colin did not see Mr Barlow standing just behind the door honing a scythe.

'What do you mean, Colin? What's all this about?' he asked sternly.

'Oh, Mr Barlow, I did not see you,' Colin exclaimed in dismay.

'What has Simon done that he is in danger of being arrested?'

'We ought to have told you, sir,' Simon said. 'I am a Frenchman, an escaped prisoner of war.'

Mr Barlow gave a gasp. 'Simon!'

'I should explain, Mr Barlow, that I have never taken arms against this country. I was a merchant returning from Scotland to France when my ship was captured and I was made a prisoner. I am anxious to get back to France because my wife is ill.'

'I see,' Mr Barlow said slowly. 'Well, it explains a lot which made me think hard; why you were working as a farm labourer and yet knew so little of farming; why your tongue was not even quite like a Highlander's tongue, aye' — and here Mr

Barlow chuckled — 'and why the missus said you had manners like a young lord.'

'Mr Barlow, I must get away from here at once,' Simon said urgently. 'If I am found here, you could get into trouble for sheltering me.'

'Aye. I suppose you're right,' Mr Barlow said, looking troubled. 'I had not thought of that.'

'I will go into the house and say farewell to Angus and Mistress Barlow and then I must go at once.'

In Angus's bedroom, Mrs Barlow was very distressed when she heard Simon's story. 'Why did you not tell us when you first came here, Simon?' she asked.

'I am ashamed, Mistress Barlow, that I did not,' Simon said with deep regret. 'It was wrong of me to let you run the risk of trouble on my account, but I thought a day or two would see me on the road to the coast again. We did not know Angus was so sorely hurt then.'

'But for me, Simon, you would have taken ship at Whitehaven by now,' Angus said, very troubled.

'Oh, Simon! You must *not* go to Whitehaven,' Colin remembered. 'Bethia, the gipsy girl, said that folk were watching for you there, too.'

'What will you do now, Simon?' Angus asked anxiously.

'I am not sure — another port, maybe,' Simon said vaguely. 'I shall manage, never fear, but I must get away at once.'

'I wish you had told us earlier, lad,' Mrs Barlow said, then turned to her husband. 'Listen, Thomas, I have a plan in my head. Could you get Simon to Penrith secretly?'

'I might, lass, but wouldn't that be taking him right into danger?' the farmer asked.

'No, you are wrong there, Thomas. Penrith is the very last place where these men will be looking for him. Once you get Simon to Penrith, I think I know a way that he might be smuggled out of the town. What about Charles and Chloe Cotsworth and their travelling theatre?'

'Aye, you've a head on you, missus,' Barlow said with admiration. 'I never thought of them. They're old friends and they might oblige. It's a bold plan, though.'

'Come down to the kitchen and talk to me while I cut meat and bread for Simon's journey,' Mrs Barlow said.

Simon advanced to Angus's bed. 'This time it is really good-bye, Angus,' he said sorrowfully. 'I hope your head heals soon and you have a good journey home with Colin and Donald.'

'Wait, Simon! I have been thinking —' Angus said quickly, then he turned to Colin. 'Colin, would you like to go with Simon and see him safely aboard a ship? Two of you could keep better watch for the rascals than one.'

'Oh, Angus, do you mean it?' Colin cried, his face lighting up.

'Yes. I should like to know that Simon was safe and on his road home. You could bring us word again, Colin. It is only right. Simon did not think of his own safety when he stayed to help you to bring the herd to Catterlen.'

'But, Angus, will you be all right if I leave you?' Colin asked.

'Of course I will, with the good Mistress Barlow pouring broth into me and not so much as letting me lift a finger. I'll soon be on my feet again now. If you get Simon aboard a ship quickly, then come back and join us here. If we have already set out, then follow us to Carlisle on the stage coach.'

Mrs Barlow called then from the kitchen. 'Simon, I have a meal ready for you.'

Simon took his leave of Angus. 'Good-bye, then, Angus. We shall meet again, I promise. May Heaven bless you for all you have done to help me.'

'God be with you, Simon,' Angus said in a deeply moved voice. He beckoned to Colin. 'A word before you go.' Colin came back to his bedside. 'You have the money safe in your kilt?'

'I have.'

'And you still have the smaller amount in gold in your sporran?'

'I have seven guineas in gold,' Colin told him.

'If you should need any of it to get Simon a passage on a ship, then use it. I will make it right with my father. He will not grudge it when he hears what Simon did for us. Be careful, now, and keep out of trouble.'

'I will do my best,' Colin promised. 'Good-bye, Angus.' He grasped his brother warmly by the hand and then turned and ran down the stairs after Simon.

'Mr Barlow, can you smuggle me into Penrith too?' he asked excitedly as soon as he reached the kitchen. 'I am going with Simon.'

'Aye, I think I can manage the two of you under the load of hay,' the farmer said.

'Under the hay?'

'Yes, the missus has suggested it will be a grand chance to deliver a load of hay to the George Inn. You will travel on the cart under the hay.'

'Here is meat and bread done up for you in this kerchief,' Mrs Barlow said. 'It will save you from showing yourselves in the town to buy food.'

'You are very kind, madam; I can never repay you,' Simon said gratefully.

'Aye, you can,' Mrs Barlow said practically. 'You can be kind to any of our lads who are prisoners in the hands of the French.'

'I vow I will be that, madam.'

'Sam and Ned are loading up the hay now. Simon, it would not do for them to see you hide under the hay, for they might give it away to the searchers when they come. No, it would be better for them to see you depart quite openly. When you get to the little wood that is on the other side of that hill there, hide among the bushes. I'll pull up there and take you under the hay,' the farmer directed.

'Good-bye, Mistress Barlow; I thank you and kiss your hands,' Simon said, bowing low.

Mrs Barlow stared after the two of them as they crossed the farmyard and then looked at her work-reddened hands and a tear dropped upon them. 'Did you ever, now! No one ever did that to my hands before,' she said to herself, as she waved them a last farewell as they turned up the farm lane.

Mr Barlow rumbled along the lane with his cart of hay, straight from the yard where the farm hands had been loading it, so that they could bear witness, if need be, that no one else travelled with it. When he reached the wood, he pulled up, just within a lane going down into the bushes, and Colin and Simon scrambled on top of the load and pulled the hay over themselves.

'If you hear me whistling a tune, it'll mean there's danger at hand,' he warned them. 'Then get down well under the hay and keep there.'

They proceeded for about a mile along the road leading to Penrith when Mr Barlow began to whistle his favourite tune: 'When first I went a-waggoning, a-waggoning did go'. Instantly Colin and Simon wriggled down deeper under the hay. A couple of hundred yards further along a man hailed Mr Barlow.

'Hi, there, man! Are we on the right road to Catterlen?' It was Laidlaw.

'Aye,' Mr Barlow replied in laconic country style, his hat pulled well down over his eyes.

'Has Barlow got any Highland drovers staying at his farm?'

'Eh, man, Highland drovers are always coming and going. Barlow deals in cattle, you know,' the farmer said impatiently.

'Is there one of them there who speaks like a foreigner — like a Frenchman?'

'Nay, lad, all you Scotchmen speak queer-like to me,' Barlow told him. 'But ye'll need to ask at the house. Maybe the farmer's wife can tell ye more about them. For all I know the drovers may have left there by now.'

'Come on, men, hurry!' Laidlaw said, motioning to the two or three men he had with him.

The cart rumbled along again. Barlow waited till he was round a bend and out of sight and hearing of the rascals before he looked over his shoulder and said: 'You can lift your heads from the hay now. The

"You can come down now"

rogues are making for Catterlen as hard as they can pelt. Well, they'll not stay long if I know the missus! They'll get the length of her tongue. We'll soon be at Penrith now, so keep under the hay when we come within sight of the houses.'

The cart clattered into the inn yard of the 'George'. Barlow backed the end of it against a barn and then he called to Simon and Colin: 'You can come down now. Yon's the hay loft for the stables. Here's a couple of pitchforks. Get busy shifting the hay into the loft; I'm going into the inn. If you've finished before I get back, stop in the loft till you hear me whistling again.'

Colin and Simon forked up all the hay. Simon was a little awkward at handling the fork at first but he soon learned under Colin's experienced teaching. They had just finished when Mr Barlow came back into the inn yard whistling 'The Jolly Waggoner'. He beckoned them out of the loft.

'You can come down now. There's no one about the yard. Follow me up this passage and into the room at the end.'

At the end of a flagged passage, Mr Barlow rapped sharply upon a door. 'Come in!' a deep voice invited them.

Seated before a small table was a tall middle-aged man with a flowing head of grey hair, and a most distinguished appearance. Lounging upon a sofa by the fire, an untidy sheaf of manuscripts in her hand, was a very pretty fair-haired girl, her curls bound by a blue ribbon. Her handsome blue eyes had a slightly calculating expression, and her mouth looked petulant, except when she smiled. She was about a year older than Colin, though she looked almost grown up. There was a distinct resemblance in features between herself and the gentleman at the table, which proclaimed her as his daughter. The gentleman looked hard at Simon and Colin.

'Mm! So these are the two you've been recommending to me as extra hands for my theatre, Thomas?' he asked.

'Aye, Charles,' the farmer said. 'This is Simon Chisholm, and the lad is Colin Cameron. This is Mr Charles Cotsworth and his daughter, Miss Chloe Cotsworth.'

Simon bowed low. 'My duty to you, sir. Your servant, mistress.'

'Good day to you, sir. Good day, mistress,' Colin said politely.

'*La!* How quaintly the boy speaks!' the girl giggled.

'And you, Simon Chisholm, you speak — er — *quaintly* too,' Cotsworth remarked with a sharp glance at Simon. 'Your clothes would make you seem a seafaring man.'

'I hope to join a ship at the coast, sir.'

'Oh, you do! Well, now, I have a travelling theatre company and my friend Barlow here has persuaded me I need one or two extra players and baggage hands. I have need of an actor who might — er — play a *Frenchman*, perhaps?'

Simon nodded. 'I see you understand about me, sir. It is better so.'

'I will not offer you wages,' Cotsworth went on, 'but you can travel with the company. We are going towards the coast and you will have your food as payment for your services.'

'We are content with that, thank you, sir,' Simon replied.

'And you, boy? What can you do? You've a fine sturdy leg. Can you dance?' Chloe asked with a charming impudence.

'Only my own Highland dances, mistress.'

'Do you hear that, Father?' Chloe cried with delight. 'Can you blow the bagpipes too?' she asked Colin. Colin nodded. 'Oh, but this is amazing!' Chloe said, clapping her hands. 'And can you sing?'

'The songs of my country, that is all,' Colin replied.

'Father, are you listening?' Chloe exclaimed.

'Aye, my wench.'

'Then he's the very lad to play the bagpipes when we play *Rob Roy*. Do you agree, Father?'

'You run on fast, my girl. Well, we'll try him. Here's a set of bagpipes we use in the play, when we have any actor who can blow them. Show me what you can do.'

Colin inflated the bag and played a plaintive Highland tune, 'O Can ye Sew Cushions?', upon them. At the conclusion Chloe clapped her hands again.

'But that will bring the house down,' she declared.

Colin looked positively alarmed. 'Oh, no, mistress! I assure you the ceiling is quite safe. I did not blow my loudest.'

Chloe threw back her head and laughed heartily. 'Oh, you silly lad! Don't you understand anything at all? I meant that the applause, the clapping, would be like thunder.'

'For *me*, Mistress Cotsworth?' Colin asked amazed.

'That's enough of your teasing, lass,' Cotsworth said peremptorily. 'Have you never seen a theatre before?' he asked Colin.

'Never!'

'*La*, would you believe it!' Chloe exclaimed.

'We are playing tonight in the big barn belonging to the inn. Our baggage carts and horses are in the stables. Tonight, when the performance is over, we must take the road for Keswick, for we cannot afford to lose time on our journeys. We open in Keswick tomorrow,' Cotsworth told them. 'You and the lad had better keep to the loft till then. Once the audience has left, you can help us to load the baggage carts and travel on them.'

'Excellent, sir,' Simon agreed.

'Well, I'll be going back to Catterlen now,' Mr Barlow took his leave. 'Any message for your Aunt Barlow, Chloe?'

'Give her my dear love and tell her I am peevish that she did not come to see me play Juliet this time. But you can tell her that, if she will have me, I will come to stay with her again in the summer.' Chloe spoke like a little queen dispensing her favours.

Barlow gave an affectionate tug to one of her golden curls. 'That will make your aunt right glad, I know. She's rare fond of a lass about the house, having none of her own. Well, good-bye, Chloe.'

'Good-bye, Uncle Barlow.' She kissed him prettily.

'Good-bye, Charles, and thank you for this help,' Barlow said, shaking the actor warmly by the hand.

Colin and Simon followed the farmer out to the inn yard and said good-bye, thanking him from the bottom of their hearts. Then they climbed into the loft and stayed there behind the hay till it was full dark, and the bobbing lanterns showed that the people of Penrith were on their way to the play. In the darkness of the loft they munched their bread and cheese and listened to the hoarse shouts of the men at the door urging the folk to come to the performance.

Afterwards they heard the strong voice of Charles Cotsworth declaiming his part, and Chloe's clear musical tones; the murmur of other actors' voices, followed by a burst of clapping. This went on for a long time, and then there came a thunderous applause and after it the people came pouring out of the barn like bees out of a hive, and they knew the play was over.

Once the inn yard was clear of folk, Colin and Simon came down the ladder and lent a hand to store the stage properties and curtains in the baggage cart. It was with amazement that Colin lifted a golden throne and carried glittering spears and swords into one of the wagons, together with the long dark curtains.

Charles Cotsworth told his men that he had taken on extra hands for a short time, and no one seemed to think it strange, for actors came and went a great deal, Cotsworth often picking up small-part men here and there. So, at last, when all was ready, Colin climbed into the covered cart and sat with his legs dangling over the tail-board, while Simon took the horse's head and the cart rumbled out of sleeping Penrith and along the moonlit road over the hills to Keswick.

The travelling theatre jogged along at a quiet pace. In front went the other baggage wagons and the caravan in which Chloe and Cotsworth slept and travelled. Sometimes Simon led the horse, sometimes Colin did, and so the night wore on. At last, when dawn was striking the rugged sides of Blancathra, they rumbled down into the valley of Threlkeld and into the market place at Keswick just as the townsfolk began to stir.

The tired players climbed into the baggage carts to take a short rest before beginning the work of setting up the theatre. Simon and Colin were just preparing to settle down for a sleep among the curtains stowed in their cart when Colin thought he heard a strange sound inside the wagon.

'What was that, Simon? Did you hear someone sneeze?' he asked.

'Perhaps it was someone in the next wagon?'

'I don't think so. It came from this wagon,' Colin was sure. 'Simon, I am convinced there is something hiding behind that great throne. I am going to look.'

He climbed on to the wagon and began thrusting the stage properties aside with Simon's help. When he came to the throne near the back of the other things, a figure jumped from behind it and tried to elude Colin. Colin made a successful grab.

'I have you! Come out! It's no use struggling!' he cried, pinioning the person by the arms. It was a girl, who struggled to get free.

'Let me go! Let me go!' she cried in a panic.

Colin dropped his hold at once. 'Bethia!'

'Who is it?' Simon asked sharply.

'It is Bethia, the gipsy girl who warned us about McQuaid.'

'What are you doing here?' Simon asked her with some suspicion.

Bethia was sobbing a little. 'I have run away from my people, the tinkers,' she said. 'I cannot go back to them. They will know that I gave you warning about Laidlaw and McQuaid coming to the farm.'

'How *can* they know?' Colin asked.

'McQuaid told my uncle he had seen me talking to you at Falkirk Tryst, Colin, after you had taken the bull from them again. My uncle took hold of me to beat me, but I said boldly: "And was I not telling the fortunes at Falkirk Tryst, and did not the young lad cross my palm with silver? Here is his sixpence." So neither McQuaid nor my uncle was sure if I had told you about the bull. My uncle let me go, but he threatened that if he found out I had been near you again, it would be the worse for me.'

'And yet you dared to come to warn us even after that?' Colin said in wonderment.

'Yes, for I overheard them say they would rob you of the money you had got for the cattle too. They knew you must be carrying it, you and your brother. They meant to take the Frenchman so that you would offer them money to let him go.'

'So that was their wicked plan! They were going to blackmail Angus and Colin into giving up their money and pretend to let me go!' Simon exclaimed in anger.

'Yes. I dare not go back to them now. They would know I betrayed them, when they had been at the farm.'

'How did you know we were with the strolling players?' Simon asked.

'When I left the farm, I hid in a thicket in the wood, for I did not wish to meet Laidlaw and my uncle on the road back to Penrith.'

'Was that the same road where Simon and I waited for the hay cart?' Colin asked.

'Yes, I saw the farmer take you under the load of hay, then I waited till I heard Laidlaw and the others go past. Then I crept out and ran as fast as I could after the hay cart. I was just in time to see it turn into the inn yard. When it was quite dark I came back among the crowds and hid behind the baggage carts. Later on, when you were running backward and forward with the stage things, it was an easy matter to slip inside this wagon and hide behind that great chair,' Bethia told them.

'But what will you do now, Bethia? Where will you go?'

Bethia shrugged her shoulders. 'Oh, I am used to fending for myself. If I can ride on the wagon to Cockermouth, where the theatre is to go next after Keswick, I can soon tramp my way into Workington, where the coal mines are. There's plenty of work for lasses down the coal mines, carrying the coal, so I've been told,' she said bravely.

'But that is hard, terrible work. Children like you toil from five in the morning to seven at night in the darkness below the ground!' Simon said aghast. 'It is a dreadful life for the young.'

'It is all I can do, sir. I cannot go back to the gipsies now,' Bethia said plainly.

'We must do something for Bethia at once, Simon. Do you think Miss Chloe would help her?' Colin suggested.

'Yes, surely she will, if she has a heart at all,' Simon agreed.

'We will go to her caravan, then, and ask her,' Colin decided. 'Come with us, Bethia.'

They made their way to where Chloe's caravan was drawn up in the little market square close to the Moot Hall, in the upper part of which the performance was to take place that night. Colin tapped timidly on the door of the caravan. To the first knock there was no answer and he had to tap again. This time the door opened about six inches and a tousled head of curls was thrust out.

'What do you want?' Chloe asked.

'Could you speak with us a minute, mistress, please?' Colin begged.

'Why, it is the Highland boy!' Chloe exclaimed in surprise. 'I'm hardly awake yet. Come back when I've had my breakfast.'

'Mademoiselle, please, we need your help,' Simon implored her.

Chloe rubbed her eyes. 'I am half-asleep yet! What is it, then?' Suddenly she caught sight of Bethia standing behind them.

'Who is that girl with you?' she asked sharply.

'Her name is Bethia,' Colin said.

'Is she a gipsy?' Chloe asked, turning up her nose a little.

'Yes, mistress,' Bethia acknowledged.

'We have come to ask your help for her, Mistress Chloe,' Colin pleaded.

'What? For a gipsy? Oh, no! You must send her away. I cannot do with gipsies!' Chloe cried with distaste.

'Please, mademoiselle, listen. Bethia saved us from our enemies in Penrith. She dare not return to the gipsies now. Could you persuade your father to let her stay with the company and work for you?' Simon asked humbly.

Chloe tossed her head. 'Why should I? I am not very fond of gipsies.'

'Oh, Mistress Chloe, please help us,' Colin begged.

Bethia drew herself up a little proudly. 'There is no need to beg for me, Colin. I will go away and be no more trouble to you.'

'Then we *must* find some other way to help you, Bethia.'

They were just about to turn away when Chloe called: 'No, wait! If I ask my father to let the girl stay with us, will you play the bagpipes and sing your Highland songs here at Keswick for us and at Cockermouth where we go next?'

Colin hesitated. 'But why do you wish that, Mistress Chloe?'

'Oh, just because it will be a novelty that will make the crowds come to the theatre, and if we take a lot of money, then it will please my father, and if he is pleased, then I can ask him for a guinea for a new dress,' she laughed.

'It is not a thing I have ever done, but if it will please your father, who has helped us so much, then I will do it,' Colin agreed stiffly.

'Then the girl can stay with the company and help me to dress for my part and she can sell oranges and sweets at the intervals in the performance,' Chloe decided.

Bethia nodded. 'I would rather earn my bread than do nothing,' she said a little coldly.

'There, then, that is all fixed,' Chloe said gaily. 'I will tell my father all about it. Oh, never fear, he'll do what I say!' she added with the assurance of a spoilt child.

In this way Bethia, too, joined the company of the

strolling players, and Colin was pledged to play a part in the performance, a thing which filled him with misgiving and yet made his heart beat more quickly at the thought.

The Barnstormers

That night, after the first part of the play was over, Charles Cotsworth came before the curtain.

'Ladies and Gentlemen, for a diversion between the acts of the play we have brought here a young gentleman famed far and wide for his singing, and for his music on the bagpipes. It has been an enormous expense to us, but nothing is too good for our audience in Keswick,' Cotsworth flattered his audience. Colin, trembling in the wings, heard this surprising statement with great astonishment. Cotsworth drew him forward to face the people, and Colin wished the stage would open and let him fall through. 'Ladies and Gentlemen, the only and original Highland Laddie!'

There was a perfunctory applause and Colin stepped forward and with the bag thrust under his arm and the mouthpiece to his lips, his fingers leaped into a gay Highland dance. In a moment the audience were tapping to the music with their feet. It was almost as if they were dancing. When Colin had finished there was loud and warm applause, and cries of 'Encore!'

Colin set his pipes down gently on the stage and announced simply: 'Ladies and Gentlemen, if you will listen, I will sing you a Highland song, one of the songs of my home.'

His voice floated out, clear, with the sweet notes

"Ladies and Gentlemen, the only and original Highland Laddie!"

of a bird as he sang a Highland lullaby, one that his mother had sung to him as a child. As he thought of her, all his heart was in the singing. There was a spellbound silence in the hall, then, as the last note faded away, a spontaneous burst of clapping and even cheering.

Colin bowed awkwardly, trying to imitate Cotsworth, and stepped into the wings where the actor awaited him, delighted. 'Well done, lad!' he cried. 'Well done! Listen! They are calling for you to sing again.'

'It frightens me, all the clapping of the hands.'

'Nonsense, boy!' Chloe said, giving him a little push forward. 'That shows the people like you. Wasn't I right, Father, to make him perform?'

'Oh, perfectly right, Chloe, my love,' her father said with fond admiration. 'You have a head for the stage business, right enough. You know what will draw the crowds. Listen, Colin! They want you back. You will have to give them an encore.'

'What is that?' Colin asked, bewildered.

'You must go and sing to them again.'

'I do not understand it,' Colin said. 'It is a small thing to do, to play my pipes and to sing as I have always done at home in Drumbeg, to earn so much praise.'

'Go and sing to them again, Colin, and I will treat Bethia kindly indeed for this,' Chloe said persuasively.

Once more Colin went to the centre of the stage and sang to the people, this time a boating song of the islands with a lovely lilt to it. Again the audience applauded and applauded. It seemed as if they could not have too much of this simple Highland lad with

a voice like a lark in spring, and within himself Colin
felt a strange power growing, the power to hold and
delight those who listened to him. It was like nothing
he had ever known before.

During the three nights that they played at Keswick
the Moot Hall was full and folk even had to be turned
away. Every night the play was changed, and it amazed
Colin to watch Charles Cotsworth play one part after
another, never at a loss for a word. The actor was a
great favourite with the Keswick people, and there was
always a queue of theatre-goers to buy tickets. With
her winning clever ways and her mop of golden curls,
Chloe was as great a favourite as her father. It was only
when she was off the stage that she appeared spoilt and
self-willed. Though Bethia waited on her hand and foot,
she could not always please Chloe, though she bore with
her whims with great patience.

Although it was a strange new world to Colin, he
was happy enough in the company of these travelling
actors whom the country folk called Barnstormers.
He grew to like the little old town of Keswick set by
its lovely Derwentwater, for the mountains crowding
round it reminded him of the far-away Highlands.

When the third night's performance was finished,
once more the company stowed away their properties in the wagons, the curtains, the furnishings
and the great golden throne, and set out for ancient
Cockermouth. The way wound along by gentle Bas-
senthwaite Lake and was pleasant indeed. At length
they came to the wide gracious main street of the
little town, and there they played for two nights in a
barn belonging to the Bluebell Inn. Once again Colin
scored great successes.

After Cockermouth, they travelled to Maryport. Maryport proved a little town of mean houses where black-faced miners dwelt. Here Charles Cotsworth rented a hall belonging to an institute.

It was at Maryport, on the second night of their performances there, when Colin had just finished playing the pipes and singing between the acts, that trouble caught up with him and Simon once more. He had just left the stage when Bethia appeared breathless behind the scenes, still carrying her basket of unsold oranges.

'Colin! Mr Cotsworth!' she cried, terrified. 'They are down there in the hall with my Uncle Peter.'

'Who?' Cotsworth demanded.

'McQuaid and Laidlaw. The men who are hunting Simon.'

'Are you sure?' Colin asked her.

'I am certain. I was just going among the people after you had played to them when I caught sight of Laidlaw. They are sitting on the very back row of the benches near the door. They must have come in late, for I am sure they were not there when the play began.'

'Did they see you?'

'No. I was in the shadow and they were watching you.'

Mr Cotsworth beckoned Simon over the stage behind the closed curtain. 'Simon, McQuaid is here in the audience with Laidlaw and Peter the Gipsy. You must leave the company at once.'

'I will go this minute, sir. I do not want you to have any trouble.'

'I will come with you, Simon,' Colin said.

Cotsworth laid a detaining hand on Simon's sleeve. 'No! Wait! Let me think. Simon is due to go on the stage and speak his part now at the beginning of the next act. If he does not appear the rogues will be scouring the town for him within the next five minutes. You would not stand the ghost of a chance, man! No, we must play for *time*, somehow.'

'I know what we must do, Father,' Chloe said with her usual decision. She had joined the group and heard what Bethia had to say. 'Colin, you must go before the curtain and thank the people and say you hope to play for them again, and announce the last act in the play. If we can trick those men into believing we do not know they are there, they will wait till the play is over before they seize Simon. They will not want to make an uproar in the theatre and set the folk against them. The only way out of the hall is through that main door. They will wait for Simon there when the show is done.'

'The wench is right!' Cotsworth declared. 'Go on, Colin. Do as she says. It will give me time to *think*.'

Colin went on stage to make the announcement and then came back to Charles Cotsworth.

'Simon, you go on in your turn and speak your part as usual, but come to my little room as soon as you leave the stage,' Cotsworth said. Simon nodded and the actor turned to Colin. 'I am due on the stage in three minutes, so listen carefully, Colin. You must take off your kilt and put on yon ragged breeches and jacket hanging there.'

'Yes?' Colin listened carefully.

'You see this black paste here? It is the lamp-black

I use when I am playing Othello. You must rub it over your face and hands.'

'Yes, sir.' Colin's voice sounded surprised.

'Be as quick as you can. Simon comes off the stage before I do. Tell him to put on his seafaring clothes and to rub the black stuff over his skin too. Waste no time. I will explain later. I must go on the stage now. I shall soon be back.' He disappeared into the wings.

Quickly Colin changed into the ragged clothes which were used in one of the plays, and put the gold from his sporran into the pockets. 'There's no time to take the bank notes out of the kilt,' he said to himself. 'The pleats are stitched too tightly. I'll take the kilt with me rolled into a bundle. Now for the lamp-black!'

By the time Simon joined him, Colin was already sufficiently disguised to make Simon start, and hardly recognize him.

'Into your seafaring clothes, quick! Then rub this stuff on your face as I am doing,' he told Simon.

Simon hastened to obey. He looked into the glass. '*Tonnerre!* What a pretty pair we look! But how are we to get out from here? The only way is straight through the hall. Do we just march boldly out in our black faces as if we were hiding behind them?'

Mr Cotsworth came hurrying into the room. 'You're ready? Good! Where's the lamp-black? It's lucky the coat I'm wearing on the stage is a tattered black one.' He began to black his face too. 'If anyone stops us, we are three coal-miners going to work a shift down the mine. Leave me to do the talking.'

'But how do we get out?' Colin asked. 'This window has iron bars across it.'

'There are no bars to the window in Chloe's room. Come quickly. Chloe is on the stage now, but Bethia is there. We'll take a lantern with us as miners would do.'

They tiptoed behind the stage back-cloth to Chloe's room and pushed up the window quietly.

'I will go first through the window and make sure no one is about,' Cotsworth said. 'When I miaow like a cat, you follow me, Simon, and then Colin. Bethia, you must shut the window after us.'

'But what will happen to Bethia, sir?' Colin asked.

'Don't worry. We'll look after her. There's no time to talk now,' Cotsworth said as he dropped agilely through the window. There was a minute's silence, then a cat's miaow.

'You next, Simon,' Colin said, assisting him through the window.

There was a thud outside as Simon dropped on the ground.

Quickly Colin dipped into his pocket, putting his wrapped-up kilt on the table while he did so.

'Here, Bethia! Take this guinea from me,' he said.

Bethia backed away, her hands behind her. 'No, no! I cannot!'

'Yes, you must!' Colin said, seizing one of her hands and pressing the guinea into it. 'It might prove useful. Good-bye, Bethia! I shall not forget you. Make your way back to Catterlen. Angus will help you.'

There was a miaow outside.

'Good-bye, Colin. Good-bye and thank you,' Bethia said.

Colin mounted the table and climbed through the window after Simon. There was another slight thud and then the sound of rapidly retreating footsteps. For a moment Bethia stood staring into the night, then she shut the window.

Ten minutes later Chloe came rushing into the room. 'That's the curtain down at last, thank goodness! Did Simon and Colin get away safely, Bethia?'

'They went through yon window with your father ten minutes ago.'

'I tried to spin out my bows before the curtain to give them a chance to get away. But why have you been weeping, Bethia?'

'It is because they have gone and no one was ever kind to me before,' Bethia said defiantly.

'Silly child! You should *make* people kind to you like I do!' Chloe said with a note of scorn. 'Well, you had better be packing my dresses in yon big hamper. We move on to Whitehaven tomorrow. But what's in that bundle on the table?'

'I thought it was something belonging to you,' Bethia said.

'I do not carry my things about rolled up in a dirty old curtain. Open it and see what's in it.'

Bethia opened it. 'It's Colin's kilt!' she exclaimed. 'He must have forgotten it when he went through the window in such a hurry. He was wearing dark breeches and jacket.'

'Oh, well, he'll have to make do with those. Why are you staring at the kilt as if you expected it to get up and dance before you, wench?' Chloe sneered.

'It is just that Colin set great store by his kilt. Even if he wore other clothes for the theatre, he never let it out of his sight.'

'It's no use worrying about it now. He's gone and

he won't be coming back,' Chloe snapped. 'You can leave it there. It will do to wrap round my little dog.'

'Oh, no, no! Not Colin's kilt!' Bethia cried.

'Don't be so foolish, wench! What's the good of an old tattered kilt like that? Oh, don't stand gaping there at me! Get along with packing my dresses.'

'Where will Colin and Simon go?' Bethia ventured to ask.

'I expect they will try to get a boat for Ireland.' Chloe suddenly put her head on one side. 'Listen! There are voices just outside. I'll see who it is. Keep the door closed behind me.'

She slipped outside to find McQuaid coming down the steps from the stage.

'Are you looking for someone, sirs? My father, perhaps?' she asked politely.

'I want to see the tall dark young man and the lad who played the bagpipes,' McQuaid said truculently.

'Oh, they've left already,' Chloe said with a careless air.

McQuaid looked at her with dark suspicion. 'I never saw them go! There's no door but the one out of this hall. I made sure of that.'

'Oh, but I assure you they have left, sir. Ten minutes ago at least,' Chloe said sweetly. 'Perhaps you will find them at supper at the inn.'

'I do not believe it! They are still in these rooms behind the stage.'

'Oh, no, I assure you, sir —' Chloe began.

Bethia had heard the voices on the stairs. 'McQuaid!' she cried and stood stock-still for one panic-stricken moment. 'He mustn't find me here.' She snatched up Colin's kilt, bounded on to the table, and in a second she had the window open and was through it like a cat to the ground. Then she began to run as if her life depended on it.

Behind the stage McQuaid thrust himself roughly past Chloe and began to investigate the small rooms at the back. In Cotsworth's room and the one for the actors he found only one or two people busy packing up their stage costumes. Chloe followed him haughtily. Then McQuaid came to the door of her room, shut fast.

'What's in here?' he demanded.

'That, sir, is *my* room!' Chloe said indignantly.

McQuaid hesitated, then said: 'All the same, I'll just push my head round the door, lass.'

There, with the light breeze blowing in, the window stood open.

'That window's open! And it's not barred like the others! That's the way they've gone! The Frenchie's escaped through the window!' Roughly he pushed Chloe aside and raced back over the stage into the hall, shouting: 'Quick! Laidlaw! They've gone through the window! Out into the streets and after them!' They tore into the street and took the road to the harbour.

Ten minutes earlier Charles Cotsworth, with Simon and Colin, had taken the road to the harbour too.

'Where are we going, sir?' Simon had asked him.

'Down to the coal wharf. Tonight a coal boat will leave with the tide for Belfast. Offer the skipper who sails her a gold piece and he will give you a passage aboard,' Cotsworth panted. 'Down this lane here! It should lead to the waterside.'

But when they reached the wharf, there was no ship there! Cotsworth was dumbfounded. 'She cannot have sailed, surely?' he cried.

'What are those lights across the water? Is that a ship?' Simon asked, peering through the darkness.

'Plague take it! I've come to the wrong wharf!' Cotsworth cried aghast. 'That's the ship lying on the other side of the river! We must get round to her at once.'

'Which way do we go?' Simon asked, turning about.

'Back into town and over the bridge! It's the only way. Oh, this loses precious time! The play will be over, and those men will be wondering why we are not there to take our bow with the rest. Hurry! Faster yet!' Cotsworth urged them.

When they reached the street again, however, the people were already leaving the hall and a crowd was coming towards them.

'Make your way quietly along. We must pretend to be miners coming from our work. It's our only chance. Keep moving steadily towards the bridge over the Ellen River.'

At last they reached the bridge that spanned the river and led to the wharf on the other side.

'Once we're across, I'll feel easier in my mind,' Cotsworth said. 'We haven't far to go then.'

'Look! There are three men approaching the other end of the bridge,' Colin said in a low tense voice. 'One is McQuaid, I'm certain.'

'Keep on walking towards them, say nothing and leave all to me,' Cotsworth instructed them in a whisper. When they came abreast of the three men

Cotsworth greeted them with a broad Cumberland tongue. 'Good neet, lads, a grand neet!'

They were almost past when McQuaid swung round. 'Wait, man, we'd like a word with ye.'

Colin's heart almost stood still, but Cotsworth answered calmly: 'Ah well, what is it?'

'You've just passed the crowds coming from the theatre. Did you see a tall man and a lad with him?'

'Aye, mony a one in yon throng!' Cotsworth laughed.

'This lad was wearing a Scotch kilt,' McQuaid told him.

'You sound a bit of a Scotchman yoursel',' Cotsworth remarked.

'Aye, you're right, but did you see a lad in a kilt?'

'Come to think, I did!' Cotsworth exclaimed. 'He was with another fellow. Hurrying he was, too!'

'Which way did he go?' McQuaid asked, excited.

'I think it was down by the water on t'other side o' the bridge,' Cotsworth took McQuaid by the arm and pointed. 'Over yonder, see, man?'

'Right! Come on, Laidlaw, or we'll lose the Frenchie yet!' McQuaid cried. They rushed off in the direction Cotsworth pointed.

'My faith, that was a close thing,' Cotsworth said, mopping his brow. 'I thought McQuaid had recognized us when he stopped us.'

'I saw him turn and look after us in the moonlight as he ran,' Colin told him, a little troubled.

'Aye, and he'll soon find out I've sent him in the wrong direction, and he'll think about us again,'

Cotsworth said soberly. 'And we still have our bargain to make with the master of the ship. We'd better run now.'

Panting, they came abreast of the coal ship. Cotsworth called: '*Pride of Larne,* ahoy! *Pride of Larne*! Is anyone aboard?'

A head was put over the side and an Irish voice asked: 'What are ye after, now?'

'Is the master of the ship aboard?' Cotsworth asked.

'Sure he is! I'm the master. What are ye wantin'? If it's a job, I've all the hands I want.'

'It's not a job. It's a passage to Ireland,' Cotsworth told him.

'And I'm giving no free passages, either! Not to a lot of dirty miners!' the skipper retorted. 'There's no coal-mines in Ireland now. So there's no job for ye there at all.'

'Will ye listen to me, man?' Cotsworth cried urgently. 'We're willing to *pay* for our passages.'

'Och, why didn't ye say that at the first?' the skipper asked. 'What are ye willin' to pay, now?'

'Would a guinea be of any use to you?' Cotsworth asked.

'What? For the three of ye and all the meat ye'd eat? Think again, man!' The skipper spat into the water.

'A guinea from each of us, then,' Simon put in desperately.

The skipper eyed him craftily. 'Ye don't talk like a sailor, though ye're dressed like one! Ye're sure in a mighty hurry to get away from Maryport?'

'Leave this to me, Simon,' Cotsworth said sharply. 'Have you a dinghy you can tow astern?' he asked the skipper.

'Yes, I have, but what of it?'

'If you will take all three of us aboard and beat round the headland and put me ashore in the dinghy at Risehow, while you take this gentleman and the boy to Ireland, then there'll be a guinea from each of us when we're landed, and a spare one for your crew, maybe. Come, man, four guineas for an obligement that costs you nothing!'

'Very well, then, it's a bargain,' the skipper agreed. 'Come aboard. Watch your step on this plank, now.'

Just then there was a yelling from three men who tore round the head of the quay and made for the ship.

'There they are!' McQuaid shouted. 'Just going aboard that ship! Stop them! Stop them!'

'If you want your money, Captain, cast off your ropes as quick as you can and push off from the land,' Cotsworth cried.

The skipper took in the situation at a glance. 'Let go the rope, Patrick!' he called to his deck-hand who sprang to obey him. 'All hands to push her off! Then up wi' the sails!'

Colin, Simon and Cotsworth all lent a hand to push the ship away from the wharf. By the time McQuaid and the others had come abreast of the boat, she was already a yard away from the wharfside.

McQuaid stood on the quay and shook his fist at the moving ship. 'So ye've cheated me, have ye, Frenchie?' he shouted. 'Another minute and I'd had ye fast and clapped in jail!'

'Good-bye, McQuaid! Wish me *bon voyage*!' Simon said gaily.

McQuaid snorted in disgust. 'As for you, young

Cameron, take care ye never cross my path again, or it'll be the worse for you!'

'I am not troubling much at that, Mr McQuaid!'

'Plague take ye!' McQuaid cried after them.

Aboard the *Pride of Larne* Cotsworth was congratulating Simon on their lucky escape.

'It was not only luck, sir, it was thanks to you,' Simon told him. 'But will they be lying in wait for you when you get back to the town?'

'Not they!' Cotsworth said easily. 'Even if the rascals saw through my disguise, they would never dare to attack me among the theatre folk. Besides, they'll not stay long in Maryport now you've escaped them. But how will you get back to Scotland, Colin?' he asked.

'Maybe I shall come back on the ship again once I have seen Simon ashore,' Colin said.

'Have ye money enough?' Cotsworth asked.

'Oh, yes —' Colin began, and then he broke off suddenly in consternation. 'Oh! What have I done!' he cried.

'What is it, Colin? What's the matter?' Simon asked.

'My kilt! I have left it ashore! When we jumped through the window I must have forgotten it!'

'Nay, lad, you're going back to a land where there are plenty of kilts, surely? You'll be able to get another,' Cotsworth laughed.

'But that kilt — that kilt —' Colin faltered, his voice choking.

'What about it, lad?' Cotsworth asked sharply.

'It had all my money sewn into it — all my father's money from the sale of our bull!'

'How much was that?' Simon asked.

'A hundred and fifty pounds, no less!' Colin gasped. 'I had sewn the bank-notes into the pleats.'

Cotsworth gave a whistle. 'Where did you leave the kilt, lad?'

'I think I put it on the table in Chloe's room just before we jumped through the window. I — I put it down while I gave Bethia some money to help her.'

'Then cheer up, Colin! It may be there yet,' Mr Cotsworth said encouragingly.

'Oh, Simon, I cannot go with you to Ireland now,' Colin declared. 'I must go ashore with Mr Cotsworth and get my kilt again, or how can I face my father at home?'

'Now, don't get into a state, Colin,' Cotsworth chided him. 'It's probably still lying on the table, or Chloe may have put it away in the theatre baggage. Don't worry now. It'll turn up.'

Just then the skipper came up to them. 'We're round the point now, and in a few minutes I can lay the ship close inshore and put you off in the dinghy. Are ye ready to go now?'

'Yes, if we're near to the road from Workington to Maryport that lies close to the shore. This lad is coming with me,' Cotsworth said.

'Sure now, I thought you were for Ireland?' the skipper said, looking curiously at Colin.

'I — I have changed my mind,' Colin said.

The dinghy was brought alongside. 'It is really good-bye then, Colin, this time,' Simon said, taking him by the hand.

'Oh, Simon, I am so sorry.'

'Step into the shelter of the cabin a minute, Colin,'

Simon asked. He took an envelope from his pocket. 'See, here is a letter for you. I wrote it while we were at Cockermouth. Do not open it till you get home. Promise!'

'Very well,' Colin agreed.

'And now adieu, dear lad! I pray you may find your kilt and your money again. God go with you!'

'And with you too, Simon. You are the best friend I ever had.' Colin gulped hard. 'Will you ever come back to Scotland again?'

'Why, yes, of course, once this sad war is over. I promise you I will come to Drumbeg then.'

Cotsworth touched Colin gently on the arm. 'It is time for us to go in the small boat, Colin.'

'Good-bye, Simon!'

'Good-bye, Colin!'

They shook each other by the hand.

'Here you are, skipper. Here is the gold I promised,' Cotsworth said.

'Thank ye, thank ye. Mind how ye step into the boat. Ye can pull away now, Patrick. Good night, sirs.'

Charles Cotsworth and Colin were put ashore at a point where the road runs alongside the shore and they walked very fast along it the mile or so back to Maryport, not talking at all. At last they came to the hall where the play had been given.

'I think we dare walk boldly in. McQuaid will hardly be looking for you here, seeing he has just seen you sail in a boat for Ireland,' Cotsworth chuckled.

'There's still a light in the window. Perhaps Chloe and Bethia are still there packing up the stage costumes,' Colin said hopefully.

Cotsworth strode inside and called 'Chloe! Chloe!'

Chloe appeared from the back room. 'Are you all right, Father?'

'Yes, quite all right. That was a clever thought of yours, my dear, that disguise.'

'But why has Colin come back?'

'I — I have come back for my kilt. It isn't among the things you are packing up, is it, Mistress Chloe?'

'Did you come back for your kilt?' Chloe asked incredulously.

'I dropped it in a bundle, somewhere in this room, I think,' he said.

'What was there about that old kilt that you should risk your skin to come back for it? And why should Bethia make such a fuss about it?' she asked.

'Bethia?' Colin exclaimed.

'Tell us where it is quickly, Chloe. Colin is half out of his mind about it. It had all his money stitched in the folds,' her father told her.

'All his money? Oh!' Chloe's hand went to her mouth in alarm.

'Tell me, please, what has happened to it?' Colin begged.

'Bethia! Bethia took it!' Chloe stammered.

'Bethia! Where is Bethia?' Colin cried wildly.

Chloe shrugged her shoulders. 'How should I know? She jumped through the window when I was out of the room and she took your kilt with her.'

Colin stared speechlessly at Chloe.

Cotsworth looked very sorry for him. 'It looks as if she knew about your money, I fear, my lad.'

'Perhaps she has gone to join McQuaid and her gipsy tribe again,' Chloe suggested. 'She'd be very welcome with your money no doubt!'

'Oh, no, no! I cannot believe it of Bethia!'

'*La!* You can't trust gipsies. They're as sly as foxes,' Chloe said.

'I'm afraid Chloe is right, Colin. I'm sorry. It is a sad experience for you, my boy,' Charles Cotsworth said pityingly. 'You have seen very little of a world that is sometimes very wicked. What will you do now?'

Colin was looking distressed and bewildered. 'I do not know,' he said slowly. 'I cannot face my father at home and tell him I have lost his money for the bull, and yet I must —' His voice broke in a great sob. Even Chloe felt sorry for him.

'Could you not give Colin a place in the theatre, Father?' she begged. 'The folk like his songs well, you know. Then you need not go back to Scotland at all, Colin,' she smiled, as if that were an easy solution of the problem.

'Well, Colin, how would you like to stay with the players and become a barnstormer too?' Charles Cotsworth asked a little quizzically.

'It is very kind of you — but I do not know. My duty lies in Scotland, and yet —' Colin stammered, undecided.

'Think it over, Colin. Sleep on it and you can tell me in the morning,' Cotsworth said kindly.

'Thank you, Mr Cotsworth. May I stay the night in the covered baggage cart, sir?'

'Why, yes, of course,' Cotsworth agreed. 'Good night then, Colin.'

'Good night, sir, and thank you for all you have done for Simon and for me this night,' Colin said gratefully. 'Good night, Mistress Chloe.' He turned away to go out to the baggage cart.

All that night Colin tossed among the stage curtains in the baggage cart and no sleep would come to him. He thought of Simon on the sea on his way to Ireland. He thought of his father who had trusted him with the bull, and he thought of Angus who had given the money into his care, and he was bitterly ashamed. But most of all he thought about Bethia and a lump came into his throat that she could have deceived him and stolen the money and the kilt. That was the bitterest thought of all.

Colin thought, too, of Mr Cotsworth's offer that he should stay with the company and become a play-actor, and he was half-tempted to stay. At last, however, out of all this welter of thoughts, there came the one clear thing, that it was his duty to go back to his father at Drumbeg and ask for his forgiveness. But Colin made up his mind he would go first to Catterlen again and find if Angus was still there.

So the next morning Colin took his farewell of Charles Cotsworth and the travelling players and Chloe. Cotsworth saw him go with regret, but Chloe merely pouted and said: 'I think you are very foolish, but you must please yourself,' and shrugged her shoulders. But she turned away quickly from Colin for all that, as though to hide her face.

Catterlen Again

When Bethia jumped out of the window she hesitated for a moment wondering which way to run. Then she thought that Simon would be sure to make for the harbour and try to get a ship there, so she went as fast as she could in that direction. In the darkness she mistook the turning at the end of the street and found herself on the wrong road. She retraced her footsteps to the crossroads but, to her alarm, when she got there, she heard running feet and the sound of voices, and recognized among them that of her uncle, Peter the Gipsy.

Like a little hunted animal she sought a hiding place and bolted into the garden of a large house close to the road. There she sank down among some laurel bushes and waited trembling. She heard McQuaid say: 'Quicker, Laidlaw! We don't want them to escape us this time, neither the Frenchie nor the droving lad. That lad's got the money on him for the bull. I'm sure of that.'

The sound of their feet and voices faded away in the distance, but still Bethia hid among the bushes, shaking with fear. Then she tried to gather her wits together and think what to do next.

'It's too late to get the kilt back to Colin now,' she said to herself, 'and I dare not stay here for fear those wicked men find me. I must run as hard as I can out of Maryport. I must get away from McQuaid and my uncle.'

Like a frightened hare she raced up the road and out of the town and took the way towards Cockermouth again. For almost a mile she did not slacken her speed until she felt that she was well away from the tinkers, then at a slower speed she continued on and on through the dark night. At last, when she felt she could go no further, she staggered to a standstill and gazed wildly about her for some place where she might shelter. In a field just by the roadside stood a haystack, and against it leaned a ladder.

'I'll get on top of that and pull the ladder up after me. I'll be safe there,' Bethia told herself.

Quickly she scaled the ladder and then with a great effort she drew it up after her. Now at last she felt safe as though in a tower, and decided to stay there till morning. The night breeze blew coldly on top of the haystack, and she unrolled Colin's kilt from the bundle and snuggled down among the hay with it wrapped round her. Then, utterly weary, at last she fell asleep.

When she awoke it was full daylight and the birds were twittering about her. Bethia sat up and rubbed her eyes.

'Mercy on us! It's full daylight already,' she cried. 'I must get down from here before the farmer sees me.'

She began to roll up the kilt into a bundle again, when all at once she saw a piece of paper sticking out from one of the folds near the waist. The stitching had come undone a little. 'What's this?' she cried, pulling out the paper. 'It's a bank-note for — for —' She

could hardly believe her eyes and looked at it again.
'For *fifty pounds*!' Consternation, amounting almost
to horror, filled her mind. She seized the kilt and
began to feel the other pleats stitched at the waist.
Two more of them were crisp and crackling to the
touch. Bethia sat back suddenly. She was in possession
of the money for which McQuaid and Laidlaw had
followed the drovers so far, the money for Colin's
bull! It was money that would have bought her back
into her tribe of tinkers with honour!

Bethia thought hard for a minute, and then she
said to herself: 'I know what I must do. There is
the guinea that Colin gave me. I will use it to pay
my fare on the stage to Penrith and see if Angus is
still at Catterlen. Yes, I will go to Catterlen.'

Kneeling on the haystack she braided her black
hair, tied up the kilt neatly into a bundle again
inside the old piece of curtain, with the fifty-pound
note thrust safely back and pinned inside the pleat of
the kilt. Then she let down the ladder, came down it,
and was on on her way to Cockermouth.

At Cockermouth she stopped in the wide main
street and asked a baker going home from his work,
still white and floury: 'Please, sir, can you tell me
where I can get a coach for Penrith?'

The man shook his head. 'You can't get a coach
direct to Penrith from Cockermouth, my lass. The
mountain roads are too bad for coaches.'

'How can I get there then?' Bethia asked.

'You're a young lass to be going so far alone, so
early in the day,' the man said curiously.

'I am going to work on a farm,' she told him to
satisfy his curiosity.

'Well, you could go to Carlisle by coach from here. It's not very far. If you were lucky at Carlisle, you might get a coach from there to Penrith without waiting more than a few hours. The coach stops over yonder at the Bluebell Inn.'

Bethia thanked the man and ran across the road. She waited in the shelter of a doorway, lest when the coach did come, any of her enemies should be on it, but the coach came from Keswick, though she did not know it, and the tinkers were not likely to be aboard it.

She waited a long time, but at last it came round the corner and rumbled to a halt close by the inn. Timidly Bethia approached the coachman.

'Have you a seat to Carlisle, please, sir?' she asked.

'Aye, outside on top, if you've the money to pay for it,' the man said curtly.

'How much is it, sir?'

'Five shillings.'

'I have money enough for that. Which seat is it?' she asked him.

'Nay, the money first from the likes of you, my lass,' he said, holding out his hand.

Bethia produced the guinea. 'Will you give me my change, please?'

'What? A guinea?' the coachman said and stared at it. 'Did you come by this honestly?'

'Indeed I did! It was given to me by a friend,' Bethia said hotly.

'Aye, that's the tale all thieves tell,' the coachman said, curling his lip a little.

'Indeed, I am not a thief.'

'I've only your word for it, my lass.'

'If you do not give me my guinea back I will go to a magistrate about it,' Bethia said boldly. 'The landlord of the Bluebell Inn will know one.'

This the coachman did not want, so he began to rattle in his pocket for change. 'All right, all right then,' he said. 'But my fare is double for gipsies. It will cost you ten shillings.'

'But that is a wicked thing!' Bethia said indignantly.

'If you don't like it you can find another way of getting to Carlisle,' the coachman told her.

'Very well, I will pay the money,' Bethia said desperately.

'I thought you would,' the coachman said with a sneer.

'My change, please?' Bethia held out her hand.

'My, but you're the grabbing one,' the coachman said. 'Here you are, then.' Unwillingly, he counted out ten shillings into her hand.

'And another shilling. It was a guinea I gave you,' Bethia insisted. Unwillingly, he placed another shilling in her hand.

'There! You can take an outside seat on top,' he said.

Bethia climbed up the stairs to the uncomfortable seat indicated to her, and in a few minutes the post-horn sounded, the coachman flicked the horses with his whip, and the great coach rattled down the main street and out of the town to the north-east.

It was almost three hours later when the coach drew up outside an inn in Carlisle. Stiff with sitting on the hard seat Bethia got down. There would be a coach for Penrith in an hour, she learned. She wandered about the streets of Carlisle, hungry and thirsty, pressing her nose to the shop windows, but afraid to buy even a bread roll for fear by doing so she would not have enough money for her fare to Penrith, for she did not know how much it would be, or how much the coachman would take from her over and above the fare he ought to charge. She returned at last to the inn to find a coach drawn up there and fresh horses being fastened into the traces.

'Does this coach go to Penrith, please?' she asked a groom.

'Aye, it does.'

She sought out the coachman. 'Have you a seat as far as Penrith, sir?' she asked timidly.

'Inside only, my wench. It costs more there, though,' he told her.

'How much is it, sir?'

'Four shillings,' he said, this time without looking her up and down. Bethia was thankful and counted out her precious shillings at once into his hand.

'What time do we reach Penrith?' she asked.

'About six o'clock tonight, if we meet with no bad roads and no horse casts a shoe,' he told her.

'It — it will be near dark by then?'

'Aye, my lass. You're a young girl to be travelling alone.'

'Oh, I have friends in Penrith,' Bethia told him. 'It — it will be all right.'

'All aboard the coach! All aboard the coach for Penrith!' the coachman cried, and the passengers came running from the inn where they had been taking refreshment. Bethia felt hungrier than ever.

With the resounding notes of the post-horn, the clatter of horses' hoofs, and the rattle of the coach, they left Carlisle, and soon they were following the road up hill and down dale among green fields and through sleepy villages.

When they reached Penrith it was already dark. The coachman gave Bethia his hand to alight.

'Have your friends not come for you?' he asked, staring round the inn yard.

'Oh, no! I know where to look for them,' she said, and had vanished like a flash out of the inn yard, lest he should detain her.

It was dark with a snell wind blowing as she took the road for Catterlen. She undid the bundle and wrapped Colin's kilt about her shoulders thrusting the loose note inside the pleat first and making sure it was securely fastened by the pin from her own shawl. Then she stepped out along the narrow country lane, shadowed in even deeper darkness by the thick hedges on either side. Bethia shuddered a little, looking nervously over her shoulder, as though she expected someone to be following her. At every creak of a branch she started. At last she began to run.

'I hope they do not go early to bed at Catterlen,' she said to herself; then, to her own surprise, she found herself beginning to sob. Stumbling on, she pressed in the direction of the farm.

In the farm-house Mrs Barlow was seated at the supper table with her husband, Angus, and Donald. Except for the pallor caused by being indoors, Angus was looking much better.

'Now, Angus, another plate of meat?' Mr Barlow asked him.

'No, thank you, Mr Barlow,' Angus replied, but

Donald did not need much persuasion to take another plateful.

Mrs Barlow paused, knife and fork uplifted. 'Listen, Thomas, is that a dog barking?' she asked.

'It's perhaps the farm-hands out after rabbits,' the farmer guessed.

Again the bark came. This time there was a crescendo of barking from more than one dog.

'Oh dear, it fidgets me to hear the dogs barking at night, ever since those tinker fellows came here after Simon,' she said. 'I wonder where Colin and Simon are now?'

'Don't fret, lass! Charles Cotsworth would get them to the coast all right.'

'There must be someone out there in the farm-yard,' Mrs Barlow declared. 'I thought I heard a step then.'

'Now, missus, you're imagining things.'

'Aye, it's foolish of me, I know, but I wish you'd just take a look to see that the hens are all locked up. There's plenty of queer bodies about these days.'

'Eh, there's no peace for a chap when his missus takes notions, Angus,' the farmer laughed and clicked his tongue against his teeth. 'Oh, all right, lass, I'll step outside and take a look round.'

Before he got there, there was a knock came to the door.

'Mercy on us! Who's that at this time of night?' Mrs Barlow cried. 'Don't go, Thomas. Leave the door bolted. It might be highway robbers.'

Mr Barlow laughed. 'Nay, come, lass. Robbers don't usually come knocking at the door.'

The knock came to the door again and this time

a girl's voice sobbed: 'Oh, please, please, let me in!'

'Why, that's a wench's voice!' Mr Barlow said.

Mrs Barlow was almost before him, drawing the bolts. As soon as the door was opened, Bethia stumbled over the threshold: 'Oh, please, please —' she sobbed.

Mr Barlow caught her as she fell. 'Here, help me, missus, she's fainting!'

Mrs Barlow helped to carry her into the kitchen. 'It's that gipsy lass again!' she cried when she saw Bethia's face.

'I — I am sorry, mistress — I did not mean —' Bethia faltered.

'Here, drink this, my lass,' Mrs Barlow said, holding a cup of hot tea to her lips.

'Thank you. Thank you,' Bethia said in a weak voice. 'I — I am feeling better now. It was just — I have had nothing to eat or drink for nearly two days. Is — is Angus Cameron still here?'

'Aye, I'm here,' Angus said from his seat at the table. 'Is there anything wrong with Colin? Tell me quickly!'

'No. I think Colin is safe. He went to take a ship for Ireland with Simon at Maryport.'

'For Ireland? Oh, why did he go all that way? Whenever will he be back again?' Angus cried in dismay.

Bethia thrust the bundle at him. 'I came to bring his kilt. It is here.'

'His kilt?' Mrs Barlow cried. 'Why was he not wearing it?'

'He went away disguised as a miner's lad. McQuaid

was at Maryport. In the hurry of his escape, Colin left his kilt behind. Please take it now, Angus. There is something sewn into the pleats near the waist.'

'What? The money?' Angus cried.

'Yes,' Bethia said simply.

'And you journeyed nearly two days without food to bring it to me?' Angus asked, deeply touched.

'Why, yes, what else was there for me to do?'

'Oh, Bethia! How can I thank you enough for this?' Angus cried. 'You cannot guess how much it means to us all, especially Colin. Oh, what can I do for you in return?'

'It seems to me the best thing you can do just now is to draw up a chair to the table for the lass, while I make some broth hot for her,' Mrs Barlow said practically. 'And after that, my lass, we'll find you a bed, for you look fit to drop.'

'A bed? But I have never slept in a bed in my life!' Bethia exclaimed in alarm.

'You poor bairn! Then it's high time you did! You could do with a bit of mothering, I'm thinking,' Mrs Barlow said kindly. The next moment Bethia was sobbing in her arms as she had never done in her life before.

Sad and troubled as he was at the loss of the kilt and his money Colin's heart began to lift again as he set his face towards the high hills. There was always something in the power of the mountains to make his spirit soar. He had got a lift in a carrier's cart from Maryport to Cockermouth, but from there he took the shorter route across the hills by way of the Whinlatter Pass to Keswick. That night he slept in a wood near Portinscale, snug among the bracken, in spite of the stiff breeze that blew among the peaks and whistled over Skiddaw.

The next day came the long slow pull over the mountains by way of Threlkeld and then over the wild moors past Scales Inn and Troutbeck Inn till at last he came to Greystoke with its ancient church. Here Colin sat for a while on a long flat tombstone like a table top and ate some bread and cheese he had bought in the village. He was not now more than three miles as the crow flies from Catterlen, but his way went by winding green lanes and wooded paths, so that the distance was half as much again. At last he came over the heath and saw Catterlen's friendly house rosy with the setting sun upon it amid its gracious pastures. As he came into the farm-yard, old Donald was just coming with the pails from the evening milking.

'Mercy on us! It's you, Colin!' the old man cried.

'All right! All right, Donald!' Colin laughed. 'Don't drop the milk pails now. I am not a ghost.'

Donald set down the milk pails and ran towards the house shouting: 'Angus! Mistress Barlow! Look who's here!'

Angus came running out. 'Colin! Colin! It's really you! But we thought you had gone to Ireland?' He gripped Colin by the arm as though he would never let him go again.

Mrs Barlow came bustling to the door. 'Colin!' she cried. 'Where's Simon?'

'He stayed on the ship for Ireland. I — I had to come back.' Colin faltered a little and a look of shame crossed his face.

'Oh, Colin, it's good to see you safe!' Angus cried, overjoyed. 'You do not know how I have blamed myself for letting you go with Simon to encounter all kinds of dangers. Oh, it's troubled sore I've been —'

Colin cut him short. 'Before you say any more, Angus, there is a thing I must tell ye — a terrible thing!'

'What is it?' Angus asked.

'I have lost the money for the bull,' Colin told him, hanging his head. 'I left it sewn in my kilt and — and the kilt is lost. How shall I face my father now? How shall I face him when he trusted me?'

Mrs Barlow, standing behind Colin, signalled to Angus with her finger on her lips that he should keep silence.

'Come into the house, Colin,' she said, drawing him in by the arm. 'Nay, lad, say no more just now. It must be too long a story to tell on an empty stomach. And that's true for you, Angus, too. *You will please me by saying nothing to Colin yet*,' she spoke with emphasis. 'Come and sit at supper, all of you.'

She led the way into the house and pushed Colin into a chair at the table. 'Now, sit you there, Colin! My, you look weary, my lad!'

The door opened and Mr Barlow came hurrying in. 'What's this? Colin's back? Why, lad, it's good to see you. I'm not the only one who'll be pleased too,' he added with an air of mystery.

'Sit down, man, and carve the meat. There'll be time for chatter afterwards,' she said pointedly. 'The lad's hungry.'

'Why, missus, haven't you told him?' Mr Barlow said in surprise.

'Ssh! In a minute! Wait till he's set at his food,' she hissed in her husband's ear. Then she said in a louder voice: 'We could do with some more butter. I'll call the wench from the dairy.' She lifted her voice: 'Bring some more butter and cheese, lass.'

A voice from the dairy answered happily: 'Yes, mistress!'

Colin started: 'Who's that?' he asked.

'Our new lass,' Mrs Barlow said, amused. 'Here she is.'

Bethia came into the kitchen carrying the butter and cheese.

'Colin!' she cried when she saw him sitting there.

'Bethia! I never thought to find you here!'

'But surely you would know I should be bringing your kilt to Angus, Colin?'

'My kilt!'

'Why, yes, you remember you left it behind at Maryport?'

'Oh, yes, but I never thought you would —' Colin began, and then came to a stop, confused.

'You never thought I would leave it lying around in the playhouse for anyone to pick up, surely?'

'Oh, Bethia, I am not certain what I thought,' Colin said, bitterly ashamed that he should ever have doubted Bethia. 'Oh, that you should bring it all the way to Catterlen!'

'It was easier to bring it to Catterlen than to take it all the way to Drumbeg, silly lad!' she said.

'Would you have done even that? Taken it to Drumbeg?' Colin asked, astonished.

'With all that money sewn into it? Indeed I would!' Bethia declared.

'So you knew about the bank-notes in it too? Oh, Bethia, what can I say? How could I think —'

Mrs Barlow interrupted before he should betray himself. 'Are we to get any supper tonight or not?' she demanded. 'Come on, Bethia, set down the butter before you drop it, wench! And you, Thomas, how long are you going to stand there with the carving knife in your hand as if you were turned to stone? Pass the bread, Angus. You can all talk when you've eaten and not till then!'

After supper, when all Colin's adventures had been told, Angus turned towards Mr Barlow. 'Now that Colin is back with us, Mr Barlow, I think we should take the road north again as soon as he is rested.'

'Och, I'll be fine after one night's rest,' Colin declared.

'You're surely not thinking of setting off yet, Angus?' Mrs Barlow asked.

'My head and my ribs are healed now, thanks to you, mistress. It is a long journey back to Drumbeg and we must go afoot because we have the pony with us. I want to reach home before the winter frosts make the roads difficult.'

'Aye, I can see the sense of that, Angus,' Mr Barlow observed.

'Besides, my father and mother will be anxious because we are so long in returning. So, if Mistress Barlow will forgive us, we will be on our way tomorrow.'

'Very well, though we'll miss ye, Angus,' Mrs Barlow said with a sigh.

'You can tell your father he can be proud of his two sons,' the farmer said. 'I wish our son had taken to farming, but he did not; though, mind you, he is doing very well as a lawyer in Kendal. We never had a daughter, more's the pity!'

'Aye, more's the pity,' Mrs Barlow lamented, 'for I like a lass about the house. Well, Bethia, and what's to happen to you?'

'You have been very kind to let me rest here, but I must go tomorrow, too,' Bethia said sadly.

'So soon? Why, lass, are you going back to the gipsies?' Mrs Barlow asked.

'No, I could never go back to them now.' Bethia shook her head.

'Where will you go, then?'

'I must find work to keep me. They say there is plenty of work for girls in the cotton-mills in Lancashire. I will go there.'

'That you will not, my wench!' Mrs Barlow said firmly. 'The children who work in the cotton-mills are little better than slaves!'

'Perhaps I could find work in the fields. I would like that better, but the winter is drawing on,' Bethia said doubtfully.

'Would you like to work on a farm, Bethia?' Mrs Barlow asked sharply.

'Indeed I would. I like well the animals,' Bethia said wistfully.

Mrs Barlow looked straight at her husband. 'Well, Thomas, are *you* thinking what I'm thinking?'

'You know as well as I do, missus, that it would go badly with me, if I didn't think as you do!' he answered drolly. 'But I'm with you in this, sure enough.'

'Then will you stay and live with us as our daughter,

Bethia, and help me about the farm?' Mrs Barlow said at once.

'Oh, Mistress Barlow, do you mean it?' Bethia asked breathlessly.

'Of course she does, Bethia!' Mr Barlow said. 'The wife's fair sick to have a lass of her own she can talk to — one that she can trust.'

'Oh, then I'll stay gladly, with all my heart,' Bethia cried. 'Oh, thank you! Thank you!'

'Oh, Bethia, I am so glad too,' Colin said. 'I had been troubling about what would become of you.'

'I think we shall all go away with lighter hearts now,' Angus smiled.

The next day the three of them, Colin, Angus and Donald, took the long road north again, and parted from Mr and Mrs Barlow and Bethia with many a backward look and wave of the hand. Though it was such a tiring wearisome journey, they went with light hearts.

It was twelve days later that they reached Drumbeg, and already the first winter snows were white upon the mountains of Glen Coe. At last they came to the low white-washed farm-steading that was home to them all. As they came in, the three of them with the pony and the two dogs, Rob and Sim, the other farm dogs set up a great barking. Mrs Cameron dropped the spoon with which she was stirring the broth and asked her husband: 'What is that great stramash outside with the dogs?'

The door opened and in rushed Colin. In a moment his arms were round his mother, and they were almost laughing and crying in the same breath. James Cameron took Angus by the hand, and Donald too.

'Mother! Father! Oh, it's good to be home,' Colin said.

'Aye, thank Heaven you're back, my lads! We were beginning to fear that something ill had come to ye,' his father said thankfully.

'Angus did have an accident when the cattle stampeded,' Colin told them.

'What's that?' Mr Cameron asked quickly.

'Oh, but I'm fine now,' Angus said jauntily. 'Mistress Barlow looked after me well, Mother, but I'll tell you all about that later. But how is your leg, Father?'

'The bone's knit, I'm thankful to say, and I can get around all right, though I still hirple a bit. It was coming to look for you I was, though, if ye'd been any longer,' he told them in a mock-angry voice. 'Well, Angus, did ye sell the beasts at a fair price?'

'Aye, we did,' Angus said with a little air of triumph. 'Nine pounds ten for each o' the stirks and the bull fetched — well, Colin can tell ye about the bull, for he sold it.'

'A hundred and fifty guineas, Father!' Colin said with pride.

'What? You tell me that? I cannot be believing it!' James Cameron cried. 'It is making a joke you are!'

'It is quite true, Father,' Angus said quietly.

'Here is the money sewn into my kilt,' Colin said, taking his mother's scissors and cutting the stitching.

'My, Colin, but you're the clever one to bring the money safe like that all the way. I'm pleased with ye,' James Cameron said.

'It was not always safe, Father. Once it was lost,' Colin's honesty forced him to say.

'Lost?'

'Aye, it is a long story,' Colin said.

'Then draw up your chairs to the table, and you can be telling us when you have eaten. Let the story wait till then,' Mrs Cameron said.

Long after the lamp was lit the story of their adventures went on and on, until it was nigh bed time.

'And that is how Bethia gave us back the kilt again, Father,' Colin came to an end at last.

'She is a fine lassie, that one. I am thinking Mistress Barlow is the lucky woman,' Mrs Cameron said, staring into the fire.

'Aye, it's a big adventure you've had, my lads, a big adventure! But ye've come through it well, and what is more, you have kept your good faith and your good name as drovers,' their father said proudly.

'I am glad you were able to help yon fine man, Simon, French though he be,' Mrs Cameron said.

'Oh, Mother! I almost forgot!' Colin cried. 'Simon sent you this.' He drew the little flat parcel from his pocket. 'He said it was to be a fairing from both of us from Carlisle.'

'For me? What can it be?' Mrs Cameron cried, as with excited fingers she untied the string. The shawl tumbled out in all its folds of silken loveliness. 'A shawl! A silk shawl, no less! Oh, no, this cannot be for me!'

'Who else, then?' Colin laughed.

'No one has ever given me a silk shawl before, not even your father!' she cried, near to tears. 'It is a shawl such as the fine ladies wear. It is much too grand for me. I can never wear it!'

'Oh, yes, Mother, you will! You will wear it when the minister comes to visit you,' Colin suggested.

'Oh, no! It is too good even for the minister, though may I be forgiven for saying it! I shall put it in a drawer and whiles I shall be taking it out to look at it and my heart will be glad that my son brought it home for me from his first droving,' she said with pride.

'But, woman, it's for *wearing*!' her husband laughed.

'Oh, never fear, I will be wearing it for the grand occasions, for the weddings and the baptisms, you will see, but for nothing else except, perhaps, when your Frenchman visits Drumbeg, Colin,' she decided. 'But what is that letter that is lying on the table there beside it?'

'Oh, yes, it is a letter Simon said I was not to open till I got home,' Colin told her. He broke the seal, and as he read his eyes grew wider and wider. 'Oh, what is this?' he cried. 'Listen!' He read aloud:

'To Colin Cameron:

As a token of my great gratitude and our abiding friendship I would like you to buy yourself a keepsake with what is enclosed in this letter.

May God's blessing go with you always, and I pray that we shall meet again.

Ever your true friend,
Simon de Conceau.'

Colin turned over the enclosure. 'Oh, look! It is a bank-note!'

'Let me look, lad,' James Cameron cried. 'Why, it is for fifty pounds!' he cried in awe.

'Whatever keep-sake will you buy with fifty pounds, Colin?' his mother asked.

Colin knew at once what it was to be. 'I know! With fifty pounds I can buy a small herd of young stirks. With them I will become a farmer and drover like you, Father. I will follow the drove roads and make my fortune, maybe. Then some day I will go across the sea to see Simon again.' Colin's face glowed. 'I think Simon would be liking that, aye, and Mr Barlow too, if I mind well always what he told me.'

'What was that, Colin?' his father asked.

'That a good name for honesty and good faith is worth more than gold to a droving lad,' Colin declared.

How the Story Ended

'Well, Ian, that is the story of how I took my first drove on the long grassy roads to England,' his grandfather concluded.

Ian drew a deep breath and let out a long sigh. 'Oh, Grandfather, that was a fine story, and I liked it most because it was a *true* story about you.'

'Aye, laddie, it's true right enough. Well, it's taken a few nights in the telling. And now you had better be off to bed if you are going with me to take the drove to the rail-head at Falkirk tomorrow and see the beasts put on the train for England. Changed days from the old drove roads!'

'Oh, could I, Grandfather? Could I really?'

'Well, perhaps you'd better ask your grandmother first,' his grandfather laughed.

'Oh, you'll say "yes", won't you, Grandma?' Ian begged. '*Persuade* her, Grandfather!'

'Don't you think the lad might go with us this once, Beth?' the grandfather said in a coaxing voice. His wife raised her white-haired head with a smile and her dark eyes rested lovingly on the boy and her husband.

'Well, yes, I think he might,' she agreed.

Ian regarded her curiously. 'Grandma, there is a thing I wish to ask you. Grandfather calls you "Beth".

I never thought about it before, but is it short for Elizabeth?'

His grandmother chuckled a little before she answered. 'No, dear, it is short for *Bethia*,' she told him.

'Oh, Grandma!' Ian cried with wonder and delight as he realized all this meant.

Grandfather Colin Cameron chuckled too. 'Aye, it was surprising how often, when I grew older, my droving business took me to Catterlen to see Mr and Mistress Barlow, and — er — *Bethia*! Or maybe it was not so surprising after all?' he said, looking proudly across the table to where Bethia sat, her lovely white-haired head bent over her knitting.

For my dear friends
Helen and Bill Girvan
who encouraged me to write this book

Other Kelpies by the same author

THE DESPERATE JOURNEY

ESCAPE IN DARKNESS

FLASH THE SHEEPDOG

TURK THE BORDER COLLIE

HAKI THE SHETLAND PONY

SEAL STORY

If you liked this story then why not
look out for other Kelpies. There are
dozens of stories to choose from:
ghosts, spy stories, animals and the
countryside, witches, mysteries and
secrets, adventures and many more.
Kelpie paperbacks are available from
all good bookshops.

For your free Kelpie badge and
complete catalogue please send a
stamped addressed envelope to:
Margaret Ritchie (K.C.B.),
Canongate Publishing Ltd.,
17 Jeffrey Street, Edinburgh
EH1 1DR.